Myrrh
&
Mayhem

LAURIE ALBERSWERTH

MYRRH & MAYHEM

A Jude and Audie West Mystery

Bear Write Media

St. Louis

This book is a work of fiction. Names, characters, places, and incidents are products of the author's imagination or are used fictitiously. Any resemblance to actual events, locales, organizations, or persons, living or dead, is entirely coincidental. (Also, the author is aware that, as of the publishing date, no Jeep is rated to tow the Wests' travel trailer. She has hopes for the future.)

Copyright © 2025 Laurie Alberswerth

All rights reserved. This book, or parts thereof, may not be reproduced in any form without written permission except in the case of brief quotations embodied in critical articles and reviews.

Cover design by Laurie Alberswerth

Cover illustrations by Michael Alberswerth and Laurie Alberswerth

Title font: Odachi, used gratefully with permission from creator Mehmet Tugcu

ISBN (paperback): 978-1-960550-06-4
ISBN (ebook): 978-1-960550-07-1

Published by Bear Write Media, St. Louis, Missouri, USA

START AT THE BEGINNING WITH THE WESTS!
Bones & Bloodlines (Book One),
available on Amazon.

***

Want a sneak peek at Audie's notes as she and Jude begin Book One's adventure?

Go to LaurieAlberswerth.com for a FREE download, plus access to the author's monthly newsletter.

Never miss news about our intrepid duo and their quest to unearth the roots of every family tree.

Dedication

In Technicolor memory of Grandma and Grandpa Grabin, whose holiday traditions string every bead on our Christmas tree.

To Michael, who can take the vaguest request ever and create a noose out of a wreath. (Audie's mind-reading skills have nothing on you.) In a book full of artists, I'm proud it's your work adorning the cover.

Acknowledgment

My thanks to the First Missouri State Capitol State Historic Site and the interpretive specialists who let this author ask way too many questions on an accidentally one-person tour. I can't believe it took me this long to visit a place so critical to Missouri's early days. With the exception of a particular piece of decor in the governor's office, I've kept the site's description as accurate as possible. (I wouldn't want to offend my fictional historians.)

"Art is a lie that makes us realize truth."

-Pablo Picasso

Chapter 1

The man in the top hat and cape—not even trying to hide the heavy winter coat beneath—held a triangular fragment between mittened fingers.

"A shard of broken glass is three times sharper than a stainless-steel scalpel," he declared with the drama of a fellow wearing a top hat. In the strobing glitter of the street's gas lamps, the shard pulsed in yellows and oranges.

"That comparison is based on obsidian, formed by the rapid cooling of lava. When it breaks, each edge becomes a razor because of its atomic structure. But glass as we know it, like this piece here, is every bit as deadly. Beer bottles, jelly jars, decorations such as stained glass—how many of you have sliced yourself open on the remnants of your favorite flower vase?"

Within her coat pockets, Audra West clenched her fists. Through the wool gloves, she felt the thin engravings left by trying to hide that figurine of Mom's she'd toppled at age seven. Vita, a decade older, had been horrified to find her in a messy pool of blood and tears. She'd cleaned the cuts, wiped the eyes, and taken the blame for the accident, putting aside money from her drugstore job for weeks to replace it.

Thank God for big sisters.

The icy wind gusted, and Audie nestled closer to Jude. The crowd around them wasn't much of a crowd. Convenient, that. And not surprising. Her husband's hand rested on her shoulder, more relaxed than it'd been in ages. Also not a shocker. When he'd suggested the ghost tour, he knew a Thursday night in mid-December wouldn't attract throngs. Those had come and gone two months ago, when self-respecting spooks put on a show for anyone who had the slightest inclination that the afterlife was a hip and happening place to be.

But just because the masses yearning to see apparitions had moved on didn't mean the specters had. They lived—unlived?—here year-round, or at least Stuart Morrison would like his ticket holders to believe they did. He wouldn't have much of a business otherwise. According to Vi, Stuart was the new kid on the St. Charles block, though he'd been performing these melodramas for almost three years. The original ghost guide—OGG?—had prowled the local streets for twenty-seven, and his patrons only grew in number as interest in the paranormal increased. Seeing an opportunity in the unseeable, Mr. Morrison carved out a niche for himself with shorter programs that were—*how shall we say?*—less concerned with historical accuracy.

Embellished was the word Vita had used.

"So why do we care about the science of glass tonight?" From out of his rucksack, Stu pulled a homemade rag doll, straw-colored yarn flopping above its wide eyes and full baby lips. He lifted it so everyone could see. "Meet Tina."

"Hello, Tina."

Jude put out his palms as Audie raised an eyebrow at him. "What? I was being polite."

At the front, Stuart bowed. "Tina is happy to make your acquaintance, sir. But, alas, the friendship will be a short one."

With a lightning-fast stroke, he slashed the shard across the doll's linen neck. "Darling Tina has fallen victim to the murderous Nathaniel Silvain."

At once, a flood of red beans spilled from the gash, crashing like angry raindrops on the two-hundred-year-old cobblestones. The group gasped and stumbled backward, a man nearest the carnage hopping away as if the legumes were genuine blood spatter.

"Really, Stuart?" Vita muttered. To Audie's left, her sister shook her head and crossed her arms.

"He sure knows how to play an audience."

How many of these dolls did he have at home? Or was the same one mended and reused weekly? There's a script for Hollywood: the soul of a toddler is trapped inside her toy with the makings of a decent chili. Every seventh night, the peeved poltergeist is released in a public reenactment.

Ick.

Stuart stowed the doll in his sack, more ragged than it had emerged. The spilled blood would rattle into the gutter if it wasn't first munched by the horses pulling carriages tomorrow.

Rest in peace, Tina. You've left us too soon.

Happy chatter from the opposite sidewalk disrupted the theatric moment, and their escort through the Great Beyond frowned. A quartet of carolers they'd enjoyed earlier tried and failed to quiet their laughter as they scurried past, heading for a bar still open this late on a weeknight. A longstanding tradition, the Holidays of Hope players were a huge draw for the city each December, and a worthwhile one to boot, with its proceeds going to the nearby children's hospital. They'd be hard at it again tomorrow, especially as the last weekend before Christmas got underway.

God bless us, everyone.

Stu cleared his throat and roped their wandering attention like a wayward bull. "We've heard some gripping tales tonight, but there's a reason I save Tina for the end. It happened in the building before us."

Jude leaned behind her. "Hey, Vi. Any decapitated toys ever show up in your display cases?"

"Not yet. If one does, it could model some of my earrings."

Practical to a fault.

"This building," their droll docent continued, ignoring the peanut gallery, "now houses a trio of artisans, like so many others along Main Street."

"Artisans," Jude whispered. "Aren't you fancy?"

"Don't you forget it," Vi replied. Thank heavens she'd learned long ago how to handle her brother-in-law.

"But in 1821, this was a boardinghouse used by members of Missouri's shiny new legislature. A year before, the arduous Missouri Compromise had passed, and the path for our statehood finally cleared. The first General Assembly formed in the summer of '21, laying the groundwork for official entry into the Union that August. For the state capital, the founders decided to create a centrally located community from the ground up, now known as Jefferson City. But in the five years before its completion, the fledgling government needed a place to meet. The representatives of St. Charles, then a frontier village about twenty-two miles from St. Louis, offered space above the Peck Brothers Dry Goods Store for free. As the state had no money, they accepted the offer. If you haven't yet, visit the First Capitol Site, run by the Missouri State Park system." He gestured down the road a block.

Jude shielded his eyes from the flickering lamp and squinted toward a brick structure that looked much as it had centuries ago. "We should do that," he said.

Vita nodded. "Yes, go sightseeing. You guys need this vacation."

Like no one would believe. Three insane family-tree cases in less than two months? Who knew genealogy could be so dangerous?

"But back to our story." Right. Tour guide. Audie hoped he'd wrap this up before hypothermia had them joining Tina at the Pearly Gates. "Fifty representatives and eighteen senators journeyed here from their districts. They met in the summer, after planting and before harvest, as most of Missouri was agricultural like today. Imagine the heat and humidity—hard to do tonight, I know—in these old masonry buildings. No air conditioning, heavy clothes, and only a couple of outfits per person. The reps, sometimes traveling with their wives and families, would have little with them for their stay, and laundry wasn't as easy as tossing a load in the Maytag."

Jude wrinkled his nose. "Pleasant."

"Be happy he isn't slashing Raggedy Ann."

"Raggedy Tina."

Shifting from foot to foot, Vita exhaled the last of her patience into a cloud of frozen condensation. "Stuart—the sharp, pointy glass?"

His gray beard had been brown when he started his speech, so her complaint was valid.

"I'm getting there."

Thank goodness this was the final stop of the night. They'd already heard about such total fabrications as the Carpenter's Apprentice and the puppy poltergeist of Lewis and Clark's Newfoundland, Seaman. If he didn't get a move-on, they'd be here when Santa shimmied down chimneys next week.

They'll also be chipping me out of ice in another ten minutes. Somebody needed to sew those chemical hand warmers into full body suits.

Stuart stepped to the short, wrought-iron fence in front of the white clapboard building and its lawn. "It was July 28, 1821. Representative Clarence Richards, from Chariton County in the center of Missouri, was living here for the legislative session with his recent bride, Josephine. As wasn't uncommon in the day, Josephine, at twenty, was less than half Clarence's age. Her family had been thrilled when the politician—and his money—swept the lovely lass away from her hardscrabble life on the farm in his constituency. Despite her rural upbringing, she was learning the skills required of a lady of means and was said to be an elegant accompaniment for Representative Richards."

"Read: scared and docile," Vita grumbled.

A Marik daughter, Josephine was not.

"On this sweltering evening, Clarence arrives at his temporary home after a long day of ironing out the many details of a fledgling state. He quickly finds the happy abode to be anything but." Their narrator's tone softened for dramatic effect. Nice. "The boardinghouse seemed deserted, darker than it should've been. The shutters were drawn, and the place was stifling. He lit an oil lamp in the entryway and stepped inside, calling out for Josephine, who usually awaited him in either the parlor or the rear family area. She didn't answer. His uneasiness mounted with every step he took."

A door slammed a block away, and the whole assembly flinched.

"'Josephine!'" Stuart cried. "Something crashed to the floor. Was that near the kitchen? He raced toward the noise.

There, he found a sight he wouldn't forget as long as the Lord gave him life.

"His fresh-faced bride lay on the sofa, her skin white as porcelain, her eyes vacant." Jude's arm tightened around Audie's shoulder as she shivered. "Her throat had been slit from ear to ear, a red sticky sheen covering her summer dress and her wavy brown hair.

"Above her hovered the son of the devil himself, Nathaniel Silvain, a French-Canadian glassmaker originally from Quebec. He lived next door with his wife and two small children at his shop. Well-known to Clarence, Silvain had even been commissioned by the legislator to produce a special clock for the governor's office at the Capitol building. He'd taken pity on the industrious man striving to provide for his family. Silvain stood still as a statue in Clarence's lantern light, holding a glistening shard of his own glass in his hand, dripping with the blood of dear Josephine."

"Clarence cried out for help and dove at the murderous fiend. Imagine the glow in the room growing brighter, the shadows starker, as more lanterns descended onto the cursed spot. The men wrestled a crazed Silvain until he dropped the bloody weapon, and they hauled him away."

"Why did he do it?" asked a woman off to the right. Every eye ogled the building, where only single, orange Christmas candles—the electric ones, not those ready to burn the place down if given an ounce of freedom—illuminated the wreaths hanging from red velvet ribbons against the panes.

"Why, indeed. The best bet was lust. Our precious Josephine was a youthful beauty, and Clarence testified he'd caught Silvain leering at his wife on more than one occasion."

"With his own family right next door?" Another woman clucked her tongue.

"For his part, the killer was struck speechless. The guess was that he had had some sort of psychiatric break. He must've gone to the house to force himself upon the unlucky woman. Legend says he used a pretense to visit her. Clarence had ordered a stained-glass panel for their first anniversary, a spring scene because that was her favorite season. Silvain had delivered it to Clarence that noontime at the legislature, and he claimed he wanted to see how she liked it. It gained him access. And her trust."

A cluster near them shuddered.

"When she turned him away, he destroyed his own glass creation and used it to kill her. The next day, as residents learned what had happened, he swore to his family and the judge that he had found her like that. 'Dead as a doornail,' as Mr. Dickens would say. Then who had killed her, everyone demanded, if not the bloody, delirious man who stood over her body with the weapon he himself had made? It was ludicrous to think anyone but Nathaniel Silvain had been the murderer."

"So what happened?"

"Silvain, of course, was hung. He protested for weeks before comprehending the further harm it did to those involved. He even begged them to let him finish the clock for the governor's office. At first, they refused, but Clarence ultimately petitioned for him to do so, an act of pure selflessness. He said he'd like Silvain's soon-to-be-widow to have bread, at least for a while."

"I don't know that I'd be that generous," Jude murmured.

"If I'm the dead woman on the couch, do whatever you feel is right." *I'd be beyond caring.* "But no reason for that unfortunate wife to suffer any more than necessary. The frontier wasn't an ideal place to be a young mother with a husband executed for murder."

And when is the ideal time and place for that?

Hmm.

A man in his twenties, who hadn't looked up from his phone throughout Stuart's soliloquies, said, "I thought he was a glassmaker, not a clockmaker."

And they say screen use kills focus.

"Interesting tidbit." *No, no, no. No tidbits.* Her toes had begun to tingle, despite the extra socks. "Back then, clocks were taxed, but paintings and decorative glass were not. Does everyone know what a banjo clock is?"

"Those old ones with a round clockface at top, a kind of skinny section, then a wider rectangle thing at the bottom?" Phone Guy was more surprising by the minute.

"Exactly. A painting was often added at that base, covering a narrow storage box or nook. Then the item was considered artwork and not a clock, and therefore not taxed. Nathaniel had an excellent reputation as an artist. He made fantastic stained glass and had provided windows for two churches and the homes of some of the St. Charles elite. For the governor, he was designing a rectangular glass piece to be fitted where you normally find the painting on a banjo clock."

"Stuart," Vita piped up between blowing on her fingers. "Is there a ghost on your ghost tour?" She knew there was. The woman operated a business out of the building where the murder happened, for heaven's sake. She whispered into her sister's ear. "Now I remember why the other guy wasn't too upset when Stu edged into his turf."

Stuart ran a hand over his face and adjusted his cape wearily. "Vita, I love you more every day."

"Simon will be happy to hear that." Her husband, away on business until the twenty-third, might like the break.

"Yes, so, the ghost. Can anyone guess?"

If I say Josephine, can we move this party along?

"The dude who was executed?"

Good grief, people.

"While that may be more terrifying, I think the truth is equally horrible."

Truth? *We're using that term generously today.*

"Each night since July 28, 1821, Josephine Richards has walked these cobbled streets. She is the most consistent spirit of any here in the historic district, always seen in her pale-blue dress, curls brushing her dainty shoulders. Before you imagine that as a peaceful scene, consider this: her head is perpetually cocked to the side, unable to support itself, and the smell of blood follows her, emanating from where the offending glass protrudes from her delicate neck."

A much stronger collective shudder that time.

Audie looked up at Jude. "Ol' Stu sure nails the pressure points, doesn't he?"

"I wish the souls we're paid to chase down would be so accommodating. If they all took an evening stroll, we wouldn't spend half our lives in libraries and courthouses."

"Bah!" came a shout much closer to Audie's ear than was really necessary. The crowd spun. "Don't let this scammer fill your heads with superstitious hogwash."

The man was on the short side, mid-fifties, wearing fashions straight out of 1800s *GQ*. A long-tailed frock coat, a scarlet double-breasted waistcoat, and black slacks laid the foundation, with a pocket watch hanging from a silver chain. A top hat similar to

Stuart's completed the ensemble. Puffy curls protruded over his ears from beneath it, matching an unruly mustache and beard. His only acknowledgment of the weather was an emerald scarf wrapped snugly above his ascot.

That look… why was it so familiar?

Their guide rubbed at the bridge of his nose. "Glen, how can the Ghost of Charles Dickens have a problem with a program like this?"

Of course! How could she forget photos of the famous author, especially the wild facial hair? Was the hat covering a receding hairline too?

"I'm trying to picture him wearing that get-up at the casino down the street," Jude mumbled. She could hear his smile.

The resurrected writer glared at them for passing notes during his grand entrance. "St. Charles has a rich, *real* past you should be sharing, and a prosperous future."

He must be running for mayor.

If he snags a baby to kiss, I'm finished.

"As we've discussed,"—Audie could imagine those discussions—"I always include the days of old. Where do you think the wandering souls come from?"

Vita leaned in, covering her mouth to avoid her own scolding. "Stu's just aggravated Glen won't fork over the money for a ticket. Plus, it's funny for Dickens to call us a fine city when we're in the middle of the worst rash of burglaries the district has ever seen."

That's news. "Big stuff?"

"No, petty theft. Mostly sentimental tidbits from window displays. But two months now, with no leads. Not terrific for his fair town's reputation."

"Your patrons," this Glen fellow continued, emphasizing the word with dripping sarcasm while his tall hat bobbed, "should be learning about people like Louis Blanchette, our founder, and the shop owners who outfitted Lewis and Clark for their great expedition from our river bank." Yep, definitely mayor material. "It's the pioneer grit we should be talking about, not this garbage regarding—"

"Excuse me!" An airy female voice piped up behind Jude, and the folks at the rear turned a few degrees further. Audie found herself eye to eye—unusual for her height—with a girl in her late twenties. She wore a heavy puffer coat that had seen too many winters and a purple knitted stocking cap with a pom-pom on top, braids hanging down from the earflaps. "I'm so sorry, but can I get through, please?"

"Hey, Fran!"

"Vita! I didn't see you there."

"Don't mind me." *Sure, now he's impatient.* Stuart would be haunting the bar himself before the evening was over.

The new girl cringed. "I didn't mean to interrupt."

But Vita waved off Stuart Morrison's personal angst. "What are you up to?"

"I left a list in the shop. I'll want it in the morning."

"Stu," Vita called out. "Fran is a glass artist too. You should be happy to have Nathaniel Silvain's modern-day equivalent stopping by in the middle of your story."

Fran stepped through a breach in the company and pushed against the squeaking iron gate. "Just don't hang me for murder, please," she laughed, then headed up the walk to the door. The jangle of her keys carried in the thin, crisp air.

"Where were we?" Stuart asked a woman wearing a Kansas City Chiefs coat.

"Sullying the reputation of our beloved home," Glen yelled over his shoulder as he began to move away.

"That was my plan all along," Stu shouted back. "I always wanted to be a sullyer." He returned to his congregation and inhaled from somewhere near his frostbitten arches. "Josephine Richards haunts the streets. She's been seen at the cemetery where she's buried, at the Catholic church up the road, and around the Capitol building. But mostly, she's spotted right here, at the old Simpson Boardinghouse—"

"Now the DFV Boutique, 10 a.m. to 7:30, six days a week," Vita plugged cheerily. "Not to be confused with the DMV, of course. We're a lot more fun."

Their leader clasped the iron fence so hard, Audie worried he'd use it to spear her sister. "—searching for the life she lost. She looks in on people like you and me who still travel this land of the living. Alone, in pain, suffering."

Light flooded the left window of the boutique, and again the group jumped.

"That's only Fran, sweeties," Vita said. "No spooks here to—"

A soul-stealing scream slashed the electrified atmosphere like that surgical scalpel. Stuart spun toward the building.

Vita forced her way through the pack, Audie clinging to her sleeve and Jude close behind. They reached the fence as the door of the shop blew open.

Into the glow of the gas lamps staggered young Fran, hat missing, dark splotches painting her coat. Stu fumbled with his flashlight until it focused on the frantic woman. In her hand, she held out a single triangle of glass, dripping with deep red blood.

Chapter 2

Audie hovered at the edge of the window, in the small welcoming space where shoppers might leave umbrellas, rest on a settee, or cool off in a Midwestern August. The street-facing rooms had been dimmed so the world couldn't see inside.

But that didn't stop her from peeking out.

From between the window jamb and the holiday wreath, she took in the chaos. The entire population of St. Charles, St. Louis, and the surrounding municipalities blocked Main. Where Stuart had sung for his supper two hours ago, there were now shoulder-to-shoulder reporters and overly exuberant spotlights.

Fingers touched her back, and she leapt like a jackrabbit, spinning around with both fists raised. *Yes, because I'm the next mosquito-weight boxing champ.* Jude slid away a step.

"I come in peace."

"Good heavens, son." She retrieved her heart from where it had landed on the neighbor's roof and eased aside the lace curtain to resume peeping. It caught on something. A tiny loop snagged on what must be one of Fran's stained-glass pieces, slanting the hanging artwork a few degrees. Gingerly, she lifted the material away and straightened the art. No need to cause more damage tonight than had already been done.

"Sorry, I thought your Spidey senses heard me."

Activity filled the next room, the section boasting its artists' offerings. Vita's hand-crafted jewelry anchored one leg of the three-point layout, accustomed to happy lighting, refined beauty, and the oohs and aahs of impressed shoppers. Instead, the flash of a CSI camera strobed like a disco ball.

"Are they making any progress in there?"

"I guess. You know how it goes."

Why? Why do we know how it goes? How many dead bodies do we need to be adjacent to?

Wait—*recently* dead bodies. Long-dead was in a genealogist's job description.

Wasn't this supposed to be a vacation?

Vita materialized in the doorway to the foyer-slash-sitting area. The Simpson Boardinghouse had been renovated sixteen times since its establishment in 1804, and she'd led the way for the latest round of changes. The historic preservation board only cared about the outside appearance of the buildings. As long as the aesthetic from the cobblestone streets was right and the general architecture wasn't transmogrified or some such nonsense, the interior had more flexibility.

Just don't tell the honorable Mr. Dickens, er, Glen What's-his-face.

Vita's voice—calm, contained—cut into Audie's wandering thoughts. "You two don't have to stay here in the dark. The body's covered up and will be gone soon. The police say it's okay to come in with me. They've done what they need to do."

"Already?" Audie's fingers slid between Jude's, and she trailed him toward her sister.

"I told them I needed my emotional support people. And I guess procedures are different when the death is a, well…"

Suicide. Not saying it didn't make it any less true.

But what a way to go.

Jude said, "The city's sure been through the wringer. Burglaries, now this."

Audie caught the downturned corner of her older sister's lip. "The burglaries were a nuisance, yes, but it's been almost entirely worthless stuff, things that were easily concealable."

"You haven't had a problem, have you?" Jude rephrased himself as they stepped through the passageway and into the shop proper. "Before tonight, I mean."

"In two months of it, no."

Someone had cranked the lights in here up to eleven, the comforting aura of nostalgic gaslight and handcrafted wonders replaced by the need for sharp vision. Members of law enforcement moved in and out through the open back door. No wonder the ambient temperature was subarctic.

The store's wares were in such contrast to the white body bag lying zipped on the floor, it was nauseating. Racks of colorful scarves filled the corner farthest from the center of current attention. Thank heavens, because the mist of blood painting what must be Fran's workbench and her display case would've ruined every scrap of the dyed fabrics.

Vita's corner seemed to have escaped harm as well. Her case and counter overflowed with unique pendants and earrings, mostly silver, some bronze, some gold. Intricate wire designs adorned with beads and gems chimed as heavy shoes in disposable booties crossed the wooden flooring.

A woman wearing the cap of a patrol officer poked her head in through the rear door and addressed a man in a suit. "The morgue van is here."

A soft whimper drew Audie's attention to the right. Fran looked like a lost puppy, sitting on a bench against the opposite wall. Her coat lay draped over the seat beside her, folded to hide the fresh stains. She stared at her hands. At least someone had had the common sense to get her washed up.

"The blood came off pretty easily," Vita murmured. Of course, it would be Ms. Big Sister to the World doing the washing. "The coat is going to be a different story."

The trio skirted the bagged body and approached Fran. "Sweetheart, I've got some coffee brewing. It'll be ready in a minute."

She lifted a round face, but Vita may as well have been explaining nuclear physics. Once hidden by the now-missing knit hat, Fran's short-cropped hair was neon blue at the crown. It faded to ivory by her ears, accenting lobes lined with studs up to the arc. A red turtleneck, perfect for the season, stuck out from her denim overalls, cuffed at the ankles, with matching Converse high-tops. Like her outerwear, they too had been around the block, but nobody could say they weren't festive.

Audie picked up the coat and tucked it behind the old dining chair beside the bench. No one needed to be using the stains as an inkblot test just then. She perched on the seat's edge, Jude coming around to her side. It was hard to avoid looking at the body bag, but she tried. Her eyes fell on the glass art zone, hoping the joyful chaos of colorful rods, kaleidoscope ornaments, and an animal scene straight out of *The Glass Menagerie* would distract her rolling stomach.

Alone near the workbench sat a soft-sided tool bag, screwdrivers and a box cutter poking out from narrow pockets. Audie's hope for calm called it a day when she realized those weren't Fran's initials stitched on the side. The tools were more appropriate for a handyman than fine crafting.

They awaited an owner who would never return.

Vita settled down beside her trembling partner. "Does Trenton have Lizzie?"

Fran shook her head, once more studying her hands. It took two tries and a throat-clearing to get words past her lips. "Penny, my neighbor. It was only supposed to be for a few minutes while I ran over here for my list. But I called and told her what happened, and she's keeping Liz overnight."

"Perfect." She gestured to the Wests. "Fran, this is my sister, Audie, and her husband, Jude. I don't think you've met yet?"

She offered them both the best forced nod she could manage.

"Fran expanded from a home hobby to a business with us about six months ago. We're so happy to have her and her beautiful creations." Vi rubbed the woman's back, straightening the overall straps like she did for Connor when he was in preschool.

But the poor girl shuddered. "He didn't agree," she said, tilting her head toward the floor.

There, a twelve-inch-square glass panel lay in ruins. A few feet away, a single fragment rested by what must be the right side of the body. What a choice of weapon.

"It was a work in progress." Probably why he chose it. Close at hand, convenient. "He broke it to get to the edge, and…"

Yeah.

Three times sharper than a stainless-steel knife.

The blue-haired pixie had found her vocal cords, but the tremor they sprouted grew worse as her words flowed too fast. "There was so much blood. I've never seen so much blood. He—"

Vita pulled her into a hug. "I'm sorry, sweetie. But it's okay. You're okay, now." She cringed and amended herself. "It's over."

Except for the cleanup, that is.

"Do you know who it is, or was?" Jude had taken to pacing along the short wall. She couldn't blame him. The energy in here had lit every nerve on fire.

Vi inhaled deeply and frowned anew. "His name was Kurt Boulton. He's a jack-of-all-trades, doing general maintenance for us and lots of other businesses. Some cleaning, some fixing."

"Some stealing," Fran mumbled.

Jude paused at a turn, head cocked. Vi's lips pursed. "Apparently, he was our local thief. I guess he makes the most sense out of anybody. He had keys to every building because we all used him."

"But we used him because he was so trustworthy," Fran argued. "I haven't been here long, but he always acted ready to help. I don't understand."

There was a lot of that going around.

Vi motioned toward the body bag. "The police found a drafting set and a pocket watch from 1875 in his tools. Both had been reported missing this morning. One was in the front window of the architect's office across the street. The watch had hung on a wall at the cycling shop a couple doors down."

"Then… I'm confused." Jude wasn't the only one.

"What they told me…" Fran fought her inner turmoil like the prizefighter Audie wasn't. "What they told me was that an empty bottle of whiskey was near Kur—the body. It had rolled under my workbench, so I didn't see it at first." She squeezed her eyes shut. She didn't want to see any of that ever, ever again. The evidence marker for the bottle rested beneath a sort of lateral file on wheels, only instead of paper or folders, it contained one-foot-square stained-glass panels of a variety of colors and designs. "The liquor was on his breath. That, I noticed. They think he was going to burgle our place next—burgle, is that a word?—but the booze and the guilt got to him. He was holding one of my photos of Lizzie…"

And there came the tears. Another Big Sister bear hug. Audie didn't mind sharing.

Propped up on the glassworking bench were three four-by-six frames, each a snap of a curly-haired pixie. In one, the kindergartner wore a St. Louis Cardinals jersey and matching ribbons in her hair. Dots of red that had nothing to do with baseball dotted the outside of the protective pane.

"They said he'd been divorced for ages. I never knew that. He has a daughter he hasn't seen in, like, twenty years. Didn't know that either." She turned raw eyes to Vita, mascara smudged on cherubic cheeks. "How could we not know that? He was a man. He was hurting. Maybe he wouldn't have stolen those things if someone had treated him better."

"Sweetheart, we do the best we can."

She'd known. Vita would've known about the divorce and the daughter. If anyone could peel the armor of someone's life without letting them realize what was happening, it was her sister. *And Jude says I'm the empath.*

Must be genetic.

Two people wearing jackets that read St. Charles County Morgue entered the room with a gurney. One was a woman no taller than Audie. As they hoisted the body bag, she had no problem.

Apparently it was true about lifting with one's legs.

The man in the suit watched them strap down the body and roll it out of the building. As the photographer packed away her gear, the presumed lead approached their corner. "I don't think I've met you two yet. Detective Adrian Flores."

Audie reached out her hand, dead-fish white compared to his vibrant bronze. Jude did the same.

"We're wrapping up for now."

"Good." Fran wiped at her eye.

But Vita had caught the qualifier. "What do you mean, for now?"

"It looks like a simple case of suicide." He grimaced as soon as he said it. "I didn't mean simple. Suicide is never simple. But there was no forced entry of the building and no weapon found other than the glass by his hand, which looks appropriate for the wound."

Thank heavens Fran had grabbed a different remnant of her smashed creation when she'd run outside. Her fingerprints didn't need to be on the actual makeshift scalpel.

"But?" Jude voiced the word they all heard unsaid.

"Yeah, but." The detective's phone buzzed. He gave it a perfunctory glance and stowed it in his pocket. "First, you've got a biohazard on your hands."

"The authorities don't take care of that?"

"No, but we'll leave you with information on professionals who will. Your business insurance should cover the cost."

Sure, because indie artists always pay for the comprehensive crime-scene-clean-up package.

"And second?"

"The official cause of death is pending a medical examination. The M.E. has to make the call and sign off."

"How long will that take?"

"At minimum, a few days."

"Well," Vita exhaled, "we'll get the place cleaned, then we'll be able to stay occupied with Christmas sales while we're waiting." Audie watched her sister mentally calculate which rug from the house could cover that awful patch until it was properly sanded and restained.

"That's the thing." Flores must've chosen a knot in the wall three inches above Vi's head to address, because he couldn't look the ladies in the eye as he broke the worst of the news. "You can't reopen until we get everything sorted out."

"What?" Audie caught Fran's arm as she started to jump from her seat.

"I'm sorry, but if it turns out to be something other than suicide, this is a crime scene. Technically, it's a crime scene anyway, and it has to stay that way until the official ruling."

"We can't sell during the last seven days before Christmas?" Vita, too, looked stunned. "Do you have any idea how busy we are at this time of year?"

"And only at this time of year?" Fran was beside herself, pulling at the lowest of her earrings. "No, I need this money. We can't close now. I've got rent to pay, Christmas gifts for Lizzie. We can't go without a paycheck just because somebody decided to end it all in the middle of our shop!"

"I know. But it's not up to me."

"Can't you gather any evidence now and be done with it?"

"No." A hush fell on the room, the most quiet they'd heard since the ghost tour's abrupt conclusion. "Folks, I really am sorry. If somebody's already despondent or struggling, the holidays pile it on. In Mr. Boulton's case, you add in the guilt from the thefts and too much alcohol?"

The shock of the shutdown painted Fran a sickly green, and she searched the detective for answers and hope. "If Kurt was the thief, what's he been doing with the stolen stuff?"

"I've already spoken with my colleagues about the thefts. They've been watching the markets like a hawk, but nobody's seen any movement of the pieces. Private buyers aren't ruled out, of course. But we're heading to his apartment after we finish here. There's the possibility that he didn't steal the items to sell them, or at least not yet. We hope to find his stash there."

Pausing beside Audie, Jude asked, "He didn't leave a note or anything?"

"They don't always," he said, looking more tired than his age should've made him. Law enforcement service must count like dog years. "It's impossible to understand what's going through another person's head. If he felt that much shame, he might not have wanted to ponder it at the end." He shrugged. "I can't help but think he might've liked you ladies, and that kept him from nicking anything from here. Your shop was one of the lucky few he hadn't hit."

Fran's tears restarted. "Yeah, we're lucky all right."

Vi gripped her hand. "Don't worry about a thing, Frannie. Nobody's having a crummy Christmas on my watch."

"Or ours," Jude added. "We have contacts inside the elf union."

The policeman saw his chance and turned to make his escape. A loud commotion out the back door froze him in his tracks.

CHAPTER 3

Officious voices rose to shouts as they argued with someone about yellow tape. They lost that battle in the opening volley.

"I'm not staying behind any silly tape, yellow, red, or polka-dotted, young man. I have friends inside, and I will not stand out in this cold one second longer. Now, scoot."

Detective Flores and Jude hurried toward the door through which Kurt Boulton had been wheeled, but Vita called them off.

"That's Darla, the D in DFV. She's with us."

An older woman with long, narrow braids, a flowing skirt beneath a maroon parka, and a floral lacquered cane appeared in the doorway. After one scrutinizing stink eye, daring them to try her, the men chose a life of peace. As she stepped between them, she nodded with approval. "Glad somebody's got some sense around here."

She scuttled toward her business partners as fast as her three legs allowed. "Are you all right?"

"We're okay, Darla." Vi spoke for both of them, because Fran was blowing her nose. "I'm sorry I hadn't called you yet. How did you know to come?"

"Honey, have you seen the street out there? We're the lead story on every channel." She unbuttoned her coat, fired up from parting the Red Sea. "We'd just gotten in from the church pageant. There I was, plopped on the sofa with Lionel, researching that shibori dye technique I was telling you about? The man starts shaking my arm like he's having a fit or something. Well, I lost the website I'd finally found, so I was plenty irritated, but then I saw what he was blubbering about. There, on the big screen, is our building, lit up like Christmas!"

She paused, remembering the month. "You know what I mean. I got my shoes back on, and that Vin Diesel fella would've been proud of my driving skills. First, they're blocking our rear lot, then they didn't want me walking anywhere near the shop. I couldn't go out front with those goofy newspeople acting like Jimmy Hoffa had been dug up in here. How many reporters does it take to say the same thing? Some sad soul ushered himself out. End of story."

Jude resumed his pacing—expanding the route now that a certain handyman's earthly remains had moved on—and Audie stood to offer her seat.

"No, no, I'm fine."

"She's not going to sit again," Vi patted the cushion, "so you might as well take it."

The newcomer hesitated, but then removed her canary-colored bucket hat and eased onto the cushion with her left leg stretched out straight.

"Darla, this is my sister, Audie, and her husband, Jude."

"Pleasure to finally meet you—not under these circumstances, of course. But your sister talks about you all the time."

"That could go two ways." Jude tried for his no-fail charmer smile, and it failed before it hit his eyes, sabotaged by the aforementioned circumstances.

Darla chuckled. "Don't worry. I think she only tells the good parts. Some folks are like that. And some don't tell anything but the bad." She played with the brim of the hat on her lap and quieted. "They didn't say on the news who it was, Vi."

"Kurt Boulton."

The woman's deep brown eyes widened.

"Not only that, but he was apparently the one pinching antiques up and down Main."

Darla's mouth hung open for all of two seconds before she snapped it shut. "I won't believe it. Mr. Boulton was too nice of a man."

"Nice doesn't always mean innocent." How often had they learned that lately? People acting one way in public, a monster behind closed doors…

Dr. Jekyll and Mr. Hyde weren't the final entry on that list.

Audie's wandering hubby had paused by the counter flowing with a rainbow of fabrics. Agitated fingers picked up a photo frame. "Are these your children?"

It broke the horror of the moment. He excelled at that.

"Yes." Her face softened for the first time since she'd arrived. "That's my son, Ronald, his wife and their two children. The older boy, RJ, was a shepherd in the pageant tonight. It's why I was hustling to get out of here earlier." The idea that she might've met the thief-slash-dead man at the store obviously crossed her mind, and she hurried on, pointing to a second frame. "And that's my girl." Another pic had been tucked into the corner of the glass. "The family's had a population boom."

"Twins?" He brought the photos over. The original shot showed an attractive woman in her late twenties beside a man who could've doubled for Denzel Washington in the actor's early days. It was a forest pose, both sitting on a log in far nicer clothes than Audie would've worn out there, but complementing the autumn foliage. In her hair, she wore one of her mother's scarves, reminiscent of a watercolor painting. The two held each other's eyes and hands like they were the last people on earth.

The smaller snapshot had the same couple in a hospital, now beaming beside a pair of incubators.

"Preemies." Darla's eyes glistened. "So new, they're still in the NICU. The worry those angels have been causing! First, Rachelle was on bed rest for weeks, then they had no choice but to take the babies early. The medical bills stack up with each fresh crisis, and they're running out of paid leave." She raised her chin and shook it off. "But it'll be okay. They came into an unexpected windfall that'll help. Lord knows Lionel and I can't give as much as we'd like." Her thumb wiped at a microscopic water droplet on her cane until Audie worried for its lacquer, and she reset herself, turning to Vita. "Kurt really...?"

"It was Fran who found him."

The youth of the group had gone radio silent, and even now only conjured up a kind of chant. "That glass, my glass."

Darla's eyes landed on the center of the floor. "Lord have mercy."

Agreed.

Wait—where did the detective go? Audie heard him outside, talking about getting into the victim's apartment.

Victim? Is that what we call someone who took their own life? They certainly suffered. They certainly felt a compulsion they couldn't stop, and they weren't in a rational state when they made the decision.

Victim fit.

She understood better than anyone in that room. Pain, guilt, an oppressive weight like Mt. Everest resting on your head and chest. Death beckoned. And, oh, for that escape? Why wouldn't you take it? Why wouldn't you end the suffering and bathe in the utter relief?

Because life was sacred, painful or not. And while she understood the compulsion, she prayed for the strength to cling to it.

The temptation would never slip away, though.

"Audie?"

She forced her eyes from the bloody constellation on the rustic floors and turned to her sister. "Yeah?"

"Boy, you'd wandered off. I asked if you were ready to go back to the house."

"Sorry. Yes, whenever you are."

Darla rose from her chair, accompanied by popping joints, and hobbled to her racks. "Not that it's the important part, but my things seem to have weathered the storm."

"The police are shutting us down until the M.E. rules on the cause of death."

Unlike the others, she immediately nodded. "That's what they'd do on *CSI*. Lionel watches so many of those shows, I had to order him to stay home tonight. He would've been all up in the detectives' business, asking about fingerprints and DNA and the rest of that stuff that makes us think we're Columbo."

Fran had gone as white as her platinum locks again. Darla grimaced.

"Frannie, let's get you out of here, okay? Do you want to stay at our house tonight? Is Lizzie taken care of somewhere?"

"She's at a friend's, thanks. And, no, I just want to go home." She extracted herself from Vita and got to her feet. Immediately, she swooned.

"Yeah, baby, you're fine on your own." Darla rolled her eyes. She backtracked to the bench, plopped her hat on her head, and offered Fran an arm. "I'll drive you anyway, okay? I didn't see your car outside."

"I'm parked on Main."

"No problem. We'll get it tomorrow."

Fran's second try succeeded. She steadied herself with a sniffle.

Jude snapped his fingers, hazel eyes brightening like an Edison bulb. "The car! Audie, you and Vi stay here. I'll run up to the house and bring the Jeep." They had walked the four blocks from Vita and Simon's to start the ghost tour. They'd need to circumvent the press and then suffer frostbite to walk home after seeing a dead man.

Unless, of course, St. Jude was on the job.

God bless the boy.

"Tonight, I won't complain," Vita accepted. "I'm sorry Simon's not here to help. He's going to want to come home when I call him."

Audie knew that face. She wouldn't call until tomorrow, and then she'd play it down so it didn't sidetrack him from business. Vi could handle it. Of course she could.

Or thought she could.

Sometimes, that was all she needed.

"We should tell Connor."

"Absolutely not."

"Vi, he's only a few miles away."

"On the other side of the river."

"There is a bridge, you know." Several, actually.

"He's been working too hard, getting his ducks in a row before the company shuts down between the holidays. Plus, he's been trying to perfect Grandpa's sausage recipe for Christmas Eve." She cringed at her sister with knowing eyes. "The poor child will never get it quite right. It can't be done."

"It's like Grandma's recipes," Audie agreed. "He left out some key ingredient without telling anybody, and he's laughing from heaven while we wonder about the magic."

No matter what, a Marik meal would never be mediocre.

Jude twisted his charcoal gray scarf around his neck, zipped up the ebony leather jacket, and pulled on his matching gloves.

"Please don't get hit out there while you're wearing Batman's wardrobe."

"Give me ten, fifteen minutes. I'll pull up at the rear, away from the cameras. Maybe some will have lost interest and gone home themselves by now."

"Thank you, hon. Text me when you're here. I don't want to be hanging around the windows."

"And what was it you were doing in front?" She gave him the expected smirk. With a grin, he slipped outside, telling the remaining officer he'd return shortly for the ladies.

"The man does like black, doesn't he?" Darla watched after him. Between her attire and Fran's, they'd fill a perfect painter's palette.

"Hopefully, that'll make him harder to spot by scoop-hungry journalists."

Audie helped Fran into her coat, and Darla gasped. "Honey, I'm taking that right off you when we get to your place. I'll have it clean by morning."

"No, Darla, I don't need you—"

"You need me more than you know," she retorted. "As does Lionel, but he hasn't learned that yet either. Vi, I'm sure I'll talk to you tomorrow—or rather, today." Audie glanced at the wall clock. Friday had tiptoed in when they were otherwise occupied.

"Do you want me to call our insurance, or are you going to take care of it?"

"I'll call and let you know what they say. Drive safe out there."

"Will do." They, too, disappeared into the night.

The Marik sisters stood alone in the room where Kurt Boulton had passed from this life to the next. The unsettled atmosphere seemed like something Dickens himself would've written, and a ghost would soon spring out of the floorboards.

Hmm. Less Dickens, more Poe.

"You got a saint for this situation?" With the crowd gone, her sister's words carried extra weight.

Audie began counting on her fingers. "St. Dymphna, patron of mental illnesses. St. Dismas, patron of thieves. St. Homobonus, patron of business owners."

"You made up that last one."

"Did not."

Vita side-eyed her, but little sister didn't flinch.

"Fine. I think we need them all. Real or not."

As he cut through the alley to the street above Main, Jude buried his fists in his pockets. The wind blew harder now than it had when Stuart regaled them with the saga of Josephine, Clarence, and Nathaniel. How many deaths would that building see? The years weren't in its favor, of course. Statistically speaking, any building over two centuries old could've had deaths occur within its walls.

But a brutal murder *and* a suicide?

Both with glass shards as the slicey thing of choice?

Obviously, Mr. Kurt Boulton knew the story of the legislator's wife. If he'd been in St. Charles long enough, he'd probably seen her ghost, or Stu would insist he had.

What drove him to the thefts? And why were the poached items worth pennies? Was he a lousy thief?

Better question: why do I care? This had nothing to do with him and Audie or even Vita, since they weren't burgled. Kurt's crime spree had ended, so as soon as Detective Flores and Company found the buried treasure, the whole sad escapade could be boxed up and put away as just another grim story.

We've seen enough grim stories lately to last a lifetime. They did not need to stick their noses into any new ones.

He reached the first empty intersection, scoped out all directions, and hurried across the street. Good. Nobody was tracking those leaving from the boutique's back door. A couple more blocks and he'd be at their home away from home.

What the—

He swallowed the last word, certain Audie could still read his mind at this distance, and dove behind the next bush of practical size. Down the hill, something large, flowy, and as dark as Stuart Morrison's top hat had... floated?... into the road. The shape stopped dead at the center and gazed up the incline.

Directly toward him.

Nope, we are not doing more weirdness tonight. Jude darted out of his hiding place and walk-ran the next block, his head on a swivel. At the intersection, there he was again. Or she. Or it or they. Three raccoons in a coat?

The creature—entity—was tall. Maybe four raccoons.

Another block. This time, the whatever-it-was peered from some evergreens in the side yard of a home. It continued to study him like slides under a microscope.

Or an ant to be incinerated with a magnifying glass.

"Absolutely not." Jude spun on his toes and sprinted, his calves reminding him why Monsieur Blanchette called this area *Les Petites Côtes*, The Little Hills. He wasn't to his in-laws' street yet—no reason to lead the phantom to home base. He looked over his shoulder, once, twice… but now, nothing was there. Backtracking, he turned left, then dropped behind a wooden cutout of Kris Kringle himself. The bowl full of jelly lent decent coverage for surveillance, but he was once more alone.

Had he imagined it? Was it somebody from the Holidays of Hope? Or a bored kid playing a prank?

He stayed behind the cutout, giving his lungs a chance to catch up, until he remembered the prevalence of doorbell cameras and nonchalantly retook the sidewalk. Over his pounding heart, he couldn't hear much, let alone footsteps.

Do phantoms make footsteps?

Not helpful.

He continued on, climbed another few blocks, turned right, and eventually rerouted in the proper direction. Turning the last corner, he was never so happy to see a certain high-mileage Jeep. Inspecting every shadow, mailbox, and inflatable reindeer, he sprinted like an Olympian and leapt behind the wheel, locking the doors. He checked each mirror, sank into the seat, and exhaled.

CHAPTER 4

The overstuffed chair in their attic bedroom would've had anyone else dozing in nanoseconds. But Audie didn't expect it to work its magic on her, even with multiple handmade afghans thrown into the mix.

Not tonight.

With her legs curled beneath her, she settled her head onto her forearm. Through a shadowy, sideways lens, she watched Jude roll over in the bed for the fifth time in the last two minutes.

Yeah, she couldn't stop seeing the shattered glass and the bloody spot either.

She should call Fran—that girl wouldn't be sleeping a wink for days.

Incoherent mumbles rose from the restless husband as he pushed at the blanket and flipped again. Usually, he was so spent by their typical day, the Sandman would've been collecting unemployment. She tuned out the furnace, the fancy clock on the dresser, and her own bullhorn of inner turmoil to focus only on what kept him from dreamland.

When he bolted upright with a soul-sucking gasp, she half fell off the chair. Snagging a toe on a crocheted loop, she stumbled across the floor and onto the bed beside him.

"Jude!" She put her hand on his shoulder, and he spun toward her with manic, unseeing eyes. "Honey, it's me. It's okay, it was just a dream."

Slowly, the veil between sleep and wakefulness lifted. But his breath came in slivers. He leaned forward, running unsteady fingers through the hair that had dropped across his left eye. Around his neck, the wyvern medal swung like a pendulum. "Oh wow."

She rubbed his upper back, feeling the coin-shaped scar tissue remaining from another terrible night. Cloaked by a covering of tattoos, it was funny to run across it by touch.

Not funny ha-ha.

"Are you okay?" The house remained quiet, so hopefully Vita hadn't woken downstairs. After their sisterly rehashing of the evening's awfulness, the two had only turned in an hour ago.

Jude held his forehead and stared toward his knees, blinking too much. "Yeah. I'm okay." He reached to her hand and squeezed it without making eye contact. "Sorry I woke you."

"You're hilarious. What was the dream?"

He paused, then just shook his head.

Her thumb ran across his knuckles. "After tonight, I'd be surprised if it was sugarplum fairies."

He tried to laugh. It didn't work. "Sorry."

As she lowered him onto his pillow, his skin felt clammy, and he pulled his right arm behind his neck. She laid down too, facing him. The blinking slowed, but he continued to contemplate the rafters.

Nobody's eyes were closing soon. Too many spirits were walking.

* * *

"Sounds like you were visited by the Ghost of Christmas Yet to Come."

Jude plated a stack of pancakes onto a Santa serving platter and turned off Vita's stove. When faces had formed in the batter's bubbles, he knew they were done.

Not his normal cooking strategy. But it hadn't been a normal twelve hours.

"The creepy one that foretells of Tiny Tim's demise because his dad's boss was a miserly cretin?" He hadn't told them about the phantom chase when they'd gotten home—it had been horrendous enough already. But when Audie had pressed more about his nightmare this morning, he decided to spill the beans on his experience.

Beans. Tina the Beheaded Ragdoll.

Oof.

The chase had been unsettling. Disturbing.

But it wasn't as disturbing as the dream.

"Yes, him. Or her. Or they." Audie sipped her coffee while her sister made lists of things to do that day, now that her regular schedule had been derailed by one Mr. Kurt Boulton. "Your description matches. Flowing robes, unseen face, unearthly movements."

He carried the platter and a spatula to the table, then returned with the maple syrup. He'd have the carbs burned off before he ate them. "Is that supposed to make me feel better?"

"Absolutely not." Vi set aside her notepad, and Jude slipped breakfast onto the plates of both Marik daughters. "I'm just glad you escaped. I never get service like this."

Audie admired the golden brown frisbees without touching them. "Do you think he was chasing you?"

"I don't know what else you'd call it." He pulled out his chair and sat down to a stack twice as high as the ladies'. He missed cooking for Simon, Connor, and Becca.

Ten percent of him was happy there was more for himself.

"So this phantom thing followed you?"

Jude chewed through a bite of spiced apples larger than he should've taken and put up a finger to pause questioning until he swallowed. It took longer than polite, but he didn't plan to die by cinnamoned fruit. No need to add to the spectral head count.

"Followed? Stalked? I don't know. It was tall, dark, and not so handsome, but I couldn't see any details. Where it emerged from the ether was the one street not blazing with Christmas lights."

Vita frowned, reaching for the syrup. "We're supposed to stay relatively historic around here. Giant inflatable snowmen, made in China, were not a staple of decor in 1820 Missouri."

"He didn't approach you, did he?" A fluffy wedge had made it as far as Audie's fork. Progress.

"No, but I didn't give the dude an opportunity either." He hadn't climbed under their warm covers until 2 a.m., and then after that dream... A tremor shot through every vital organ, and he pushed away from the table, going back for the coffee pot. "Can I top anyone off?"

"Drinks all around, please." Vita raised her mug. Handmade, with painted pine trees and a snow scene, it must've come from another talented craftsman a few blocks down the hill.

"You haven't heard from Detective Flores yet, have you?" Audie asked.

Her sister grimaced. "I've been informed the police had to sleep sometime too."

"I guess they'll find the stolen items at Boulton's place." He finished pouring duties. "I wonder what the deal was. Do you think he was waiting to sell the stuff later, when the heat was down?"

Audie grinned. "The heat? Better make sure the fuzz doesn't give you a bad rap in the ol' slammer, Al Capone."

He raised the syrup in her direction. As he enjoyed living, he did not follow through.

Vita, accustomed to their antics, ignored them. "I guess everything will be back to normal soon enough. I'm glad folks will get their things. Half the stores on Main had been burgled. Most items were decorative, but they meant something to someone." She put down her fork, considering the flapjacks. "You know, I'm not complaining about the shop being closed, because that'd be crass. A man we knew personally took his own life, and in a gruesome way, a week before a major religious holiday." She paused, lifting her eyes to examine the stained-glass lamp hanging over the table, and sighed. "But we really need to be able to open."

Christmas, year-end taxes, shop rent—the bills she must have. "Whatever we can do to help, Vi."

She cut him off. "No, that wasn't what I meant. Simon and I are fine, hon, but thank you. I'm lucky. I've got long-standing clients who buy regularly. I have products in a few other stores around the county. And, of course, Simon's job isn't peanuts." No, the chief data analyst at a major biotech firm doesn't need to be supported by his wife's creations, however expertly made. "It's Fran I'm worried about."

He took another bite, one more suitable for genteel company. "Tell us more about what she does."

"She's a glass artist, of course, but that covers a spectrum. She excels at them all, or at least the ones she has the workspace to handle and the upfront money to kick-start. An uncle taught her when she was in her teens, and she's only gotten better. Glass beads, stained glass, cane glass. Lately, she's been researching dichroic glass."

"Sounds like something from a sci-fi movie. Does it fuel rockets?"

"I'd like to see that one. The way I understand it, dichro, as the cool kids call it, is a technique where two layers of glass are fused together to form the finished product. I assume voodoo is involved. In some, the resulting colors or picture are different, depending on how you look at it or how the light hits it."

"Okay, so maybe more fantasy than sci-fi."

"They've found evidence of it as far back as a goblet in the fourth century. It's green if viewed from one direction, blood red in the other." She bit her lip at her own word choice and hurried on. "Yes, a wizard would like her merchandise. The process became easier to do in the 1960s, but it's still no simple project. Her collection has been selling well, but she just joined Darla and me this year. She was lucky our place is still growing its roots; we had room for another maker." Vita laughed. "You should've seen how excited she was when the F for Fran went into our name. But now, her third of the rent is an expense she didn't have. And with Lizzie and the divorce…"

Audie cringed. "Messy?"

Vita reached for her mug and frowned. "Trenton is the definition of a schmuck. Fran will be the first to tell you their marriage went off the rails because of things they both did. They married young." Her eyes flitted to her sister, who didn't look away. "But that's not always a problem, of course. Then they had Lizzie, who is the cutest thing you've ever seen."

"I loved that photo down at the store. I hope it wasn't ruined."

"It looked like just the frame and glass were stained. It should come off. And if not, I know what I'm getting her for Christmas. Fran has worked so hard with what she's got and is such a natural mom."

"Is the shop her only income?"

"Heavens, no. We may be 'talented artisans of the fair city,' per the Ghost of Charles Dickens, but it's impossible to support a family on what we sell, especially early in a career. She's a veterinary assistant at a clinic nearby. After high school, she enrolled in college, but never finished. No attention span for the book stuff. But you should see her with the pups and kitties. The woman has a way about her."

"A five-year-old must love that."

She nodded. "Fran occasionally takes Lizzie over there on her off-hours, which aren't many. She'd been thinking about getting her a rabbit for Christmas." Her brow creased.

"So what's this Trenton do?"

"A lot of nothing, if you ask me." Vi took a bite of pancake, and Jude worried for the fork. She calmed as she chewed. "That's not true and not charitable. He did earn a degree—business, I think—and he does accounting for a manufacturing plant over in St. Peters. But in the evenings and on weekends, he thinks he deserves his 'me time.' The boy has forgotten he has a child, that the child needs clothes and things for school and the love of her father."

Love of a father. How quaint.

Cut it out, you. No projecting today.

Yes, sir.

Besides, the tot in that picture was cuter than you were at that age.

Truth.

"What does he do in this me time? Because I'm picturing excessive manscaping."

Vita laughed and almost knocked over her coffee, which would've been tragic. "If only. He plays with his little friends and games. He's a gamer. When did that become a verb? I'm too old for this new world." She finished her plate, surveyed Jude's, and stole a piece from his.

"I can make more."

Vita grabbed his arm as he rose. "Don't you dare. I'd like to fit into a decent dress for Christmas Eve Mass." She examined her sister's stack, still mostly intact. "Besides, I know an unused stockpile."

Audie smirked at her and took a bite to prove a point.

Vita continued, nonplussed. "It leaves the parenting to Fran and has her stuck in a marriage where she's neither loved nor appreciated. Now that they're divorcing, she needs every penny she can scrounge, because she doesn't want Trent getting sole custody."

"A judge would favor him?"

"He has parents nearby, and she doesn't, so he's got support in terms of babysitting and such. And he's the higher wage earner."

"He *wants* custody?"

Vi's drop earrings—products of her own making—rattled as shook her head. "Only to spite her. He's a real stand-up guy like that."

He felt his wife's gaze on him and found those gray-marble eyes sending out silent appreciation. He flushed. "Why is it so hard for some people not to be a jerk? To take care of those you claimed to love?"

"Let's put it this way: he wouldn't have been dodging midnight phantoms to spare his wife and sister-in-law a freezing walk home." Vita paused. "Now I'm sad about pilfering your pancake."

"You're housing us. I think we're square." He'd hit the jackpot with this family.

"Nonsense." She dismissed him and gathered plates. Well, two out of three. In an optimistic corner of her soul, she held faith that her sister would finish a meal again someday.

Not likely, but thanks for playing.

"So, it comes down to her needing that shop open for this last week of the Christmas shopping season. We get lots of traffic drawn in by the Holidays of Hope crew."

"Other than the carolers, I guess there's a Dickens vibe going on?"

"Actually, Glen Armquist is the sole Dickensian, and he's freelancing, you could say. The group shuffled him out last go-around after he raised a holy ruckus, complaining the wassail vendor's recipe wasn't certified by the official wassail consortium or something."

"Sounds like he ought to be playing Scrooge."

"He'd win an Oscar. I guess he means well, but you know, maybe he doesn't. Anyway, we've got plenty of Santas from around the world, the highlight being Père Noël—Father Christmas, French-style, since St. Charles was founded by the French."

"So, no Bob Cratchit, no Tiny Tim…"

"And no three ghosts," she said, nodding. "Whatever you saw doesn't match any of the costumed characters this year."

Grand.

Vita plucked a dish towel off the oven door, tossed it over her shoulder, and began running the tap. "It's crazy, from the day after Thanksgiving to Christmas Eve. But it's also fun. I'll never tire of hearing the music, so long as they keep a healthy dose of the traditional carols, preferably sung with harmonies."

And there's the difference. Radio stations playing the same five '90s songs plus the rocking Brenda Lee had led to his annual boycott of the all-holiday programming.

"I wish you'd hear something about reopening." Audie took two more bites and pushed away her plate.

"I don't suppose you have any brilliant ideas to get us moving sooner?" The elder Marik didn't turn from the sink, but the hope in her tone was pronounced.

"Despite our last few jobs, we are not a deputized branch of law enforcement."

Vita shrugged and tested the water temperature. "It was worth a shot. In any case, you're supposed to be on vacation. I'm going to do a supply run this morning. I'm getting low-ish on solder, and if we're dead in the water at the shop, I might as well be doing something productive." She looked to Jude, who had taken her towel. "How are you two planning to fill the day?"

He immediately gestured toward the table. "Please consult my social secretary."

The gray marbles went for a spin. "I've got more titles than a library. Anyway, Stuart mentioned the old Capitol site last night. I don't think I've been in there since I was in grade school. It might be interesting to see it with adult eyes."

Vi plunged the first dishes into the sink. "There's so much to learn. Even locals don't realize our fledgling state government took its first steps here."

"Can you imagine senators today in a hot upstairs room above a hardware store?"

"I'll bet the pontificating was shorter."

"I wouldn't be so sure. Politicians are politicians. Have you ever read some of James Madison's stealthy notes taken during the Constitutional Convention?"

Facts. And if Lin-Manuel Miranda could make a blockbuster musical about the founding of our nation, there was drama aplenty.

"The museum is small, but you can get a tour of the building itself for a few dollars. They've done wonders with the place since the State Parks took it over in the 1970s. I hear they're focused on improving their historical accuracy now."

"Be still my beating heart." His wife was drooling more for that than for his homemade hotcakes.

Rude.

"You know," Vita said, giving the platter she was scrubbing more attention than it required, "if you two settled down here, you'd make a perfect ranger for the site. You could expand their research, bring in additional artifacts, give tours."

"I'd have to stand on a ladder for folks to see me on the tours, Vi. But I'll keep that in mind."

He glanced out the kitchen window, but found no pigs flying. At present, the camper and the nomad life suited them fine. Vita knew it. She only wanted her sibling to be happy, and it was the one thing she couldn't provide.

"I'm just saying."

"I know what you're saying. And I appreciate it, Mom."

As their laugh faded, Jude watched from the side as Vi's expression dimmed a degree.

"Speaking of Mom."

Audie reached for her mug. "I know. I'll go see her."

Jude began drying the plates with more fervor. He didn't want to be in the middle of this one.

"You don't have to. You know she won't remember."

"It's Christmas. She's our mother."

"I'll go on Christmas Eve before church. You don't need to go on the holiday. Make it a quick stop. We'll bake her some cookies. If she's eating, she'll be distracted and won't ask about—"

The sentence stopped mid-air. Jude, reaching to place the skillet on its shelf, barely breathed.

She won't ask about Ollie.

"I should be used to it by now. And it's not her fault."

Not her fault that the Alzheimer's had stolen anything later than eighteen years ago? Yes, but at what cost? That meant the only spouse of Audra Marik's that Irina remembered was Oliver Garland, dead for all but one of those years. Jude himself wasn't a blip on her radar, and Audie had told him to stop trying. Whenever he'd shown up, edgy black hair, tattooed arm, leather coat, she'd acted like he was the devil incarnate and been scared and judgmental. Nobody needed that. He'd styled the fringe more conventionally, covered the ink, borrowed some of Simon's business clothes—it didn't matter. She didn't understand what happened to Ollie. She didn't understand who this strange man was with her secondborn. She didn't get that her perfect son-in-law was so long gone and her daughter broken in so many ways.

It wasn't a good thing.

But it was Christmas. And Audra West wasn't about to miss visiting at Christmas. "I'll go in the next couple of days. It'll be fine."

"I'll go with you."

"No, you're busy enough. And you see her more than I do."

"Sweetie, it doesn't matter anymore. She doesn't remember."

"I don't mean for her sake, but for yours. You've got the harder load."

Vi waved it off. "The community she's in is awesome. We're lucky."

Jude lifted the last plate from the sink rack and spun the towel around it. Audie stood and slipped her mug into the water just before Vi could pull the plug.

"I promise to do the next batch." She squeezed her sister's arm, winked at her husband, and headed toward the hall staircase. "I'll be ready to leave in a few."

Vita clicked her tongue. "She's going to need twelve layers out there today."

"We'll make plenty of cocoa stops." Jude took the last-last mug, dried it, and slipped it onto its peg. He stared at the winter moonscape painted on the side and dropped his voice. "Vi, can I ask you something?"

"So long as it isn't the family chili recipe, yes." She stopped, putting one hand on her hip and the fingers of the other tapping at her lips. "Hang on, you came up with that recipe, so go ahead."

He smiled, the pressure of the question fleeing. "That story last night, about the state rep and his wife?"

"Unfortunate Josephine? Yes?"

"Was that legit? Or mostly so? Stuart told some whoppers."

"That's putting it mildly. But yes, that's his one factual tale. Stu adds drama—I think he's a frustrated actor—but politicians were involved, so maybe it was more melodramatic than even he could make it." She took his towel, wiped her hands, and leaned back against the counter. Her study of him was almost as piercing as her sister's. "Why?"

"Just curious." Yeah, she didn't believe it. That's okay, it wasn't true. "Then since you practically live at the scene of the crime, have you ever seen her?"

Now the woman's eyes widened. "Seen Josephine?" He blushed as she tilted her head at him. "Jude West, I think you've got phantoms on the brain."

He laughed it off. "I do. Forget I asked." He gave her a peck on the cheek, then turned to follow his wife toward the attic.

It's silly, ghost guides and fools like us going on tours like that. Harmless entertainment, though. Right?

Yesterday, he would've agreed. But the woman with the crooked head who'd reached out, begging, pleading, in his fitful slumber, had managed to change his mind.

Chapter 5

A parade of cars, SUVs, and an F-150 rolled through the intersection of South Main and Jefferson as Audie huddled at the curb with Jude.

"Only a single pickup. Not our normal day out." One gloved hand drew the short straw and had to relinquish its cozy pocket to shade her eyes from the morning sun. The sky was a vivid blue while the windchill announced the season with obnoxious enthusiasm.

"We aren't in rural Missouri anymore, Toto." As the last vehicle passed, they stepped into the shadows of old buildings lining the bumpy street. Jude snagged her hand before it reclaimed its burrow. She wouldn't complain; he had a better internal furnace.

"Only for a little while. I can hear the camper calling."

"It has access to a phone line in the Nelsons' storage barn?"

"It was in the fine print of the rental agreement."

"That farm is very accommodating."

They reached the opposite curb and turned right. The goal: a brown State Historic Site sign swinging from short chains a block away. "At least we're getting better about packing for Vi and Simon's."

"Only two trips to the trailer so far."

"Progress, not perfection."

Audie found herself tugged backward.

"Speaking of perfection…"

The good-looking fella attached to the end of her arm had paused to study a plate-glass window filled with German meats and other European delectables. An aroma of sage, pepper, and pork wafted out to them.

"You cannot be hungry."

He glanced at her sideways. "Have we met? Besides, one doesn't have to be hungry to appreciate the finer things in life."

"They're not open yet. We'll stop by after lunch with Vita, and you can resupply my sister's refrigerator."

"I'm eager to try Connor's attempt at the sausage recipe."

It was guaranteed to be delicious and served with an overflowing side of nostalgia—bundling up after the Christmas Vigil Mass and stepping into the snug kitchen of Grandma and Grandpa Marik, a thousand scents and colors, blinking faux candles on the tree…

It didn't matter if her nephew nailed Grandpa's recipe. Everything was right in the world.

Either a stray cloud or the pall of last night reminded her otherwise.

She inhaled through frozen nostrils, and her beloved hubby, thinking she just wanted to get out of the cold, abandoned his gawking to resume the walk.

At the bookstore across the street, the double doors wore wreaths created from old book pages. The bakery beside it advertised yule logs in a variety of flavors—classic, red velvet, vanilla, mulled spice, and pumpkin. *Order now for pickup by Christmas.* A few stops away, a carriage driver adjusted the nose bag on a stunning sable horse. His cart's red velvet seats—not to be mistaken for the yule log innards—could've carried couples between the French colonial homes for holiday gatherings. On this Friday, it awaited its first tourists. From beneath plaid wool covers, they'd listen to tales of Glen Armquist's fine city while the driver earned extra cash for grandkid gifts.

But the local handyman would be miss it all.

Her arm was tugged again. "Jude, I promise, you're not going to starve."

"No, goofy. You're passing the site."

Oops.

The door stuck as Jude pushed, finally exploding open with a crash of sleigh bells. The unlucky woman behind the desk fumbled with glasses knocked askew by their less-than-subtle arrival.

"We've got to get that thing fixed." She settled the wire frames on her face and reconfigured her soft white bangs into a presentable condition. "Welcome to Missouri's First State Capitol. Are you here for a tour?"

The space was loaded with souvenirs—sweatshirts that read 'Show-me State,' mugs with the latitude and longitude of St. Charles, an entire wall of books written about the regional lore. "Yes, please."

"Wonderful. Ranger Quinn will be starting one in about ten minutes. Tickets are five dollars."

"What a deal." Audie fished the money out of her crossbody purse. The hobo bag was resting at the camper for the next couple of weeks. No need to haul her whole genealogical office along while on vacation.

"It's a steal, isn't it? Have you visited us before?"

"I have, but about a hundred years ago. I grew up across the river in St. Louis County."

"I'm a newbie," Jude added. "Ohio's capital moved around like a game of musical chairs for its first thirteen years. I want to see if Missouri was any more put-together than my home state."

Edith, per her official name tag, must've regained her full visual senses because her eyes lingered on Jude a smidge longer than necessary. His magic seemed to be working today.

Like his magic ever doesn't work.

But with minimal rest and bad dreams to boot, he's still radiating that much… Judeness?

The boy had a gift.

"We've got a small museum. You can check out the displays and our ranger will find you when he's ready to start."

"Fantastic, Edith. Thank you."

Once more with the blushing. "Anything you need, sweetheart. You know where I'll be."

Sure, assuming she doesn't have a heart attack when this Quinn fellow opens the door shortly. Audie slipped around a display of postcards, plush animals, and colonial-style toy drum kits—those lucky parents—and through an arched entry.

"Boy, when she said small, she wasn't lying."

The area was maybe ten feet by twelve feet. The framed posters and the glass exhibit cases were curated to professional standards but tried to cram two hundred years into a shoebox. Jude squeezed around her and poked his head through a side passage.

"There's more here, but that's all she wrote."

"Fortunately, we don't have to kill much time."

A green arrow pointed to what she hoped was the starting line and not somebody's idea of messing with a fellow historian, because that would be mean. The placard listed comments made about St. Charles in its earliest days by folks who saw the settlement as nothing but lowly frontier, a place not suited for the civilized.

That lowly frontier was furnishing your fancy fashions. No more had she thought it than she came upon a pedestal housing a gentleman's top hat. The sign explained it was made from beaver pelt. *Like I said.*

The beaver trade was a funny story from what she remembered. White Americans and Europeans decided the material was *trés chic*, but they weren't patient enough to wait out the beavers in their homes nor smart enough to take down the large mammals when the opportunity arose. They became middlemen for Native people who had the skills but not the markets. That dam-building critter, plus raccoon, mink, fox, and deer, built this and many other burgs along the Missouri River with the fur off their backs. Had it not been for a change in style in the 1830s, when silk became the more popular material, the beaver would be extinct today.

A certificate to her right, adorned in swooping calligraphy, caught her eye. It honored a certain Mr. Clarence Richards of Chariton County.

Clarence Richards… who was—?

"Oh!"

From the next room, Jude asked, "Did you say something?"

She stepped closer to the framed document. "Josephine, the slain woman from last night's talk?"

"Yeah?" Just hearing her name made him sound queasy.

"Her husband received a commendation about a month before her death. 'For honorable and upright service to his community after the PL Chevenard Warehouse Fire.'" She skimmed the wording, then moved on to the explanation beside it. "'The warehouse, located at the north end of town, was a major storage unit for pelts arriving from upriver. The building suffered a raging fire on June 15, 1821, leaving stores here and portions of the clothing market back East in shambles.'"

"Our boy Clarence helped put out the fire?"

She raised a finger to the type. "No word about that. But his home county is also along the Missouri, in the middle of the state, and they had a solid fur trade too. He arranged to get supplies from his area brought here fast, selling them at a significant discount so businesses wouldn't go under and the fashion business wouldn't look elsewhere while St. Charles was recovering."

"What a swell guy."

"It's signed by the acting governor, as this was still two months prior to statehood."

At least Mr. Richards had one win before that summer's end. The remainder would not be so pleasant.

Audie joined Jude in the second space, which was no bigger. A special exhibit on slavery filled most of the walls. The city and its neighbor of St. Louis had a sad legacy where race was concerned.

"Man, check out this newspaper ad for a fugitive slave." Her husband leaned over a children's 'Touch This' display of arrowheads to read a reproduced print above it. "'A liberal reward offered for the return of runaway known as Cicero. Missing from the Weimer farm since 27 June. Thought to be traveling to the river and then north. Must be delivered in adequate physical condition.'"

"May God have mercy on our souls." Her ancestors weren't in the United States when that ad had been written. They escaped Eastern Europe at the turn of the twentieth century, running from their own tyrants and oppressive governments. But the toll on people of color in this country?

"Good thing we're known as the Cave State. The next poster says some caves nearby were used to hide enslaved folks on the run."

Audie crossed to his side, combing through her mental card catalog. "Missouri entered the Union as a slave state. That's why they had to wait until Maine was ready to join the country and the Missouri Compromise was hammered out, to even things out again."

"It sounds like somebody doesn't need my tour."

Behind her, a tall man with rich umber skin stood in the doorway. He wore the tan and olive-green uniform of a State Park Ranger like he'd been born into it. The brown campaign hat was the icing on the cake.

"Not in the slightest. I know how much I don't know."

"That's half the battle. I'm Quinn Thackeray, head ranger at the First Capitol Historic Site. You two have tickets for the tour?"

Jude reached into his jacket and produced the slips.

"Perfect. Looks like you're getting the private version this morning."

"That's useful, because she asks six thousand questions." He grinned as his wife smirked at him.

"And he asks the rest. Slow day?"

He motioned for them to follow him out through the gift shop and held the persnickety door as they passed onto the sidewalk. "We'll be busier after lunch and then especially between Christmas and New Year's when hosts need to get the relatives out of the house."

"I think that's when I came to the site for the first time, during school break," Audie laughed. "Mom must've had enough of Vita and me."

"Vita? You don't mean Vita Klein, do you?"

"The same."

"That's your sister?" The man stopped so fast she almost ran right into his back. "You're Audra?"

"Call me Audie, but yes."

His expression warmed from professional-friendly to friend-friendly. "And you must be Jude." He reached out a hand and shook both of theirs. "I've heard so much about you two and your genealogy research."

"Vi likes to talk."

He laughed. "But it's flattering talk. I'd love to sit down and have a conversation about your favorite history sites in Missouri or the strangest cases you've had."

"They're coming fast and furious lately." The wind whipped at Jude's black bangs, and he brushed the hair out of his eye. "Blundered into another one last night."

Thackeray's hand shot to his heart. "That was Vita's store, wasn't it?" His lips pulled tight. "The whole neighborhood's horrified. I've heard bits of the story and saw what was on television, but they never get the details straight. Vita wasn't the one who found Kurt, was she?"

"Do you know Fran Gill?" His nod was accompanied by a wince. "We were with Vi on Mr. Morrison's ghost program—I promise it was for fun, not facts. We'd reached the shop and the tale of Josephine Richards, when Fran came by to pick up something inside."

He lowered his voice. "Did Kurt really use a piece of glass?"

"Unfortunately, yes." What would've been fortunate?

"That seems... dramatic, doesn't it?"

Jude shrugged. "We didn't know him."

"I did. And I've seen his tool bag. He had plenty of stuff that would've done the job." Their guide resumed walking, albeit slower. "I always thought Kurt was a pretty decent guy. Some problems like everybody, but decent."

"What problems?" It was out of her mouth before she could resist. Jude shot her a look, and she blushed.

The man smiled gently. "He had his share of demons, I think. But the thefts, those were surprising. I guess you never know."

"Apparently not." They arrived at the beginning of a two-story structure, built with reddish-brown brick, rows of windows on both levels, wooden doors, and a pair of arched pass-throughs. "Nothing from the site here was stolen?"

Their leader's eyes flitted up to the second floor and down just as fast.

"You *were* burgled?"

"Let's get on with the tour," he deflected. "I'll tell you more upstairs, okay?"

"Of course."

Another look from her hubby. *Yeah,* she agreed silently. *I might've died of curiosity before then.*

Chapter 6

The ranger pulled himself straighter and launched into the script he'd recited a thousand times. "We're standing in front of the Peck Dry Goods Store, completed in 1819 by Charles and Ruluff Peck, brothers who moved here from Vermont to restart life on the frontier. They built it to house their shop and themselves as two bachelors. The left half of the place was owned by a carpenter named Chauncey Shepard. The upper floor was being used only as storage and not for much of that.

"As you already know, the Missouri Compromise led to our acceptance into the Union in August 1821. Missouri had many slaveholders running its farms and wanted to be entered as a slave state, but that would've shifted the country's uneasy balance. Maine was also being considered for statehood. It took three years of wrangling before the Compromise was struck. With it, states north of the Mason-Dixon line would be free, and those south could choose slave or free, except for Missouri, which was automatically slave."

Jude frowned. "Lousy legacy."

At least hubby's birthplace had been on the right side of these morals. *Go Buckeyes.*

"Agreed, but it's a fact. Border disputes with free Kansas led to some of the bloodiest action of the Civil War and its buildup. But all anyone seems to be taught is that the Battle of Bull Run was also called Manassas and that there were two of them."

Note to self: create a program of critical Show-Me facts and list it as a complimentary service of West Genealogy LLC. "Stuart told us some of what happened on his tour last night, how this building was chosen as the temporary government home."

"Stu is up on that part of his history, I'll grant him that." *And only that.* "It's funny—they almost couldn't give the site away. Nobody wanted to use it until the local delegates offered it for free. So while plans progressed for a whole new city south of Columbia, fifty representatives and eighteen senators traveled here to develop this place into something more than the Wild West. Governor Alexander McNair was elected in August 1820, beating William Clark seventy-two percent to twenty-eight."

Jude leaned forward, blocking the wind. "William Clark? As in, 'Lewis and?'"

"The same."

"What did McNair have on somebody so famous? I've never even heard of McNair."

"As always in politics, there's a lot to the story. One factor was that McNair was popular with those who had money, while Clark was seen as a tad too friendly with the native population."

"Lovely."

"You're telling me. Anyway, let's head through this arcade here, where the carriages dropped off supplies or senators, and then go upstairs to where the legislative action was."

Ranger Quinn sure excelled at his craft, as Audie could hear the clop of horseshoes echoing off the bricks in the wide opening. Movement over her shoulder made her turn. She stifled a laugh as a horse and carriage marched by with its first passengers of the day.

Now that is timing.

The forty-foot corridor opened onto a broad lawn before a modern street, the Missouri River flowing in the distance.

Sweeping his arm across the area, Thackeray said, "The Peck brothers used this yard like all typical homesteads did: to feed themselves." Fenced in, the expanse held a garden, an animal pen, and an outbuilding for smoking meats or making soap. "The road down there? That's Riverside Drive, with Frontier Park bridging the gap between it and the river. But in the 1820s, the river ended at the bottom of the yard. Twice a year, the Missouri would flood to the doorsteps here. Monsieur Blanchette, St. Charles' founder, specifically built on this bank so that people could flee into the hills during floods. These days, the Army Corps of Engineers regulates it to the channel you see now."

"It still floods though, doesn't it? Every spring, Vi is telling us how the park is shut down for a few weeks."

"We are a river town," he nodded, "for better or for worse. But there's beauty in its unpredictability too. I often eat my lunch while watching eddies swirl past. Think about life upstream and down. Imagine the Lewis and Clark expedition launching from that shore to search for the mythical Northwest Passage. All of that from simple water."

Audie touched the repaired sleeve of her coat and shuddered. After their week at Goodwin Mill last month, water would never be simple. The crashing of the creek over the wheel, the spinning stone rollers crushing anything in their path…

Jude was looking at her with a raised eyebrow.

"It's chilly," she said.

He believed that as much as he believed Stuart Morrison's tall tales.

"You're right," their guide said. "I can give my spiel just as well upstairs and indoors."

They climbed a wooden staircase that groaned at their ascent. On the second floor, he unlocked a door, and they stepped out of the cold.

The room was large and open, with five rows of spindle-backed benches arranged in two columns to their left. A spittoon sat at the end of each, and a dais in the front held a desk, chair, and a United States flag.

"This is where the House of Representatives gathered, led by the Speaker."

A pair of windows flanked the dais. "Stuart said they met during the summer?" A masonry building, limited ventilation, fifty overdressed gentlemen... *ick.*

"Right, between planting and harvesting. Because we're so agricultural, that was the best chance to gather the legislators. In that era, only white men could be elected, although they were progressive enough not to make landownership a requirement."

"Gee, how swell," Jude muttered.

"That's not to say someone like you," the ranger gestured to Audie, "or me wouldn't have been up on this floor occasionally. Blacks, women, and sometimes children visited, usually to do housekeeping or deliver messages or food. The wives of the legislators might come to watch the proceedings too."

"Building a state from scratch had to have led to some interesting discussions here."

"That's one description." The hearty laugh had his hat bouncing. "People don't change. You can imagine the spirited debates. Better yet, picture the mess caused by the fellas stuck in the middle of the benches—their nearest spittoon was over the knees of their fellow reps."

Again, ick.

He led them past the benches to the left, into a smaller room with eight tables and individual high-backed chairs. Green cloth covered the tables, and opposite was another platform and a fancier chair-desk combo.

"This was the Senate. Senators tended to be professional men: doctors, lawyers, engineers. They were expected to be more educated and take more notes, so they got desks on which to write."

"I didn't think about that." Jude peered back toward the first section. "It's kind of a free-for-all in there, isn't it?"

"Not exactly cushy accommodations. Now we'll pass through the House again to the governor's office."

They walked along a narrow hallway, past a side niche that their guide noted was likely for committee meetings. The records were vague on that account, which left Audie itching to comb those records herself. Before she could inquire about procedures for degreed archivists, they entered the last section of the floor: a decent-sized square with a fireplace, desk, chair, wood-burning stove, and multiple bookcases. Paintings of the first five governors—well, prints thereof—lined the wall.

"Why is this frame empty?" Number three held a blank sheet of paper.

"That should've been Governor Williams. He ascended to the seat when Frederick Bates died only nine months into his term. The lieutenant governor had left several weeks before, abandoning his post because he was bored and wanted to seek the riches rumored to exist up the Missouri River. So Abraham J. Williams, the Speaker of the House, was elevated to Governor.

"He wasn't happy about the promotion. An older man, he didn't want the job and beat a fast track out of Dodge. He refused to run in the special election to fill Bates' remaining term, so he was only in office for a few months, not long enough to sit for his portrait."

Jude read off the dates beside the frames. "We ran through four governors in the first five years?"

"Before we even moved to Jefferson City. Frontier life was rough."

In each painting, the sitter appeared much older than his biological age. That's what a lack of indoor plumbing will do to a guy.

Audie took up a spot near the stove, trying to fool her brain into thinking it was lit, and watched her husband orbit the perimeter. He peeked out the windows onto Main, then paused at the far corner. "What was over here?"

A faint difference in paint color outlined an odd shape of what must've once hung from the large empty nail. *How did I miss that? Bad historian. No biscuit.*

The ranger didn't answer, and Audie turned to him. His jaw had tensed.

"That's what was stolen, wasn't it?"

Now his eyes widened.

"She does that, sir," Jude said. "You get used to it."

The man hesitated, then sighed. "It can't be much of a secret if we're bringing tours in here. Yes, we'd had an artifact—about the most authentic one in our collection—mounted there. It disappeared last weekend."

"That's terrible."

"I'd appreciate it if you wouldn't spread the word too quickly. It's not a great look."

"We're a steel trap, Mr. Thackeray."

"You know the secret. You can call me Quinn."

Jude traced the vaguely triangular outline. "What was the piece? An antique like everything else that's grown legs?"

"Yes, and a doozy at that in terms of a story. You mentioned hearing about Josephine Richards?"

His tan skin blanched. "In Technicolor detail."

At least no phantom menaces had popped out from under the desk. That boy needed this vacation. It would be splendid if it ever turned into one.

"A clock was taken, the banjo clock that Nathaniel Silvain completed after he was convicted of killing Josephine and sentenced to hang."

Holy moley.

"He bought the clock mechanism from the watchmaker, but then he fitted the decorative rectangle at the base with a stained-glass scene of this building. The river flows by, and the trees are in full fall color. It shows the hills of St. Charles with chimneys and brick, and it made you ache for those days—until you think of them hanging a man and turning it into entertainment. It was a gorgeous work of art, the wood a vivid cherry, the stained glass top-notch."

Jude crossed his arms. "Am I the only one who thinks it's strange a governor would want artwork created by a convicted murderer?"

"No," the ranger agreed, "especially since it was finished at the behest of the victim's husband. Richards was well-liked in his county and had aspirations to the top seat himself, so he leaned into stoicism. He said he knew Nathaniel wasn't in his right mind when he killed Josephine. It was obvious, based on how he chose to do it.

"And already, Silvain's wife and two children would suffer by losing their breadwinner. It was Richards' benevolence that led to the clock being accepted. After Silvain stopped his protests of innocence, he returned to the project and cut no corners in its design, though he'd never see it displayed himself. It was the last thing his hands produced before he went to whichever side takes unrepentant murderers."

Yikes. Time to press fast-forward.

"Don't you have security on-site to stop thefts like this?"

"We have a few cameras, but a person might avoid them if they're paying attention. Kurt Boulton was hired by most of the building owners and shops nearby. He'd be aware of every camera angle. And he had his own keys, so he wasn't even breaking in."

"No one suspected him until last night?"

"The police talked to him, of course. He had ideal opportunity but no motive we knew of. He'd earned his living here for over fifteen years. Why would he suddenly start stealing? Gossip is that maybe he had bad debts, spending what he didn't have at the casino down the road. Lots of folks fall down that rabbit hole." He rubbed at his neck. "I'll never understand people, no matter how long I live. We're hoping now that Boulton was the thief, the cops will find where he kept his haul and we'll get our clock back."

"No word yet today?"

He shook his head. "We've been watching the online marketplaces and such, and haven't seen it show up, so maybe there's hope?"

"Always. And soon you'll have another story to share with your tourists."

Quinn laughed. "Oh right—this is supposed to be a tour, isn't it? Let's go downstairs, or I'll have you here until tomorrow."

He led them out, locked up, and sent them to ground level. There, they entered the first floor and found themselves in a recreated dry-goods store.

"We're in the Peck brothers' shop now." On the shelves were pottery vases and crocks, glass jars of beans and spices. A series of animal pelts marked with the critter of origin sat atop the counter.

"Charles and Ruluff started this place together. When Ruluff married in 1820, they continued to run the store as a partnership, but Charles moved out of the residence next door so his brother could raise his family there."

Audie ran her fingers through a pelt whose name tag was missing. "Is that river otter?"

He awarded two gold stars to the lady in the yellow coat. "We also have fox, beaver, ermine, and mink, whatever the trappers found to sell."

He went on to explain how other merchandise made it to the frontier—that it required fortune-telling by the Pecks to guess what would be needed and wanted by their customers the next year. Making that annual order entailed a long trip east. No one-click-shopping in 1820.

"Onto our final stop." Outside and then through the last door of the building, Ranger Quinn led them into the original open-floor-plan home. *And I thought the camper held it all.* To their right was a simple wooden table with a half-dozen chairs. A full-sized bed took up the opposite corner, the kind with the ropes a user pulled to 'sleep tight' while avoiding biting bedbugs. A large pot hung on a swing hook in the fireplace. Beside it sat what seemed to be an early derivation of a toaster—a pair of six-inch tall metal arches resembling intricate bookends mounted to a base on a swivel.

Audie caught Jude eying it closely. If they ever graduated to a full-size kitchen, he'd spend his entire salary at Williams Sonoma.

"Ruluff and Adeline had three children, one we believe was disabled, and they lived, slept, and ate together in this room."

"Not much privacy, from each other or passers-by peeping in this front window."

"Technically, that was the back window in those days. The buildings faced the river."

"That's confusing."

"After two centuries, a lot of things are." The guide clapped his hands. "That wraps up the nickel tour." He gestured for them to head to the front—er, back—exit. "Questions?"

"You explained everything so well. I don't think I have any."

"Doubtful," Jude fake-coughed, then grinned at her eye roll.

"Okay, I do, but it's about the long-ago days."

"Hit me."

"I've been thinking about Clarence, Josephine, and Nathaniel. It must've been an enormous scandal, a legislator's wife being murdered."

Quinn grimaced. "I'm sure it was, but St. Charles didn't have a consistent paper at the time. No salacious headlines. We were a national story because of the Missouri Compromise, of course, along with some of the really awful laws being created."

"Such as?"

"There had been promises about who could and could not vote as part of the Compromise, but the Legislature threw those out the window within the first twelve months. It led to some of the racial issues we still have.

"The murder, of course, was horrible. Silvain had been caught red-handed, covered in her blood. It was an open-and-shut case."

In the vicinity of Quinn's furrowed brow, a word hung in space. Jude plucked it out. "But?"

He hemmed, then shrugged. "I don't know. I mean, it's a certainty that Nathaniel killed her. But Clarence was a lot older than Josephine, and minutes of those legislative sessions show him to be a touchy fellow in the assembly. One could guess that in those days of women lacking rights, their marriage wouldn't have been gushing with romance. She may have felt alone, unloved. Along comes a personable, talented next-door neighbor. He's a welcome diversion, if only for conversation. I can see where Silvain might've gotten the wrong idea, and then when Josephine turned him away?"

"People do not change, do they?"

"Rarely, my friend. Or we wouldn't still be talking about leopards and their spots."

The area was teeming now, pedestrians armored against the cold, hidden behind sunglasses and impersonating the Invisible Man. Laughter rang from unseen lips as shoppers ducked into the surrounding restaurants for a midday refueling.

Lunch! The old-fashioned street clock read much later than Audie had expected. "We're supposed to be meeting Vita shortly."

"I have one last question." Jude pointed down the walk to where a set of cellar doors were cordoned off by wood railings. "Are those original to the building?"

A mischievous flicker lit Ranger Thackeray's face. "Do you want to see?"

"Not on your life." Once again, the words tumbled out without warning. *I need to get my tongue examined.* At least the blushing brought warmth to her cheeks. "Sorry. Been in a few too many creepy basements lately."

"How about you?" he asked Jude. Or was it a dare? Didn't matter. She knew what he'd say.

"Of course!" Now the same mischievous sparkle came over his face. "Aud, do you care?"

"It'll just be a minute," Quinn said. "I promise not to let the troll eat him."

"Well, if you promise."

He fitted a key in a padlock and lifted the wooden gate, then pulled up on the metal handle of the cellar door. Pulling a long flashlight off his belt, he turned to climb down a ladder. "I trust you won't close and lock me down here before you follow?"

"Rangers are licensed to carry guns. I'm not planning any high jinks."

"I knew you were smart." He backed down the rungs, and Jude followed.

"I hope you have a way of distracting the troll," she called after them. "Vi will be annoyed if you're not here to cook Christmas dinner."

"I plan to sacrifice Mr. Thackeray and run for my life if it comes to it." He winked.

"I heard that," came a voice from the below and beyond. They both smiled.

"Take notes for me," she said.

"Aye, aye, captain." He disappeared into the underworld.

Chapter 7

Within feet of entering the musty cellar, daylight solidified into charcoal.

"Where does the troll live, exactly?"

"Don't worry. He's nocturnal." A flashlight clicked on, piercing the murk lightsaber-style.

A brief rain of dirt showered down into Jude's hair. "The Peck brothers dug this?"

"It was likely built with enslaved labor, because that was the accepted way to do things then. This was extra storage and a cool location for goods sold in the shop."

As they walked farther, the ranger's beam passed over old timber shelves, some holding an occasional crate with the faded names of suppliers painted on the slats.

"I guess without refrigeration, cellars like this were the way to go."

Quinn nodded. "Caves were used a lot, too, especially by the breweries in St. Louis. We have some here in St. Charles, though not as many. The problem here is that several of ours would've flooded whenever the river did its thing. This cellar is far enough out of the floodplain that it was safe."

A narrow rectangle of gray appeared in the black ahead, five feet away or a hundred. Time and space were beginning to lose meaning. Audie was a smart woman to have stayed above deck.

"Now that the water never gets this high, we added the window there as a second means of egress in case of fire."

When they reached it, Jude prayed they'd have no need for a test. He'd be lucky to fit through. Quinn would've had no hope. Other than a spot in its center, it was covered in grime. If it opened in an emergency, he'd eat his hat.

"This is the perfect place for a thousand angry ghosts to live. Maybe local natives that didn't care for the ignorant white men taking over, or enslaved folks who decided to spend the hereafter tormenting the tormentors." He couldn't blame them. *Also, to anyone listening, I'd like to note that my family was from a few hundred miles east and never owned people.*

Huh, the one horrendous practice his father hadn't managed to use at the steel plant. Miracles never cease.

"You can't go into a building on Main without hearing stories of some specter," Quinn said.

Jude swallowed and asked as nonchalantly as he could, "Do you believe in them?" Of course he didn't. He's too rational to rile himself into nightmares. He's a Missouri State Park Ranger, by golly. A fact-lover, a truth-sayer.

But the darkness had gone utterly silent. Jude turned, trying to read the man's expression but only catching eyes.

"I've seen things. I've wondered. That sounds ridiculous upstairs, but down here? Don't you think it could be possible? Like you said. In an area with so much history, a lot of it bad because humanity swings both ways in every era, I wouldn't be surprised if somebody's on the other side, making up for some injustices."

Tiny claws climbed straight up Jude's spine, and a flash of that fragmented dream played on his eyelids. He'd take the troll now, thank you. "I'd blown off most of what Stuart Morrison talked about last night."

Quinn waved the flashlight. "Stu needs to sell tickets. Those stories get bigger with each telling."

"But the one about Josephine, that aligns with facts, right?"

"It's the most accurate of any. And I guess I'd be pretty irritated if I was Josephine, my life cut short that way."

Cut short... by a knife of glass in the hands of the artist who'd made it.

At the same spot where another man ended it all by the same means.

Shattered glass, shattered art, shattered lives.

A shattered afterlife? His eyes wandered to the only place in-focus, the egress window.

"What the—?"

He stumbled backward, his head cracking against a shelf post.

Quinn swung the flashlight to his face. "Are you okay?"

"What was that?" His hand disappeared in front of him as he pointed up.

The beam darted to the window, but the light reflected and they couldn't see out anymore. He dropped it down. "What was what?"

"In the one clear spot. A shape, dark like a hood, looking in at us."

"Down here? Hardly anyone knows the window exists. A hedge blocks it from the yard."

"I'm telling you, I saw someone." Or something. He stepped away from the shelves and probed his tender skull.

"I'm surprised you saw anything, with so much gunk in the way." Quinn moved closer, reaching up to wave some cobwebs aside.

"It was just like…"

"Like?" The tall man's voice tightened.

Okay, the park service rep didn't need to think he was trapped in a cellar with a loon. "I guess the atmosphere is getting to me." His fingers didn't feel wet—no blood from the head wound. That's refreshing, anyway. "You know, I should go up before my wife declares me dead and remarries."

Quinn chuckled. "Doesn't seem like the type racing to remarry." *You have no idea.* "Thanks for braving the abyss with me—I don't get many willing volunteers."

They surfaced into the late morning sun, and Jude raised his hand to shield his eyes.

"You survived," Audie said, smiling. Of course she was smiling. She hadn't been in the abyss.

"Barely."

Quinn's cell phone rang, and he checked the ID. "Excuse me for a second. It's the detective who's dealing with the thefts."

He stepped down the sidewalk and turned so his words were caught by the wind in the opposite direction.

Audie frowned. "Drat."

But Jude took her surprised arm and guided her even further away, whispering, "Did anybody go by while we were below?"

She examined him with those my-husband's-gone-insane eyes. "Plenty of people went by. It's a busy street."

He shook his head, and he realized how he must look because her expression changed too.

"What did you mean?"

"There's a window in the cellar, facing the rear lawn. It's dirty and way too small for an escape hatch, but I swear a shadowy, hooded figure was playing Peeping Tom with us."

"Jude."

"I know." He shoved his hands in his pockets. "It sounds like I need a tin hat. But that's twice now, Aud. Something is going on around here, and it seems to not like us—or me."

The muscle in her jaw twitched as the line above her nose deepened. She didn't argue.

"And—" *do I say it? It's Audie, yes, I say it. She'll read it straight out of my mind regardless.* "That dream I had this morning?"

"The nightmare?"

"Yeah, that. It was..." He took in the happy holiday decor, heard the carolers on the move, watched packages carried by, tied up with string. *Spit it out, man.* "It was Josephine."

Her head tilted. "You dreamt about her murder?"

"No. Her. Like, I saw her, as real as I'm seeing you. And she saw."

"Jude."

"She wore a baby-blue dress, had soft auburn hair hanging in long curls. She was pretty, delicate. But her head." He had to force down both breakfast and the urge to stop. "Her head sat crooked and her throat..." *Oh Lord.* "Her arms kept reaching out to me. One hand held this fragment of pink and black glass, with some sort of flower laid into it, like cherry blossoms. Loads of cherry blossoms."

His wife of ten years paused, absorbing the details. At least she didn't laugh. "No wonder you were so upset."

"It wasn't scary, I guess? I mean, they were flowers, for heaven's sake. Do we know what was on the glass she was killed with?"

"I'm pretty sure Stuart just said the piece Clarence ordered had a spring scene."

"My brain must've manifested that as cherry blossoms." He shrugged. "In any case, she wasn't threatening. It was like she wanted something. Needed something."

"Two hundred years after death? I would've thought most business would've been handled by now." And that from a woman who didn't believe in spirits. *Unless they're saints, but that's different.*

Is it? He'd never attended catechism class.

Before she could say anything else, Ranger Thackeray approached, wrapping up the call.

"Okay, thanks for letting me know." He stowed the phone with a huff.

"Something wrong?"

Like his hesitancy in discussing ghosts, he struggled to find the words. He, too, decided it was best to spill it.

"They've searched Kurt Boulton's apartment. There's nothing there."

Chapter 8

A crocheted scarf in enough greens to make Kermit jealous waved at them from a rear table as they entered the bustling Café Jefferson.

"We need to teach her semaphore," Jude said. Audie heard the zipper of the jacket behind her as they transitioned from Arctic to temperate zone.

Every chair held a diner, shopping bags at their feet, coats hanging where they could, and the smell of roasted squash wafting through the air. "The First Noel" played under the holiday chitchat, and the white interior of the space was awash in silver garland and round, red ornaments.

"Fortunately, the green sticks out fine."

"Leave it to Vita to be her own decked halls."

Audie skirted between tables, apologizing more than once for bumping into a purse or an elbow, but no one seemed bothered today. The horrors of last night weren't affecting the daytime visitors, and besides, it was almost Christmas.

"I thought I'd better grab us a table," Vi said from the corner seat. Jude pulled out Audie's chair, then settled into his own across from her. "How was the tour?"

Audie glanced at her husband, who gave a short shake of his head while pointedly staring at his menu.

We will not be sharing more phantom chronicles at present.

"Captivating. Ranger Thackeray told us to tell you hi."

"Quinn's fantastic, isn't he? Knows that place like the back of his hand and is thrilled to share it. I'd get so bored, telling the same stories over and over. I'd end up embellishing."

Perhaps that's where the specters originated: boredom. Of course, there were other possibilities too. When they'd stopped in a New Mexico town one year, a bookshop owner spotlighted the local ghost volumes lining his shelves.

"We're overloaded with dead people. But it's funny—about twenty years ago, somebody wrote the first book, about the hotel across the square being haunted. Soon after, every business had its own celebrity spook." He'd chuckled. "I enjoy the selling, but take into account how many of these so-called sightings happened late at night at the bar. Darn mysterious, ain't it?"

The ever-hungry half of the Wests apparently planned to eat his way through his complicated feelings regarding apparitions. "What's good here?"

Vita didn't bother reviewing the offerings. "For you, the grilled cheese and tomato soup. It sounds basic. But they use five different cheeses, with some sort of hot sauce that tastes like Cozumel, and then the soup is made with heirlooms and blended fresh daily."

"Sold."

A slim server who looked like she'd topple over if she lifted one of the loaded food trays materialized at their table. Another supernatural being? Audie didn't care, so long as she didn't wind up with ectoplasm on her lunch plate.

"Vita!" the woman cried, placing glasses of water at each setting. Where those had come from was also a mystery.

"Sandy, this is my sister and brother-in-law." Vi beamed like she was showing off a pair of prized orchids. Jude never knew how to take that. Audie simply accepted it after all these years.

"The Traveling Wilburys, right?"

Jude choked on his water. "Wests, but yes to the traveling part. Wish we had their musical talent."

"Sandy owns the cafe. This whole building, actually."

Big Sister had found another orchid to show off. Typical.

"Vi's told me so much about you. One of these days, I might come calling. My great-grandfather bought this building in 1900 when he emigrated from Belgium." She gestured to a set of three sepia-toned photographs tacked up near the cash register. The first showed the front window filled with hardware items. The farthest frame held the portrait of a sober-faced man and woman, presumably the proprietors. An image of the sign that must've hung above the door took the center spot. "But his is the longest family-tree line I've tracked. I'd love to learn about my grandmother's side. We could add some more by-gone to our cooking." She winked.

They gave their order—one grilled cheese and tomato soup, two butternut squash soup-and-salad combos. "And don't let me leave without picking up a box of apple tarts," Vita added. "We'll have them for breakfast tomorrow."

The horror on Jude's face… "Have I been fired?"

She patted her brother-in-law's arm. "Vacation, dearest, vacation."

"That *is* vacation," he pouted.

"Fine," Vi sighed. "But make something that will go with a tart."

"Yes, ma'am."

Enough sensation had returned to Audie's limbs that she could slip off the duck-yellow coat. She folded the sleeve to cover the mending she'd had to do after that debacle down in Belsever. Vita knew about it, of course. But a reminder wouldn't help their lunch conversation, or convince her to take her own break from worrying about her only sibling.

"How did you spend your morning, Vi?"

She rolled her eyes. "First, my optimistic self touched base with Detective Flores. No, we're still not allowed to open."

Jude lowered his voice, though with the racket in the cafe, it wasn't necessary. "We just heard they didn't find the stolen goods at Kurt Boulton's place."

The corner of Vita's lips pulled back. "I did too. That's worrying. I'm so glad we weren't hit, because who knows how they'll recover the things now. He didn't leave a suicide note at home, and as far as they can tell, there's no storage unit in his name or any friends or relatives where he'd dropped off mysterious boxes." She fussed at her scarf. "I'm floored that it was Kurt. And then for guilt to haunt him so badly? I would've thought it out of character." Ridges lined her forehead. "Shows how smart I am."

Jude opened his mouth to respond, but was sidetracked before the words got out. Their food arrived by another magically manifesting member of the wait staff. *Sandy must have a highly particular training regimen.* This time, a teen on college break dished out their plates. Beneath his blue apron, he sported a Missouri S&T sweatshirt.

As soon as he left, Audie leaned closer to her husband, who was already ogling the silky ribbon of cheese draping from his thick, golden toast. "What were you going to say?"

"What? Nothing."

"Nope. There was something."

He took a big bite of his sandwich and chewed it slower than usual. "It's ridiculous, but I'm stuck on this Josephine connection."

"Our resident ghost?" Vi clucked at Jude like the naive pup he wasn't. But she hadn't heard about the dream yet.

He wiped strings of dairy gooeyness from his chin. "I'm just saying it feels squirrelly, the jagged glass thing. That Josephine would die that way and then this guy goes and does the same?"

"He died by his own hand, and Josephine didn't have a choice in the matter." Vita took another bite of her salad before she looked up at him. His out-of-sorts silence—terribly un-Judelike—must've sunk in, because she put down her fork, and her expression grew serious. "I'm sorry, sweetheart. What are you saying? That she'd possessed him or something?"

He shook his head a little too hard. "No, no." *Maybe.* "Only that it's bizarre that an even-tempered fellow who everyone liked and trusted would suddenly kill himself in the same gory way."

"Not everybody liked him."

Audie's spoon slipped. "What?"

She waved the edge of her scarf again. *And she complains about my nervous pen twirling.* "For one thing, he was long divorced, and he's said that was rough for all involved. But then there's also our resident Ghost of Charles Dickens. Glen doesn't like much of anyone."

"Did someone mention our favorite curmudgeon?"

Jude flinched as a man's shape entered his periphery. He either had specters on the brain or needed to switch to decaf.

Or both.

"Derek!" Why was Vita blushing? "I, yes, I mean, I didn't—"

By now, the new arrival was grinning widely. "Ms. Vita, you're going to hurt yourself, and my uncle isn't worth that."

Vi's stammering softened into a sheepish shrug. "Still, it's the holidays. I should be more polite."

"I guarantee you, he wouldn't be."

"But he let you out of your shackles for your daily bread and water?"

The boy—tall from this angle, but most folks were from Audie's viewpoint—put out slim wrists like they were handcuffed. "I'm out on probation, and that's only if I get lunch to him before our next customer meeting."

Vi remembered she had tablemates. "Guys, this is Derek Vikander. He has the fortune to be Glen Armquist's oldest nephew and helps run the antique store between here and the boutique."

"You're an antiquarian too?" *He's pulling out all the big words now.* Jude was also diverting attention from the tomato soup he'd splattered upon Derek's arrival.

"Gosh, no, but excellent word. Uncle Glen would be pleased. I've been keeping the books for him and doing odd jobs." He squinted as he decided on the best description. "Chief Duster. I dust a lot. He's the one with the, er, vision."

"And the storefront."

He smiled, and his glasses slipped on his nose. "That too. But it keeps me busy and out of trouble." His brown hair had a slight wave to it, and a curl poked out sideways from above his right ear.

Before the end of the lunch hour, they'd meet every merchant on Main. He shook their hands, then slid his own into the pockets of his jeans. He couldn't be over thirty, possibly twenty-five.

Youngsters wherever they looked anymore. Who knew forty-three was ready for the retirement home? *We can be neighbors with Mom.*

Maybe not.

Derek bent closer to Vita. "Hey, about what happened last night. I can't believe it was Kurt."

"It's awful, isn't it? I guess he had the best access of anyone for those thefts. Such a shock, though."

"And did the rumor mill get it right? Did he really...?" The question stuck on his tonsils.

Vita contemplated the uneaten hard-boiled egg on her fork. "That unfortunate man." She turned up to Derek. "Have the detectives called you guys yet?"

He grimaced. "Uncle Glen got a message before I left. No sign of the stolen property."

"With most of the goods being antiques, your place must've been a gold mine," Jude said, managing to get a spoonful into his mouth without catastrophe.

The younger man waved off the concern. "You'd think, but no. We had a couple of old cameras in the window, displays to fit with the aesthetic around here. They weren't worth much."

"That's surprising."

"Not if you knew my mother's brother," he laughed. "He keeps most of the best stuff at his house, where it's safe from both commoners and customers. But he's upset by any of his treasures going missing, so I'd sure like to get them back."

"Vita!"

Another voice, female this time, sliced through the ambient chatter behind his head, and Jude gave up, soup dripping off his cheek. He set his spoon on the bowl's saucer, grabbed for his napkin, and pleaded across the table, "Would you please start warning me?"

Beside Derek now stood a blue-haired pixie missing her knit hat and sporting a coat that was a size too snug and even older than the one she wore yesterday evening. At least this one wasn't covered in blood stains.

"Hey, Fran," Derek said, stepping aside to let her reach the table. His smile had broadened upon her arrival, worries about Uncle Glen swept to the nearest dustbin. "How are you doing?" Then he remembered who'd made the grisly discovery, and his hand shot to his mouth. "I mean—"

"It's okay, Derek." Now she was leaning in toward Vita. *My sister, Miss Popularity.* Nothing new there. "Have you gotten any word about the stuff Kurt stole?"

"We were just talking about that. The police didn't find it and don't have any clues yet."

She groaned, her skin paling to match the platinum edges of her hair.

"What is it, sweetie? Here, sit down before you fall down."

Gloveless fingers grabbed the top of the empty fourth chair, but she didn't sit.

"No, I—. Jes—"

Audie and Vi cleared their collective throats, and the blaspheme was swallowed.

"Sorry. But…" She exhaled and began studying the garland hanging high above. Tears formed along her lower lashes.

"Fran?" Audie asked in the calmest tone she could muster. Jude would say it was lamb-soothing. She'd have to test it out on lambs someday. "What is it?"

Still, she hesitated. Vita pushed her lunch aside, already going into full mother mode. Derek got the hint and excused himself to the counter. Jude followed him to pay for their meal before Vita could. He left his chair out for Fran to fall into it, which she did.

"Oh Vita." The tears spilled, and she put a hand up to hide her face from the patrons behind her. Thank heavens Vi had snagged a corner table. "I'm in so much trouble."

Vi reached across to her forearm. "Darling, whatever's going on, there's always a way through it. Tell me. We can help."

Audie scooted out her chair. "I'll let you two talk."

"No, no. I'm sorry for interrupting." She turned to her with reddened eyes. "Vi says you're good with secrets. If that's true, you might as well hear this too."

"She's a locked crypt, love," Vi said softly.

"Crypt. Appropriate." Fran took up the messy napkin Jude had left behind and started twisting it. A set of Vita's rings sparkled across her fingers. "I did something I'm not proud of."

"Everyone does now and then. Get it out. You'll feel better."

The girl took a deep breath and dove in. "You know about Trenton and the divorce." They nodded. "A few years ago, his Great-Aunt Earline passed away, and she left this gorgeous, original Tiffany stained-glass pane to me."

Vi's eyes widened. "Real Tiffany?"

"She and her husband had traveled a lot and were pretty well-off. It was a square, about twelve by twelve inches, showing a magnolia tree loaded with blooms. Earline and I got along terrific, and she liked my work. They'd never had children, and she used to giggle with me like an old girlfriend, though she was ninety-two when she passed.

"Anyway, she'd told us she wanted me to have the panel. So in her will, we got a few bits of theirs and the Tiffany. Trenton didn't care about any of it and sold everything immediately, except for the glass which I refused to give up. It was so gorgeous, I could stare at it for days. The problem is there was supposed to be a letter that specified it was mine. Earline told me so. And the lawyer says there were other letters—official, notarized, the whole bit—kept to track the specific bequests. All the other cousins' were found, but not that one. Trent and I were still a couple though, and I figured as long as we were together, it didn't matter."

"Only, now you're divorcing."

She sniffled, coiling the napkin into an origami snake. "About a month ago, when he finally moved out—while I was at the vet's, of course—he took the pane with him. I was furious and demanded it back, but he said she was his relation and so it belonged to him."

"That's rotten."

"It gets worse." She looked like she was being waterboarded in the middle of the busy cafe. She must've found the sugar packets comforting because her eyes wouldn't leave them. "Last week, when I dropped off Lizzie for her night with him, I said I needed to use the bathroom."

"Frannie."

"I snuck into the bedroom, came across the Tiffany tossed on a chair like it was nothing, and snagged it."

"Does he know?"

"Can you believe it took that"—the search for a Santa-approved word was a struggle—"dimwit five days to realize it was missing? He searched his scummy place for a couple more before he figured out what must've happened. Wednesday, he called, saying that if I turn it over, he won't tell the cops."

"A Tiffany stained-glass, original?" Audie cringed. "That has to be worth a small fortune."

The tears fell at last, spilling into Jude's unfinished soup. "Twenty-five thousand dollars."

Holy smokes.

"I need to give it back by Christmas Eve."

"I'm sensing a 'but' here, dear."

"But I can't. You've been to my apartment, Vi. It's not exactly Fort Knox, and the neighbors three doors down are high half the time. I was too scared to keep something that valuable at home. So I had it at the shop."

"Our shop? Our safe is only big enough for the cash box."

She shook her head. "I had it filed with my glass panels, between the finished ones and the sheets I work from. It was totally camouflaged in there. I didn't think anybody would find it. And it was only supposed to be temporary."

Vita's free hand clutched her scarf. "Oh my gosh."

The woman with hair the color of the Caribbean tried to wipe at the mascara covering her cheeks, but it made things worse. "It's gone. Stolen. I noticed it yesterday morning, then tore the place apart before we opened. I know it was there at close on Wednesday. And then when Kurt turned out to be the thief, and he shows up dead…"

"Nobody knows where he stashed what he took," Audie whispered.

The girl gave up on covering her tears. "I can't even report it missing! Vita, if I don't get that panel to Trenton by Christmas Eve, I'll go to jail and lose Lizzie forever. What am I going to do?"

Chapter 9

So much for vacation.

The thought flitted through faster than a miniature sleigh and eight tiny reindeer, yet Jude immediately wanted to throw himself in the river.

That poor girl.

Vi had insisted on buying Fran a lunch to take home for her and Lizzie, then she dove straight into beg, plead, and barter mode to ask him and Audie to work their magic and help her shopmate.

Of course, she'd needed to do none of that.

He pushed his fists deeper into his pockets. To think he'd been hung up on ghosts and phantoms, letting fiction—or, at least, long-past fact—distract him from the present.

Sloppy, West. Very sloppy.

But this was a sloppy mess too. Divorces usually were. Since he hadn't been introduced to Trenton Gill yet, he was trying to keep the reflexive disdain down to a simmer. A family man should have his priorities in order, and playing video games with friends in hours he didn't have to spare failed that test. He'd give Mr. Gill a chance if they ever met face-to-face, but he had a long mountain to climb to reach Stand-up Guy status.

The sun shone brightly in the early afternoon, and lunch—what he'd finished of it—sat warmly in his stomach, making it difficult to fathom how many tribulations simmered below the surrounding surfaces. *Another two-dollar word. I'm on a roll today.* A series of thefts, the severed trust of dozens of shopkeepers trying to keep the region's lore fun and accurate-ish…

Better leave off the -ish if we ever run across Glen Armquist in a dark alley.

Hang on—could the Ghost of Charles Dickens be masquerading as the Ghost of Christmas Yet to Come?

This was getting confusing.

The nerves created by the thefts, the identification of the perpetrator, his theatrical death, and now Fran's soap opera of a life—confusing wasn't half of it. If Aunt Earline had intended her to have that one-of-a-kind Tiffany panel, worth enough to get her and Lizzie out of a bad situation, and she was only in the bad situation because of her soon-to-be ex-husband? No wonder she took it.

Was that stealing?

But if the letter wasn't found, amending the will? Nope, the eyes of the St. Charles County Family Courts System were going to see this differently. Nobody would end up happy. Not Fran. Certainly not Lizzie. Not even Trenton, if he admitted it.

People hurting others out of spite: that's got to be one of Dante's nine rings of Hell.

"You're being awfully quiet."

Jude dragged his eyes from counting cobblestones. The woman in the duck-yellow coat had been reading his mind again. What was the use of trying to hide it?

"I hope we can help."

Audie nodded. "There's a lot going on here. But all we need to do is focus on Fran. If we can get an idea where Kurt might've hidden what he stole, we're done and can return to being Wests of leisure."

Yeah, because they'd been that lucky lately.

Hatchet Bend. Belsever. Renaud. *Let's go for the Grand Slam of tragic cases, shall we?* Round out the year with a bang?

Surely, it's safer to leave the explosions to the experts on New Year's Eve.

But since when do we play it safe?

She broke into his interior monologue. "Who eats ice cream in late December?"

The next wooden sign swinging over the walk showed two single-scoop cones forming a heart. The name Lucy's Lix was painted on it in pistachio and cherry colors. "Anyone with taste buds."

She smirked. "It's below freezing out here."

He held out both hands like a scale. "Cold weather, frozen dessert. There's no debate. Plus, the scoops won't melt. It's a perfect system." On the other side of the street sat his favorite artisan shop, though its holiday decor had been supplemented with a strip of yellow crime-scene tape blocking its entryway. "The parlor is straight across from Vi's. Why don't we start there and see if they can shed any light on things?"

"And get a sample while we're at it?"

"It would be rude not to support a local business." He grinned when she gave him her long-suffering spouse look. "I'll let you have a bite."

"You're too kind to me."

For some reason, she meant it.

Oliver, you were a fine man, and I'm sorry about what happened. But I got luckier than I ever had a right to be.

He opened the door, and Audie led the way inside. It was exactly as he'd hoped. The long soda-shop counter, old-fashioned and perfect, was polished to a shimmery gleam. Glass domes sheltered a variety of flavors—the classics like vanilla and chocolate, then Rocky Road, salted caramel, cookies and cream, butter pecan, and, of course, the pistachio and cherry, settled next to one other in the same loving embrace as the business's logo. A thin woman with a gray ponytail ran an immersion blender as her partner-in-crime-and-frozen-confections chatted up a mother and child at the register.

"That'll be six hundred and fifty-seven pennies, please." He winked at the mom and bent down to the small boy, meaty palm outward. "Did you bring your piggy bank?"

The child gaped up at the man who could've played St. Nick in the Holidays of Hope cast. Tiny fingers hung in an open mouth, but he didn't answer.

"I guess I'll have to pay this once," the put-upon parent moaned. "But you owe me, buddy." The kid remained transfixed on the fellow who'd be coming down his chimney next week. That is, until Mrs. Claus arrived with a vanilla cup, hot fudge and sprinkles on top, and passed it over the counter. He took it with both hands, eyes widening even more.

There's Santa and then there's ice cream. One wasn't a going concern for another six days. One was within his grip now.

Winner.

The mother was given her mocha shake with chocolate shavings, and, with a wad of napkins the child already needed, aimed for a cafe table.

"And what can we get for you fine folks on this frigid day? Your ice cream won't melt out there, guaranteed!"

Audie refused to make eye contact with her husband.

His spleen struggled to avoid bursting as he smothered a giggle.

"We'll order in a second, but could we ask a couple of questions super quick? Do you know Vita Klein, the jewelry maker across the street? I'm her sister, Audie."

Mrs. Claus—who probably had a real name and looked like she needed some fattening up before the holiday—plopped her scooper into a bowl of warm water and wiped her hands. "Of course we know Vita!" She joined her jolly husband at the counter. "We were so happy when she and Darla and now Frannie took over that shop. I'm surprised we haven't met you before now. Your sister is an absolute dear."

"And a force to be reckoned with." The man reached out a hand. "Nicholas Ramsey. This is my wife, Idelle."

It really is St. Nick. A list of minor transgressions sent his heart racing when Santa gave him an appraising once-over. *I'm getting coal in my stocking.*

It wouldn't be the first time.

Introductions were made.

"Idelle? Then is Lucy the owner?"

Nick chuckled. "You might say that."

Idelle nudged him. "Lucy was our cat. She's across the rainbow bridge now. We were going to name this place after one of the kids, but couldn't decide which."

"So the cat won."

"The cat always won," Nick whispered behind his hand, but was smart enough to sidestep before his ribs were poked again. Idelle sighed.

"We don't have a line out the door right now. Can I get you something while we talk?"

Jude didn't hesitate. "A cup of pistachio, please, single scoop."

"I'm about frozen," Audie apologized. "I don't think I could do ice cream."

Besides, she'd already eaten this week.

"Honey, I've got the answer to that too." Idelle disappeared behind the counter, waving them toward the seating area. "I'll be there in a jiffy."

The three sat at the nearest table, Nick's joints creaking as he dropped onto one of the dainty chairs.

"So what is it you're curious about?"

Audie's soft voice sank another few notches. "You heard about what happened last night?"

The big man stroked his substantial white beard. It couldn't hide the grimace. "We're shocked. Kurt, of all people. What in the world made him do that?"

"The theft or the, uh…"

"Both. We had things taken, like a nice antique scoop and a metal sign advertising Coca-Cola. It was genuine, not one of those reproductions, but it wasn't worth much. Maybe eight inches square? I guess he tucked it into his coat. But he'd worked for us for ages, and never with a single problem."

"How long have you been in business?"

"I retired from trucking fifteen years ago. Body told me, 'No more.' Our kids were grown by then, and Idelle had been by herself at home while I was gone. So we decided we'd put our ancient bones to use and make a fresh batch of kiddos happy every day. The sugar buzz is their parents' problem." He grinned.

After-effects weren't within his jurisdiction.

His better half arrived at the table, carrying a tray. Before Jude, she set the requested pistachio with an honest-to-goodness silver spoon inside the cup. The single scoop was no more a single scoop than he was a yellow-blond Swede. Beside Audie, she placed a ceramic mug of steaming hot chocolate, complete with what had to be hand-cut homemade marshmallows. Cups of black coffee went down before her husband and herself. She took her seat and began stirring her drink with a peppermint stick.

"Now what did you two want to ask us about? I doubt it was the details of Nick's days driving the semi."

The association hit Jude like a, well, like a Mack truck. Nicholas Ramsey was a teamster, delivering goodies across the country.

All the guy needed was a hearty laugh and a belly that jiggled, marmalade-style.

Digging for a sleigh-centric joke, he came up empty due to sudden-onset brain freeze. He'd dug into the creamy green deliciousness a smidge too enthusiastically.

It was worth it.

Audie wiped foam from her lips with a pale pink napkin. "We were wondering if you'd seen anything going on over at the boutique in the last couple of nights?"

"Nothing more than the usual. The police have already looked at our security footage."

"You have cameras?"

"This may be ye olde ice cream parlor, and we may be over-the-hill, but we're not hopeless," Nicholas said, sipping his coffee. "We've got one at the front and back, watching the doors. The one out front also catches some of the street action, though it doesn't reach Vita's entrance. They have too much of a yard. Along the sidewalk here, it's easier to keep guard."

Whereas DFV Boutique has more shadows than a 1930s radio serial. *Note: start a fund for better security at our favorite jeweler's place.*

"Did the videos show anything?"

Nick whipped out his phone, started tapping at apps, and set it at the center of the table. Kris Kringle had gone high tech.

"Frannie found Kurt about what, nine-thirty or ten? And I heard Darla shooed out a dawdling customer and closed up at seven-thirty on the dot. She was trying to get to her grandson's Christmas program that started at eight, and she needed to pick up Lionel. So let's start when she leaves. I'll set it to fast forward."

They watched the view of Main Street St. Charles, lit by the flickering streetlamps. Part of Vita's long lawn was seen at the top of the screen, but the building itself wasn't. On the frozen grass, a square of light from the shop's window extinguished. The time stamp read seven-thirty and five seconds.

"RJ was one of the Wise Men," Idelle smiled.

To go from the greatest story ever told to the horror of Kurt Boulton's final act? Darla had a roller-coaster of a night.

A group of carolers entered the scene.

"I'm sorry I don't have sound on this thing, but I didn't think I needed the deluxe model."

The quartet strolled along in period-wear, as animated as a *Peanuts* special. In his head, Jude heard them going a-wassailing, whatever that meant. They greeted passers-by wrapped to the ears and then some. It was hard to see faces in the dim lighting, impossible through hats and scarves.

Time passed and the number of shoppers dwindled as the other retail stores closed for the night.

"Wait—stop there, please?" Audie's finger pointed at the lower right corner of the screen.

Nick reversed ten seconds, rerunning it at normal speed. On the sidewalk stood a familiar figure, dark-suited, top hat bolstering his diminutive height. He filled out the scarlet waistcoat more than the photos of Dickens showed—his ghost must be partaking of sweets from Christmas Present's overflowing table. He'd learned how to make the most of what he had, because he'd positioned himself up on the curb while an average-size man a few years his senior, clad in work clothes, stood in the gutter.

"Is that—?"

"Kurt Boulton." Idelle frowned. "Suffering the slings and arrows of Glen Armquist, who wants to beat the entire district into his interpretation of history."

"It doesn't look like a friendly conversation." Glen's lantern swung in his gloved hand, the face of the handyman alternating from a bright yellow to an ashy gray.

It was strange, seeing the person he'd only known in death, alive and well, if harassed. Boulton didn't flinch as the berating continued, but his eyes also didn't appear focused on Glen.

"How old was Kurt?"

"Mid-fifties. Just younger than Glen."

"Younger?" The sunken cheeks and slight hunch painted him a decade his senior. That divorce must've been rough.

But like with Fran, there were always reasons for a breakup. He wondered if he was looking at cause or effect.

On screen and despite that untamed beard in the way, it was obvious Glen never shut his trap. When Kurt did attempt to interject, he never made it past a word or two. He tucked his phone into a back pocket and began flipping a key ring with his left hand, probably the only action keeping him from throttling a Victorian author wannabe. After a minute, another figure entered the frame. This man, tall-ish, wore a striped scarf and glasses. He stepped down into the gutter, and the pair faced Mr. Dickens as a united front.

"That's Derek Vikander. Armquist's his—"

"Uncle, yeah, we met him at lunch. Doesn't look like he's siding with family."

Derek forced through an actual sentence, and Kurt's worn expression softened a degree.

"Seems a decent kid."

"Yes, but unlike Kurt, Derek's older than you think he is. Almost thirty? He and Frannie Gill went to high school together."

Schoolmates, huh? The way he deferred to her in her moment of distress... Doth love stir the youthful hearts?

Leave the writing to the ghosts, West.

Aye, aye, captain.

"Word is he wasn't a lot of fun in those days. Conceited, too much money he hadn't earned. Both his parents came from affluent families, and he didn't have the struggles the other kids did. Made him into a bully and a scamp."

"Nobody says scamp anymore, dear."

"They get the picture. Anyway, by the time Derek finished college, he'd changed his ways."

"Finally matured?"

Nick laughed, and it was almost but not quite hearty enough to validate Jude's secret-identity theory. Drat. "From what he told me one day over a cone of Rocky Road, he got his maturity handed to him. He'd been seeing this girl at the university, but she'd had it with his pomposity—"

"Another word nobody uses." Idelle smirked toward Audie, who struggled not to laugh.

"—and left him. He'd never been the dumpee and not the dumper. She found herself a better fella, and the two of them graduated, got married, and moved out to Colorado, I believe. Derek had to watch it all from a distance, with his frat brothers mocking how he'd let her treat him that way, like the girl didn't have a say in the matter."

College. *Kinda glad I missed that phase.* There'd been enough razzing on the Alaskan trawler to last into eternity.

Back on Nick's phone, a group of visitors ventured into sight and Dickens—experiencing an active afterlife—did an about-face, resuming celebrated author status. With Glen occupied, his prey seized the opportunity, and both men disappeared off screen.

"So what do you think the argument was about?" *Is it an argument if only one party got to speak?* A haranguing? A lambasting?

Nick frowned. "With Glen, who knows? It could've been something semi-serious, like a problem at his antique shop. Maybe a door left unlocked or a light left on. He's more protective of that junk than he'd be about his own children, if he had any. Has a mental inventory of every item that's been stolen from any of us. Kind of a hoarder more than a seller. Gets it from his father."

"Hoarding?"

"They called it collecting." He rolled his eyes. "A tad touched, if you know what I mean, and a 'my way or the highway' guy. Glen also might've gotten a bee in his bonnet because Kurt wasn't wearing his period-accurate flannel. The celebration of Jesus's birth will forever be ruined."

"Had Kurt worked here at the parlor last night?"

"No, we only have him come in twice a week for the bigger cleanings. We can still do most of it ourselves." Of course they could. Mrs. Idelle must have a bionic suit on beneath that green apron.

Nick reset the video to fast forward, and nothing else interesting happened for a while. They reached nine-twenty, and a large group filtered in from the north side of the camera.

"Hey! That's us!"

Stuart Morrison, his black cape, hat, and flashlight appeared across the street first, then the rest of the ghost tour groupies. Standing at the rear, outside the small crush of people, were Audie, Vita, and himself.

"You took one of Stu's tours?" Their host's narrowed eyes re-evaluated them both.

"In our defense," Audie said, fighting to keep a spot on the Nice List, "it was ridiculously cold, and the original ghost guide's outings are more accurate but much longer. Besides, there's always some truth mixed into the supernatural stories. It's once the person moves beyond the mortal plain that things get wonky."

"Now there's a word for you, Nick," his wife tapped the table.

"Love it! I'll store it away to bug you later."

There it was—the Santa laugh! *Halleluj*—

"Stop!"

The trio jumped as Audie cut in, jabbing again at the screen. "Sorry," she blushed. "But could you please go back a few seconds?"

Nick picked up the phone, sliding the progress bar.

"Run it at normal speed, will you?"

Jude leaned forward, intent on and confused by the images. There was nothing but Mr. Morrison and his specter spectators—

Holy guacamole.

"There." In what could only be described as a flit, a black-hooded shape slipped in at the base of the view, turning up at the camera long enough to be noticeable, and moved on. Nick rewound and played it even slower. When the figure paused, its face was missing.

Not in shadow. Missing.

"What in the world?"

Idelle's head tilted, and the ever-practical Mrs. Claus didn't have an answer. "It looks like the Ghost of Christmas Future, from *A Christmas Carol*, doesn't it? But I thought the group wasn't doing anything with that story this year."

"They aren't." Nick's tone was firm, but low enough to not draw the attention of the mother-child duo wrapping up to brave the outdoors. "They did away with those characters a few seasons ago. Eighteen-hundreds morality tales aren't as much of an attraction as they used to be. In any case, no one ever wanted to play this particular ghost. It's a silent role, creepy, makes the little kiddies cry."

And the big ones.

Audie had half-turned, a silent question shooting out of her eyes. He gave a quick nod.

It was the same figure he'd seen twice now. The St. Charles Phantom.

"But how is he moving so fast? That seems fast, doesn't it?" Nick scratched at his chin beneath the beard. "I don't know how you caught it."

We don't call her Eagle Eye for nothing, Mr. Kringle. Hmm, thought he would've known that.

"I was looking at the right place at the right time," she shrugged.

Sure.

"So as we're getting set at our last spot, a ridiculously spooky person in black is creeping around near where a thief has just killed himself."

"We don't know if Kurt was dead yet."

Jude's stomach lurched.

Idelle also looked incredibly uncomfortable. "Are we sure it's a, well—"

"What, love?"

"A person?" She blushed redder than Rudolph's nose. "I mean, there's supposed to be so much spirit activity here."

Her husband shook his head. "We've never believed an ounce of that."

"And I still don't. But isn't it odd? Kurt died by his own hand. Some might say it was his soul passing. Or something coming to take him… elsewhere. Other people, mind you."

Audie and Jude exchanged looks. Not their normal first thought. But in a city centuries old, with murders and hangings and slavery and who knows what else going on?

They sped through the previous two nights' recordings before a flock of students in the red plaid of the nearest Catholic grade school walked in with a dire need for dairy-based confections. Both evenings' footage had been less exciting than Thursday's, with no flitting phantoms in the frame. Kurt had come and gone like clockwork, in from the north, crossing the street to the boutique, reentering the scene to visit the next shop down the line. He'd always been alone, usually ignored as only another holiday reveler, not a man so troubled that he'd do what he ultimately did. As the Ramseys repositioned themselves behind the shiny counter, they promised to note their video catch to the right people.

I guess you don't discuss criminal matters in front of the local eighth graders, or at least not while scooping their Moose Tracks.

Once more braced for the out-of-doors, they made for Main Street. Even in this anything-but-scary daylight, Jude couldn't quite look at Vita's building the same way.

He'd just stepped down onto the sidewalk when a shove from behind launched a chain of events suitable for the Stooges. He fell into Audie, whose purse swung forward into the leash of a sweatered terrier. Its owner tripped on a raised cobblestone and nearly took flight. A remarkable set of accidental pirouettes finished with everyone on two feet (or four, as appropriate) and facing their original directions.

That guardian angel from *It's a Wonderful Life* must've been pulling extra duty today.

Jude turned to find the start of the train wreck. "Glen Armquist!"

The man, not yet in his dead author attire, looked up as he reached for the door of Lucy's Lix. No apology, no recognition of the chaos he'd caused, only a frazzled, "Do I know you?"

Audie returned to Jude's side, disentangled from Muffin the Very Good Boy. She plastered on a sunnier expression than predicted, considering the near disaster. "We haven't been introduced yet." She put out a cobalt-blue gloved hand. "Audie and Jude West. I'm Vita Klein's sister. We saw you yesterday during Stuart Morrison's ghost tour."

He could barely bring himself to touching the glove after mention of Stuart. He actually harrumphed. "I would've thought Vita's sister would've been above such theatrical nonsense."

This, coming from a dude dressing up nightly as a beloved writer's poltergeist?

"It was all in fun." Then she remembered the aftermath. "Until we heard about Mr. Boulton, of course."

It pained Armquist to come down from the parlor's top step, but a line was forming behind him now and he was forced to play the kindly king of Frenchtown. "Yes, yes, tragic. But I find it difficult to be too upset when one's conscience catches up with them." He turned the sneer into a broad and jovial facsimile of the Cheshire Cat as a particularly chic woman carrying bags from the pricier spots on Main walked by. He peeked to see if she was walking toward G. Armquist's Fine Antiques.

She wasn't.

"We ran into your nephew, Derek, earlier. You had a few things pilfered from the shop?"

The mustache derided his choice of words. "The *company* was burgled, yes. Kurt had no respect. It's outrageous that someone would pull something like that in this community."

"Outrageous? I mean, don't thefts happen in any community?" *Or have I only been hanging around the seedy spots since I left Dayton?*

"Not here, sir." Sir. *Now I've done it.* "We are better than that. Or most of us are." The glower returned to his face, much the same as when he'd been lecturing Boulton hours before his suicide.

Intriguing.

"It seems Kurt had some troubles. I find it best to give people grace on occasion."

All five-and-a-half feet of Derek's uncle quivered. "You give the grace, then. I want our history back."

Glen yanked on the door right as someone from inside pushed outward, leaving him wheeling on his heels like a helicopter. Jude caught him, but he didn't so much as grumble 'thanks' as he blustered past the fourteen-year-old with the double-scoop and started calling out to Nicholas.

"Somebody doth protesteth too much, methinks," Audie said, low, as they watched him through the large window.

"Methinks I agree. Or agree-eth."

But did it mean anything? That was the question.

CHAPTER 10

The ruckus of a thousand exuberant pooches erupted as Audie pushed into the next shop down the row. Those bricks between buildings must be lined with the greatest insulation known to man's best friend, because they'd heard none of this from Lucy's Lix.

Good thing Lucy had passed beyond the cares of this mortal world. That kitty would not have appreciated her neighbors.

"Who knew canine bakeries were the place to be?" The fluffiest golden retriever in the history of ever welcomed Jude with a leap, and Audie immediately lost her husband to the floor. He crouched on one knee and scratched at the pupster's scruff, a mutt among his kind.

The Doggy Bag was awash in fur, water bowls, and owners enjoying their own drinks and treats. Humans sat at tabletops mounted onto imitations of Snoopy's house. The place was bright and light, with walls of photos and a full-size mural of frolicking cartoon fidos.

And while her original estimate of a thousand critters may have been a tad high, the effect was the same.

The owner of the retriever retrieved her, or tried, anyway. The woman hurried to grab the trailing leash, pink and bedazzled, but her pet had found a new bestie and refused to abandon him.

"I'm so sorry," the girl flushed. "Arwen had one of the pup cups. Now she thinks the entire world is her queendom, and we're her loyal subjects."

"Arwen? If she's Elrond's daughter, she's entitled to her own elfdom, right?"

Based on the tail whacking Audie's leg every zero-point-three seconds, the queen agreed. Enthusiastically.

The woman laughed and ultimately finagled through the dog's fur to her collar. She pulled her away, but not before Arwen landed a final lick on Jude's cheek. Even the hounds fell for that man.

That or she simply liked pistachio.

"We have got to get one of those someday," he said, climbing to his feet and brushing off his jeans.

The two of them plus an animal bigger than her, living in an eighteen-foot travel trailer?

The more the merrier.

A terrier crouched beneath the nearest table, barking at Audie's ankles like they were the devil's henchmen. The resemblance to its owner was uncanny: dour and irritated with the world. At least this leash was secure. A beagle, three pugs, two corgis, and a dalmatian rounded out the cacophony.

"I'll be with you in a second!" came a voice from the rear of the space. A man about their age, brown hair slicked back and wearing an apron covered in painted paw prints, was pulling a mountainous scoop of biscuits from a glass jar. He weighed it for the stately-looking nonagenarian with the corgis and rang him up at the register. The customer tipped his fedora—houndstooth, of course—to Audie as he took his bag and entourage out into the afternoon.

The cashier automatically looked toward their feet, and not seeing any fuzzy friends, said, "You don't need to leave the kids outside. Let them join the fun."

"Don't tell him that." Audie feigned horror, nodding toward her hubby. "He'll go out and commit dognapping."

"If I could provide a better home, I'd be performing a service." But he smiled enough that the guy behind the counter didn't dial 911 and pre-report a felony.

"Are you here to buy gifts for Christmas, then? Our reindeer-shaped bratwurst chews are going over well with the furrier connoisseurs." He gestured at his full cafe.

The people and pooch snacks must get mixed up in all this chaos. *Dunking a sausage-flavored reindeer in your coffee would probably wake you up faster.*

"Actually, we were hoping we could ask you a couple of questions, but you're busy."

"Are you from the Post?" He began wiping his hands on the apron. "Idelle told me reporters were coming for the holiday grand finale, but we're not hosting any of the period activities here. Apparently, there weren't many canine bakers in early St. Charles."

That was a missed opportunity. Lewis and Clark's Newfoundland had his own statue at Frontier Park. He might've had more responsibilities than most did today, but Seaman probably would've enjoyed the occasional delicacy that wasn't squirrel.

"No, I'm Audie West, Vita Klein's sister. She's the V in DFV Boutique across the street."

"Of course! I knew you reminded me of somebody."

Another man of similar age, a little shorter and wearing a matching apron, emerged from a swinging door. He carried a tray of fresh treats and slid it into the case. How could dog food smell that delicious?

"Did someone mention Vita? She's the best neighbor we could have. That whole trio is." He closed the glass and put down his oven mitt. "The vet clinic where Fran works buys from us once a month, and Darla has a standing order for mint-flavored yum-yums for Leonard."

Jude's head tilted. "Her husband?"

Their synchronized laughter attracted the attention of the canine customers, and Audie could hear herself think. "I wonder sometimes, but no, that's Lionel. Leonard is the German Shepherd. He's about a hundred years old—"

"In human years."

"—and has terrible breath. The mint helps." He reached a hand over the register. "I'm Owen, and this is my brother, Peter. We're the paw patrol, you could say."

Introductions progressed smoothly until the bells at the door rang behind them. So much for quiet. Peter moved away to greet a sheltie and its person.

Owen waved them to the far end of the counter. "I saw the crime scene tape," he said at a lower volume. "I cannot believe the news about Kurt. Are the girls okay?"

"Shook up, of course, but all right. They can't reopen until the authorities finish with things."

He wagged his head. "The week before Christmas. That's got to hurt."

"Did you guys notice anything going on over there in the past couple nights?"

"Past couple? Why, were they burgled too?"

Quick, this one.

"No, no." Audie lied. "We were just wondering if maybe you spotted Mr. Boulton acting strangely, or carrying anything out of the ordinary, like a bigger bag? The police haven't found where he stashed the stolen goods."

Owen adjusted the neck loop of his apron. "No, but it's impossible to see the street at night when we've got our lights on inside."

Peter rejoined them, having served up a dish of something delicious because his cuff was drizzled with strawberry syrup. "I did step out for some air around eight, before we closed. I wanted to listen to the last of the evening's carolers."

"Somebody is a frustrated tenor," Owen smirked.

"Hey, I'm Pavarotti in the shower."

Jude redirected them to the track. "Did you notice anything?"

"The usual bustle as business died off for the night. And of course Kurt was starting to go door to door for his work. Some shops close up earlier than others, and he was in and out like normal. Yesterday, he left the bike shop and headed toward the boutique. The night before, I was out at the same time, but I didn't catch anybody moving around their place."

"I think Kurt only comes every few days at most places?"

"We have him nightly, because we need help with all the fur. But, yeah, that's generally right."

Owen was growing antsier as the conversation continued. He surveyed his clientele, gabbing or reading or snapping pics of their dogs with peppermint bark balanced on their noses. Convinced no one was listening, he leaned in. "I did catch something strange two nights ago."

Peter rolled his eyes. "Really? You're going to bring that up?"

"I can't help it if you have a narrow mind."

Peter rubbed his forehead. "Go on."

His sibling needed no more encouragement. "I was in front of the store after we'd locked the doors. I cleaned off our bench and was bringing in the water dishes to wash for the next day. Things were peaceful out there, it being a Wednesday, and Wednesday isn't really a busy time most weeks anyway, I mean folks don't do their shopping on a random Wed—"

"What did you see?"

Owen blushed and refocused. "Her."

"Who?"

"You know." His green eyes widened, angling his head toward the street. "Her."

Oh boy.

"Josephine Richards?" Jude's eyebrows disappeared into his bangs.

"Who else?"

According to Stuart Morrison, there were plenty of other options. "Have you seen her before?"

"Several times. I mean, we're right here and have been for the last five years. I've lost track of how often I've seen her, long before Vita, Darla, and Fran moved in."

Jude turned to Peter. "And you?"

He hesitated. "It's all a bunch of nonsense."

"But…" Owen urged, intending to stare him into spitting it out.

"Don't do that." Peter put up a hand to block his brother's giddy anticipation. *Siblings: getting on each other's nerves—and more—since the Garden of Eden.* "Yes, I caught a glimpse of something I can't describe without sounding like a loon. Only once, right after we moved in. Never again."

The disclaimers didn't dampen Owen's triumph. "Eureka!"

"What exactly did you see on Wednesday, Owen?"

His eyes sparkled while Peter's cried, 'save me now.' "A figure, over on the side of the building, between the boutique and what used to be the glassmaker's studio next door."

"Nathaniel Silvain's place?"

He nodded enthusiastically. "You know the story? Yes, the man who killed her with that awful piece of glass." He shuddered. "And then Kurt Boulton goes and does the same, only to himself."

"You watched this person go into the shop?"

"No, not through the door exactly. But it did seem to," he struggled for the right word, "pass through, so to speak."

"And it was a woman?"

"Owen, seriously." Peter tried to at least get his rising tone to drop. It didn't work, but the canines didn't care.

Owen was over his brother's embarrassment. "Who's to say what form we take once we leave these mortal bodies? With those gas lamps out there, it's difficult to see clearly. But I know it was her."

So helpful. Or not.

"And last night?"

"Other than Glen the party pooper yelling at Kurt and Derek outside, nothing unusual went on."

"And that's not so unusual either," Peter added.

"You saw that live? Any idea what Glen was upset about?"

"Knowing him, the doorknob at his store had a fingerprint left on it." Peter rolled his eyes. "He didn't like Kurt appearing to be a person from the twenty-first century. He'd prefer us confined to one of Dickens' workhouses rather than polluting his streets."

"What a jack—"

Audie's side-eye cut off Owen.

"Sorry," he reddened. "That wasn't in the holiday spirit, was it?"

That look was getting more effective and more reflexive. *Heaven help me, I'm turning into my mother.*

The doorbells rang once more. "Guys, thank you, but if I don't get Jude out of here, I'll wind up with a chihuahua in my purse."

"Nothing so wrong with that," Jude pouted.

Audie ignored him. "We appreciate the info." *Such as it was.* "If you think of anything else strange, would you give Vita a call?"

Owen took the waiting customer this time, and Peter's brow furrowed. "Why are you asking about this stuff? Kurt's death was a suicide, and he had some of the missing items on him."

Jude shrugged, trying to look idly curious. "We're deep into history with our day job. With this happening at Audie's sister's place, we're wondering if the building's backstory influenced Mr. Boulton's decisions. That's all."

"What's your day job?"

"Genealogy. Folks hire us to help fill in the branches when their hunts go cold, or when they live out of state and need boots on the ground to dig things up for them."

"Not literal bodies," Audie amended with a smile she hoped was as charming as her husband claimed it was.

"Fascinating. We've got a second-great-uncle who came home from boot camp and immediately disappeared without a trace. Nobody ever heard from him again, not even the Army knocking on his parents' door."

"That'd be a good one to chase down. There's shiny fruit in every tree."

Peter smirked. "With our family, it's more like a kook on every branch." He looked down the counter to his sibling, who was making faces at a dachshund cradled in a child's arms. "I think I've identified this branch's contender."

Chapter 11

The fire in the Klein hearth soothed more aches than Jude cared to admit he'd gathered just from hoofing it over bumpy roads. He couldn't even blame it on hauling wood from the backyard rack; for that, he was conditioned. It was like camping, only these logs hadn't needed splitting. Simon was lucky to have Connor living nearby. He might be occupied with his job and ancestral sausage-making, but the boy was nimble with an axe when need-be.

Then again, splitting wood was better than therapy, so Simon's loss.

Audie's shoulders were tense, like they were always tense, as he perched in the world's comfiest chair, kneading at her muscles. She held a mug of steaming cider that dwarfed her thin fingers and lapped up the warmth the way Arwen had licked at his face.

"Vi needs this more than I do," she said, but she didn't budge from her spot. Her sister sat opposite him on the matching chair.

"I'm glad Simon's away," she smiled. "He'd be in line too."

It's nice to be wanted. "Least I can do, since I keep sneaking into your fridge when nobody's looking."

"Darling, nobody's looking or caring. Besides, you've put most of that food there in the first place."

Audie reached around and patted his hand. "Bless you. You're dismissed. Off to your next client."

As he extracted his legs from behind his wife's back, Vita spared no time shifting down to the floor. "I may not be able to get up from here, but I'm willing to risk it."

"Pull-up service is included in every massage package."

The older of the Marik sisters was just as tense, but in a different way. Audie's was chronic. Vita's was acute.

"Thank you two for poking around for us today," she said, then moaned as Jude hit a tendon in sore need of un-sore-ing. "I'm so afraid for Frannie."

Audie set down her mug and bent forward, stretching out her legs and pointing her toes. Ripples of loosening vertebrae crackled with the embers. "We didn't get much out of your neighbors except the Glen and Kurt show. I'm glad Derek stepped in to help."

"The Ghost of Charles Dickens," Vi scoffed. "How in the world he can go around playing that role and yet be such a jerk is beyond me. It's unChristian. UnDickensian."

"Maybe he'll get haunted by three spirits." Jude started working on the right side of her neck, the dominant side that felt poised for battle. He checked over the hearth for a broadsword—nope, only a decorative iron scrollwork. Guess they were safe.

"I'd be willing to haunt him myself, always thinking people are below him because he putters among beautiful old things. I hate to tell him this, but something being old doesn't make it valuable."

"Vita, you're getting more uptight, not less."

"Oh right." She inhaled from her diaphragm, fighting down vitriol caused by their favorite snob. The bout lasted three seconds. "And it's not like he's the spitting image of Mr. Dickens. Wasn't Charles at least taller and thinner? And surely someone as famous as him would've beaten all that facial hair into submission."

"Ask the librarian."

Audie studied an imaginary bookshelf somewhere in her mind. To an outsider, it would look like she, too, was searching for the broadsword. "Dickens' mustache and beard were even more unruly in his later years. I think he was supposed to be on the shortish side, but I remember reading he had a frail build."

"Then Glen needs to lay off Nick and Idelle's cherry sundaes."

"The biggest difference is that he had a reputation as a flamboyant dresser, favoring bright colors and bold patterns. He's described as vivacious." Her squint narrowed further. "Does Mr. Armquist have an ambitious twinkle in his eye?"

"Only for pretty baubles."

"Since he's playing Charles' specter, Glen might figure the spirit world subdued him? Otherwise, he seems to be sculpting a perfect Victorian gentleman, his personal preference for a man of letters though it misses the mark by a mile."

"Leave it to him to rewrite a writer," Vita grumbled. "And he clearly missed class the day they talked about Dickens' poverty-stricken youth, how it led his ghosts to bless the lowest more than anyone."

Jude pushed down on his sister-in-law's rising shoulders. "Work with me, Vi."

"Right. Sorry."

They fell into silence, but when he glanced over at Audie, her thoughts broadcast turmoil at full volume. Not surprising. The topic? That would be a mystery until she spilled it.

After several seconds, she conceded. "Do you think any of this could actually relate to the Josephine Richards story?"

Vita's fast-twitch muscles relaunched, and he considered surrendering. Who needed relaxation anyway?

"Audra West!"

"I know, I know. It was a suicide. But I was doing some research today."

"Of course you were." Jude steered Vi's head back toward the fire and began kneading the other side.

"Did you know only two percent of suicides are by slashing, and almost always at the wrists?"

"There's a statistic for that sort of thing?"

"Sadly, yes. Two percent. The more common ways are by gun, hanging, poisoning or overdose, and jumping from somewhere onto or into something unforgiving. That's the intentional ones, of course. There are plenty that are accidental."

Vita let her head roll. "I'm stuck on why Kurt was stealing if he hadn't sold any of it yet."

"The cops haven't found a thing, huh? Black-market antiques, online, none of that?"

"No, not so much as Nick's ice cream scoop."

"So the man becomes a thief after years of not being a thief," Jude recapped. "Then one night, after being berated by the fraud of a nineteenth-century author, he gets drunk in your shop and kills himself with a shard of broken glass."

"The same means used to kill a legislator's wife two centuries ago in the same building," Audie nodded.

"To heck with the same building," Vita corrected. "It was the same spot."

"You're kidding."

"I wish I was. But in those days, our sales area was the family sitting room, right outside of the kitchen. It's exactly where

Nathaniel Silvain killed Josephine, with her husband stumbling into the bloody aftermath."

For a few moments, the only sounds were popping sparks. They'd need more logs soon. He'd also need to channel Houdini to escape from his current duties.

Always another challenge.

"It's awfully coincidental." Audie sipped her cider.

"You're implying something less voluntary happened to Mr. Boulton?" he asked. "But everyone around here knows the story of Josephine and Nathaniel. Anybody in town would be a suspect if he were killed."

"Plus the county, St. Louis county, the neighboring cities and clear across the country. The older ghost tours have been plugging that tale for decades, because it's rooted in fact. So lots of locals and tourists have heard the gory details. And it all ends with a shard of bloody glass and a slashed throat."

Audie's shiver rocked her mug. "The glass is the part that intrigues me."

"That's putting it lightly."

"Lord, not you too." Vita looked up at him with worry.

"I don't mean about ghosts," although that dream left him wanting to avoid sleep as long as possible. "And I don't think Audie means them either. But why glass? If so few suicides are by cutting, there must be better ways to do it, right in the same spot where a glass-oriented murder also happened."

"He was drunk, and it was convenient?"

He frowned, looking down at Vi's curly hair, color-matched to his wife's. "But it wasn't convenient. I mean, yes, Fran's workbench was close. But he had to break a piece to get that sharp edge, while his own tool bag sat a couple of feet away. I saw that thing. It was full of implements of destruction. Why would he risk the glass when he could've grabbed his own trusty box cutter?"

This time, the silence lasted until Vita scooted forward, her session at a close. Had they made much progress? Doubtful. "That's a valid question. And some of my tools are there, too, along with Fran's. Any of them would've been more convenient and just as deadly."

"You said this was a known event in neighborhood chronicles. I think it's worth looking into." Audie's eyes reflected the flames. The bloodhound had caught an alluring scent. It wouldn't have done them any good to call her off. "You know, out of curiosity."

Sure. Curiosity.

Another unlucky cat, destined to bite the dust at the hands of Mrs. Audra West.

Where was a masseuse when he needed one?

Three a.m., and here I am, thinking about what? As usual, too much, and as often, things of no consequence.

But that was for the best. Because ruminating on dead handymen or discouraged young women—old or modern-day— held too many consequences.

Poor Fran.

I need a distraction. I could make a chart to guess which version of Mom I'll see when I visit in the morning.

She cracked herself up.

Yeah, I'd do better predicting Jude's phantom.

In the corner of their cozy attic room, the blue glow from the laptop turned Audie's hands an unfortunate shade of dead. The neighborhood ghosts would think she fit right in. She tried to avoid too many of these midnight search sessions when they stayed at

Vita's. Her sister didn't sleep much better than she did, and for some reason, Jude was more likely to be bothered by the light in here than at the camper.

Weird, since this room technically had more square footage than their rolling home.

More space for specters? They hadn't been a problem before. But the boy had read well past his usual lights-out tonight. Didn't he know only one half of a couple was allowed to be haunted in a marriage? She pulled Grandma's afghan closer.

As softly as she could, she tapped around the online backstory of Chariton County, Missouri, represented first by good old Clarence Richards. It had only become a county the year before, though the state wasn't even a state yet. By its August 1821 induction into the country, Missouri had twenty-four counties established. Had it been the modern number of 115, the Peck Brothers' building would've burst at its mortared seams.

The county, in the north-central portion of the state, had begun as a fur trapping settlement like so many along the Big Muddy. Other similarities peppered its history, especially the loss of its first major community, Old Chariton, to a flood in 1825.

More clicking. The region became part of what's known as Little Dixie, agricultural hamlets created by those who'd moved from the Upper South and began planting fields with tobacco and hemp. She shuddered as she saw it shared a border with Saline County. After the nightmarish job in Hatchet Bend a few weeks back, Audie hoped their next several cases would head in any direction but that one. Sam's funeral had been full of the pomp and circumstance afforded a long-serving member of the US Navy. But she never wanted to hear the word hemp again, whether used as rope or for more recreational activities.

Good grief. Now she needed a distraction from her distraction.

She spent another thirty minutes searching for information on Clarence and Josephine, but to no avail. Yes, he was listed in the first General Assembly. And Ranger Quinn was right—no newspapers carried anything about the murder or the hanging. Swift justice. Well, swift punishment, anyway, if only weeks passed between Josephine's slaying and Nathaniel's swing from the rope. Not a lot of time for due process.

But this was the frontier, not *Law & Order*.

She gave in, unable to find so much as marriage records for the rising couple. She'd hoped to confirm what Quinn had remarked about the Richards' age difference. Guess she'd have to trust him. *If you can't trust a State Park Ranger…*

Gabby Tucker's bright face and perky blond ponytail popped to mind. Right. Goodwin's Mill had proved her wrong on that account too.

She closed the lid louder than intended, and under the warm quilt, her husband stirred. She went still as a statue until he settled once more onto the hand-stitched pillowcases. Setting the laptop aside, she padded to the bed and climbed in beside him. He reached an arm across her waist. She hoped they were wrong about Josephine's marriage, that before her grisly death, she'd been happy.

She also hoped Jude's imagination had simply gotten the best of him with that dream. Because the idea of a desperate woman pleading for help after two centuries tore at her heart like a thousand shards of glass.

Chapter 12

Everybody wants me taking their car, and I pick the one that doesn't have a window scraper. Audie turned up the wipers, and the fluffy flakes blew onto the Mini in the next space. *Oops.* Hopefully their scraper hadn't grown legs and walked off like Simon's.

With this being the first appreciable snow of the season, she should've known to prep better. Not all drivers outfit their vehicles for emergencies like her shoulda-been-a-Boy-Scout husband.

She verified that the bright pink poinsettia was secured in its seat, safety belt clicked, and pulled out of the garden store parking lot.

I should get a coffee.

I should stop stalling.

Like both Jude and Vita, even her conscience thought this was a bad idea and tried to protect her. This was not going to go well. It would take a holiday miracle.

The reintroductions. The remembrances of things long past, characters in her life's stage play that had been replaced despite her mother's preferences and prejudices.

"Long past?"

"Your past."

More Dickens. The man was having a busy death.

And then there's the vacant looks of other residents at the home, those further along the journey than Mom. Add in the lack of privacy, the struggling staff...

That coffee ought to be super-charged with something from Vita's "special" cabinet.

She'd opted instead for an extra dose of God, fervent and focused prayers said throughout the 7 a.m. Mass that morning. Jude had insisted on attending with her, unusual for a non-Sunday. But after that, she'd had an insistence of her own.

She would face this gauntlet alone.

The Accord passed an inviting cafe, and she had to restrain herself from turning. Her goal was only another mile down the road. And though her mother didn't have a concept of time anymore, her caregivers did. Disrespectful to be late, especially on the weekend before Christmas.

The sign for Mulberry Gardens Memory Care was festooned with boughs of green and big red bows. A resin nativity scene graced the powdered lawn in front of it. The manger awaited Baby Jesus, but only for a few more days. By now, the wise men should be packing their camels.

Parked in the shadow of a Chevy Suburban in the hopes of it blocking the precip, she tucked the plastic cover over the poinsettia. How often had Mom reminded her that a mere minute of unprotected exposure to these temperatures would kill the Christmas favorite? She pulled her knit hat over her ears—not quite as sensitive as the tropical plant—slipped her crossbody purse over her head, and pushed out into the wind.

The snow wasn't accumulating yet. The ground was cold enough, but the local meteorologists claimed this wouldn't be more than a dusting overall.

Around here, that could end up being six inches.

Then when they call for Snowpocalypse, we'll get nothing. The asphalt was slippery under her boots, and she skated to the rock-salted concrete steps.

The smell of warm gingerbread hit her as she stepped into the lobby. A bright-faced blond woman wearing reindeer antlers looked up from her computer.

"Come in out of that mess!"

Audie stamped on the mat and brushed off the top of the poinsettia's crude shower cap. She pulled it away and stowed it in her pocket for recycling later.

"How can I help you?" asked Prancer's distant cousin.

"I have a visit scheduled with my mom, Irina Marik. I'm Audie West."

"Sure, I've got you on the calendar here. You're Vita's sister? I'm Holly. I don't think we've met yet."

The woman could've offered her a plate of fresh-baked snickerdoodles while sharing something innocuous like why chartreuse is an underrated color, and Audie still would've been hit by a wave of guilt. *Vita's sister.* Vita, who lives nearby and carries nearly everything where Mom was concerned. The ever-revolving staff might not recognize Audie, may not even realize Irina had a second daughter.

Well, anymore, Irina didn't realize it either.

Caregivers with any experience understood each family's gears ran differently. And when it came to dementia, the pain of one's own mother not recognizing you or your husband or kids or knowing themselves some days was something many people simply couldn't bear. Taking care of parents is one thing. When the parent treats them like an intruder to be grilled or, worse, feared? Infinitely more difficult. The staff rarely judged. Heck, they probably had personal battles with the horrible disease themselves.

That did nothing to ease the guilt, though.

"She's having a pretty good day." Holly's antlers bobbed her namesake greenery and jingled with every syllable. The woman with her own timpani pushed a sign-in sheet across the desk and handed her a pen. "Shonda has her ready for you. You know how to get to her room?"

Of course, I know how to get to her room. I'm her daughter, aren't I?
Who hadn't seen her but a few times since last Christmas.
Blessed Virgin Mary, pray for us.

"Yes, I do. Thank you." She signed her name, as small and tiny as she felt, and picked up the plant again.

"Have a nice visit."

Hope springs eternal.

"Knock, knock." Audie tapped on the door frame and poked her head into Room 117. A woman in her early thirties glanced over her shoulder. Her cranberry scrubs complemented the mahogany of her arms and set off eyes almost as hazel as Jude's. The blue penguin socks peeking out above her athletic shoes were simply fun.

"Hello, hello! We were just getting settled for you. Irina, look who's here."

Audie hung between heaven and Hades as the woman stepped away from the power lift recliner. Okay, not that much different from September. Maybe another few pounds lost from a body that couldn't afford to lose many more. But Mom was still Mom, at least on the outside. She sat in the chair with perfect posture, an elegant black and silver sweater over her narrow frame and her hair done up in a bun. She took in the figure at the doorway, her own flesh and blood, and didn't know quite what to do with it. So she focused on what she did know.

"My word, what a lovely poinsettia. Is that for me?"

Shonda and Audie traded places carefully in the limited space.

"I'll be right out at the nurse's station if you need me, hon." That knowing look. *It didn't matter if I were here daily.* Irina wouldn't be certain who she was the next morning.

"Yes, this is for you." She set it on the wide windowsill that looked onto the courtyard of the four-winged building. Another crèche had been erected at the dormant central fountain. A white gazebo held lights that must've glittered once night fell.

"Thank you so much. What an interesting color." Was that a slight frown? Should've gone with red, with tradition. Her mother reached out and touched the pink leaves, her hands wrinkled and paper-thin, quivering like a hummingbird. Audie took off her gloves and wondered how long it would be before her own skin matched.

She slipped off her coat and sat on the chair across from her. Not for the first time, she admired how well the room mimicked the one her parents had shared at their last house. The bed was in the right place, with the same flowery comforter covering it. The television had been mounted above the dresser they'd bought when they married fifty-five years ago. In the corner stood a quilt rack, holding more of Grandma's crocheted afghans, now used regularly as their current owner grew a little colder every month. Family photographs covered a wall, in an arrangement that Audie had curated and Vita had hung while Irina was at lunch. They were supposed to help stir memories.

They didn't.

Don't ask her if she remembers you. Don't imply that she's forgetful. *Don't cry, don't cry, don't cry.*

"Mom, I'm Audra."

Her green eyes—not the gray ones of her daughters, which were thanks to Dad—darted through several stages of confusion before her temporal lobe hit the button for recognition. "Of course you are. You think I don't know my own daughter?" She smiled, and Audie smiled.

"I'm so glad to see you. I wanted to come say Merry Christmas."

"Is it Christmas already?"

"Almost. In a few days. Do you see Mary and Joseph out in the yard here?"

She turned to where her daughter pointed. "The shepherds are on the move."

Audie laughed out loud. *That, she remembers.* Her mother would repeat those words each Advent. Some things weren't lost in the sieve. Others?

"So how are you doing?"

"I'm well. This is such a nice place. There are so many kind people here. You should meet some of them before your father comes home."

A sharp stab went straight through several of Audie's vital organs. Time to brace for the rest.

"I should. Are you eating? Do they make meals you like?"

Irina waved it off with bony fingers. "They try. If they'd let me in the kitchen, I could show them how it's done. But I'm not allowed for some reason."

"Maybe the chef's crabby." *Sorry, Chef. I'm sure you're doing an awesome job.*

"Maybe." She didn't look convinced.

"She's probably sensitive. They told her what a wonderful cook you are, about your roasts and your pierogi and your potato salad.

She's embarrassed that she can't put out a meal like you can." Could. Whatever.

"I never thought of that. I wouldn't want to hurt anyone's feelings." She nodded, considering the idea. "I don't want to appear ungrateful."

"Of course not." This could be going worse. *Let's see where we can get today.* Audie pulled her phone out of her purse and launched the photo app. "Has Vi shown you her decorations? They're incredible, as always." She opened a pic of the immense tree in the living room, all sparkle and ribbons. Enlarging it, she tilted the device to her mother.

Irina adjusted her glasses for a full minute. "Vita did that?"

"Yep. Do you recognize any of the ornaments?" Audie cringed. Not supposed to ask things like that. "She used a bunch of your and dad's decorations."

A shadow crossed her face. "Well, I suppose we have some extra."

She hadn't had a tree of her own in ten years. Moving on. Audie flipped through the roll, landing on one of her and Jude that Vi had insisted on taking beside her staircase and its garlanded glory. She swallowed as she showed it to the woman who'd given her life.

"You always take such a lovely picture, Audra." Back to playing with the glasses. She must've finally focused, because her eyes narrowed. "Who's that with you? Not one of Simon's friends."

No, of course not. Simon, the corporate problem-solving genius, much in demand and currently jet-setting to his own dismay, wouldn't have friends that looked like Jude. Technically, even Jude didn't have friends that looked like him. But an abandoned sleeve of tattoos was showing and that black hair hung too low over his left eye…

"No, Mom. That's Jude." *Do I say it?* How could she not? "My husband."

The words had been said so softly, she would've wondered if Irina heard but for the discomfiture in her eyes. It kept her from responding directly. Instead, she looked toward the door. "I wish your father would get home."

Audie took the phone and tucked it away. "Where did he go, Mom?" She guessed that Sacred Heart Cemetery wasn't going to be the answer.

"He ran to the grocery store. He said we were out of that Irish cream you like."

"I could use some," she chuckled.

"So how are you, love?" Had her name escaped already?

"I'm fine. We're staying at Vita's house for Christmas, taking a quick vacation."

"That's wonderful, Audie." Ah, there it was. She relaxed a degree. "You work too hard."

"Folks are always interested in their history, so the more I can help them, the better."

The older Marik cocked her head. "Did you change departments at the library? What happened to archiving?"

Drat. Here we go. Don't say 'don't you remember'? Choose your words, choose your tone, understand.

Should talking to one's parent require a primer?

She needed cue cards.

"I left the library a while ago."

"You did? But that was such a wonderful job."

For that phase of life, yes. And I learned so much. "I'm doing genealogy research for other people. We have our own business."

We—why did I say we? Her heart fluttered on the knife's edge of panic.

Now bewilderment showed everywhere. "Surely that's only part-time. Oliver has all that education and a steady job. He wouldn't waste it to chase strangers' family trees."

Big breath. Big deep breath. "Oliver—"

"He's so good at what he does. I don't understand why they don't hire him at this place. But I'll be going home soon, so it doesn't matter. He'll help me get my strength. Then I can do more things for your father." Her eyes wandered back to the door. "What on earth is taking him so long?"

"Mom, I—"

"A physical therapist," she beamed, as always more impressed by a man's accomplishments. Sure, her girls did fine, but the husband's job was the important one, the serious one. Neither Audie nor Vita had minded that part. It was how their mother had been raised. And their respective spouses found it highly entertaining if embarrassing, because their significant others could buy and sell them in the brains department if they'd desired. *Wonderful, she's still talking.* "His parents are so proud, as are we. He's so willing to help and has those degrees and—"

"Mom—"

"Why don't you bring him around to see us more often? I mean, okay, if you're busy, fine." It wasn't fine, like the non-traditional hue of the poinsettia bracts. "But if two jobs are keeping him away, you need to quit expecting so much. A man needs rest and peace to recover."

And I'll greet him each evening with a crisp ribbon in my hair and a perfect meal on his plate, and the dog we don't have will carry his slippers and…

"Audra, are you listening to me?"

"Every word. But—"

"I don't think you are." She turned to the window, folding her arms while watching the snow gather atop Joseph and the donkey that the mother of God rode in on.

"Ollie isn't working two jobs."

"Good, I should hope not. It's all your father could do to manage one. Besides, you've got your little job, too, and aren't raising children yet." *Yet?* She turned back to her daughter, deciding that now was the perfect opportunity to bring up another impossibility and offer it as wisdom. "You've waited far too long, already twenty-five. You don't want to hold off on a family for the sake of this career of yours." The word couldn't have come out more dismissively. "I mean, Dad is proud of your schooling, but he wants grandchildren. He just won't say it." *But you will.*

"What about Connor and Becca? Are you forgetting about them?" Audie blinked, hating the tears that were trying to gather. *She can't understand. You know this.*

"Audra Garland, I do not forget things. I certainly remember my own grandchildren." Her wan cheeks flushed, those eyes as piercing as they'd always been. Why was it that part that had to survive? "Everybody tells me I forget things, and I don't. They want to make me feel stupid." She practically spat the word. "I am not stupid."

"Nobody said you were." Audie's shoulders were caving in around her chest. She fixated on a single green leaf on the floor; it must've fallen from the peace offering. *Guess I didn't keep it warm enough after all.*

"Connor and Becca are absolute blessings. Bright, kind, considerate, and talented." No argument there. "And I'll have you know their birthdays are October 28th and June 30th, respectively."

Don't. Don't...

"What year, Mom?"

She whispered it. She stared holes through that leaf as she asked, but she asked it anyway.

"What was that?"

"What year were they born? I can't remember."

Irina hesitated, the pathways traveling in too many cloverleafs, none of them the correct direction. "See? You forget things, and you don't have age for an excuse. They're eight and five. I know that, now don't I?"

One tear slipped out. "They're twenty-six and twenty-three."

In her periphery, the blanket moved from the arm of her mother's chair. She wiped her eye with the glove on her lap while the woman self-soothed by fretting at the ruffled edging.

"Now you're doing it," she accused her youngest. "Lying to me to make me feel useless. The children are in the second grade and kindergarten. Vita said she'd take me to Becca's Christmas concert. She's playing the Angel Gabriel."

And she had. Eighteen years ago. She was so cute, with her cotton-ball wings and her pipe-cleaner halo. Her lisp made her announcement to the Virgin Mary so precious that the whole gymnasium was in tears.

Much like it was now.

"See?" She was almost ripping at the ruffle. Vi had told her it was a tactile thing she'd been doing lately. A self-calming mechanism.

She didn't seem to be calming.

"If you would just bring Oliver over more often, he'd be able to tell you there's nothing wrong with me. You and this 'business' of yours—you can while away the day with this nonsense, but you're causing your husband more worry and stress. Do you think he enjoys having two jobs? No, but he does it to make you happy."

The tears had blurred her mother's face. "Please, Mom. Let's take a breath, okay? I don't get to see you a lot."

"Whose fault is that?"

"I'm not talking about faults." *I'm trying so hard not to talk about faults.*

"Two jobs. Who ever heard of such a thing? What your neighbors must think."

"He doesn't work any jobs." *I don't want to say it. Don't make me say it.*

"You don't make any sense. You need to go see Vita." Yes, Vita the Perfect. *She really is.* Thank heavens.

"We're staying with her, remember?"

"Why aren't you staying at your own house? Why do you have to drag Oliver out of his own bed? Your place is only a few miles away."

"We don't have a place—"

"Audra Garland, I have had enough of your lies!" She threw down the blanket, her weak voice finding its volume. The cover caught the frame on her rolling table. It was from their fiftieth anniversary party, which she probably thought was last week.

"I'm not lying! I don't lie to my mother." *Which is half the problem, isn't it?*

Not helpful.

But Irina Marik couldn't stop the boulder she'd sent plummeting. "You're such a disappointment, to me and your father, but he's too kindhearted to say anything. But I don't think that's a kindness at all. He's not doing you any favors, coddling you like that. And neither is Oliver."

"Oliver is dead, Mom!" Audie was on her feet now, her purse toppling off the chair, spilling onto the tiles. "He's been dead for seventeen years. A whole bloody building came down on him in the middle of the Caribbean while we were only there to help those little kids. And I tried to save him, but it came down on me too. And he died. He's buried in Lee's Summit, and I had to live through that alone. But I survived and I pushed and I prayed. I prayed until my knees bled, and God gave me the best man on earth to be my husband whom you will never remember and you insult whenever I try to tell you about him." Her hands fought her as she wrested a photo out of her wallet on the floor. "Jude, Mom. You don't remember Jude? He's the only reason I'm still alive, and you can't remember?"

"That—that hoodlum?" She folded herself into her chair as if he could climb off the paper and bite her. The slightest border of the tattoos was visible beneath his collar. "You aren't serious. You don't mean it."

"Husband. For ten years. You were at the wedding."

"I would never." And she almost hadn't, but that was a different bit of trauma. "No. No, Oliver has those sweet curls. He's such a gentle man. What are you doing, showing me pictures of freaks, trying to confuse me?" She reached for the landline on her table and picked up the handset on the second try. "I'm calling your sister. She'll tell you what you're doing is wrong. Why can't you be more like her?"

Audie wondered if she was about to pass out, color gone from the room and only static like an old TV filling her vision. But she couldn't stop her tumbling words either, though there may be nothing but ashes left in the end.

"Oliver doesn't have *any* curls because Oliver was cremated when his head was crushed in by a cinder block. The love of my life was smashed to a pulp on a dark and horrible night and because you can't remember that, I have to relive it over and over again. So go ahead and call all you want, to whomever you want if you can remember how to," *dear Lord, forgive me,* "but I don't need to hang around to hear how I'm the black sheep of the family anymore. Dad loved me. Sometimes, you did too."

She crouched to shovel her cell, a nearly empty hand lotion, and her neon yellow notepad back into the purse. Somebody had appeared in the doorway, but she couldn't care. Standing, she grabbed her coat and looked straight at the woman almost swallowed by the recliner. Her mother still clutched the receiver, but it was obvious she didn't know how to dial, let alone what the number was, or why or who she was calling. "Mom, I'm sorry that everything stops for you so long ago. But I'm doing the best that I can, like you and Dad taught us, and if you can't even manage compassion that you always said was a virtue, I can't do this anymore."

She turned and pushed out the door, past Shonda trying to offer quiet solaces. She spurned the poor woman's hand—*I don't deserve it*—mumbled soul-felt apologies, and ran down the hall and out into a day as cold as iron.

Chapter 13

The snow sure wasn't keeping the crowds away. What did he expect on the Saturday before Christmas? Every shop—clothing, jewelry, a crazily tempting chocolatier—could've used a revolving door as last-minute shoppers danced with each other coming and going. The only store that wasn't a bustling hive happened to be where he was headed: G. Armquist Fine Antiques.

Convenient for my purposes, not so much for Glen or young Derek's bank accounts. Jude had taken the first two concrete steps before his name rang out behind him.

Darla was a swirl of colors that would've made Audie jealous, which was saying something. Even enshrouded against the weather, only her maroon parka was close to a dark neutral, serving as a canvas for her bright winter accessories, cane included.

"Good morning, Darla! Wrapping up holiday shopping?"

Wrapping, get it? I'm so funny.

She waved two bags at him with her free hand. "Doing my best. I need to finish up the twins." She gestured to the baby emporium next door, then paused with a giggle. "Who am I kidding? They're already going to be spoiled rotten this first Christmas. Lionel reminds me our money plant hasn't produced any fruit yet, but I can't resist a few more boxes under the tree."

"I saw the photo—nobody could resist those two."

She laughed in agreement. "They certainly came in with a bang. It's a miracle our daughter and son-in-law have been able to pay off the medical bills so quickly."

"'Tis the season for those kinds of things."

"You know it. They have angels watching out for them."

And one of them was named Darla James.

The member of the seraphim suddenly realized where they were standing. "Honey, you're not going in there, are you? You can find much better deals at Curlings by our place. And far better quality too."

"I'm just hunting up some information, wondering if he might have intel on where antiques could be marketed on the down-low."

Her eyebrows raised. "Genealogy drying up? You're dabbling in a life of crime?"

He lowered his voice. "It's always an option. But, no, we're trying to help out Fran. Vita's desperate for her to get that Tiffany stained glass back, and we have a weird knack with this sort of thing lately." His wife, Sherlock, did anyway. Dr. Watson was usually comic relief.

"A what now?" Under her canary-yellow bucket hat, her eyes narrowed and widened at once, an unhealthy combination. She pulled her bags closer to her body, like the midnight thief—despite being deceased—would plunder them right out of her hands. "My ears are going. I thought you said Fran had a Tiffany."

"Oh! I figured you knew." And that's why he wasn't winning Best Supporting Detective this awards season.

"You said a real Tiffany? Not a Tiffany style?"

In for a penny, in for a pound. "Yeah, a square panel with a magnolia tree on it. Her soon-to-be-ex's great-aunt left it to her."

He cringed, hoping the divorce wasn't hush-hush too, and he wasn't spilling loads of Ms. Gill's dirty laundry onto Main Street. Good, she was nodding.

"Lord have mercy. It was stolen from our shop? Why was it there? Wait, Kurt couldn't have taken it that evening. It would've been found with him."

"It went missing the night before. Ironically, she'd hidden it in her supplies at the boutique for safekeeping."

The troubled expression intensified, bordering on out-of-sorts. "Wow. That sad child. First Kurt, now this. Or the other way around, I guess. Doesn't matter." She fussed with her bags and shifted her cane. "I don't know anything about it. Can't help. Unfortunately."

I didn't ask you to, but thanks... "Darla, are you okay?"

She glanced at her wrist. The watch hadn't made it past her sleeve and into view before she was exiting stage left. "Sorry, I need to run. Well, waddle. Best of luck! Tell Vi hi for me."

Jude stood on the walk, watching her move faster than he'd expected. She passed the baby store without a peek.

This city has a strange effect on people. Had one of the wandering spirits taken hold of Ms. Darla? It wouldn't be the oddest thing to happen this week.

He continued up the remaining steps by twos. As soon as he stepped through the door, the wanna-be-mayor-of-1820-St.-Charles hustled out of a rear room. When he saw the source of his anticipation, the 100-watt smile waned to a refrigerator bulb. But a customer is a customer.

"Good morning, Mister, ah, West, is it?" He reached out a hand, so much friendlier in the confines of his own four walls than he had been at Lucy's yesterday afternoon. They shook, and Jude tried to channel Audie's ever-engaging charm.

"Yes, but please, call me Jude. Business booming?" The store's current population said otherwise, unless the clientele was comprised of ninja.

"Always. Always! Though, of course, we're not as dependent on holiday sales as most of the shops." That was a relief. "What can I help you find? A gift for your lovely wife, perhaps?"

Now she's lovely. He'd been trying to shoot her with poison eye daggers less than twenty-four hours ago.

"I'll need to browse a bit." Audie would have him committed if he bought her a present from there. The rattling life of a travel trailer was not antique friendly. "But you might help me with something else."

Any expression of courtesy extinguished into the stratosphere at the same time the retailer's nephew emerged from the storeroom.

"Good morning!" His hand was out in a more congenial, less predatory manner. "You're that relative of Vita Klein's, aren't you?"

"I'm happy she still claims me." Reintroductions commenced, Glen gazing in the direction of the front door from time to time.

"Did I hear you say you needed help with something?"

"Not a purchase, Derek," Glen said, and while that may have been factual, it was nevertheless rude.

Be the bigger person, be the bigger person. "I was curious: where would one go if they wanted to get rid of some antiques in a less refined establishment than your own?" He'd referred the question to Derek because Glen had left the chat. That sure turned him around, though.

"*My* establishment. Derek dusts."

Derek rolled his eyes outside of his uncle's view. "Yes. I dust. I also do the books."

"For now," the uncle said. "I can't help it if you can't get a job with your accounting degree."

"I *can* get a job, but this suits me." He shrugged. "As he said, for now."

"Waste of an education," Glen testified, then began smoothing the pale yellow and already-smooth seat of a chaise lounge.

"I'm happy with it." He slipped into a British urchin accent. "And ever so grateful for the opportunity, Uncle."

Jude laughed, and the older man reddened.

"Sorry, Glen. Just a joke." Derek returned to Jude. "Acting lessons. Taking a few to meet people."

"Better than that bunch you're meeting at the blackjack tables." More mumbling from the obsessive-compulsive cheap seats, now straightening a perfectly upright taper candle in a pewter holder.

"True," Derek replied cheerily. Behind his hand but loud enough for Glen to hear, he added, "Though not bad for my pocketbook, since there's a shot at beating the house." Full voice, he said, "As to your question. Why are you looking for markets? Got something to sell?"

As soon as the word "no" passed Jude's lips, Glen abandoned hope and moved to shelves closer to the bypassing pedestrians. Maybe he planned to lasso them like cattle.

"You heard about Kurt Boulton and the thefts, right?" Derek nodded with a frown. "I guess because the story ended in Vita's shop, curiosity is getting the best of us. We thought we might be able to help get the place opened sooner. The police haven't found what he stole, and they're out of leads."

"They've been in asking similar questions. The illicit markets that, of course, Uncle Glen only knows because he rescues antiques from the clutches of evildoers"—Glen ignored him—"were shared, with no success."

After verifying his boss's location, he turned in the opposite direction and lowered his volume. "This whole thing has him more upset and anxious than usual. We—he—was already having a less than stellar year in terms of profit. Not that it's about profit with him—more of an antique hostage situation, with him being both the captor and the captive—but he does need to pay the rent." The taller man fiddled with the left temple of his glasses. "Maybe it's the holidays. They can make anyone touchy."

Tell me about it. *Wonder how the visit with Irina is going?* Probably safer not to wonder.

"I hope things pick up for him—for you both—in the new year. Did either of you notice anything weird the night of Kurt's death or the night before?" *Hey, West, did your brain fall out?* "Hang on—you were with Kurt on Thursday."

Derek held up both hands. "I swear I didn't tell him to break Fran's artwork and slit his own neck."

"No, I hoped not." Now he checked for Glen's proximity. "What was all that about?"

"I'd picked up a gift I'd ordered from Wax & Wicks and found Kurt caught like a deer in headlights by Uncle Dearest."

"What was the problem?"

"Nothing, as usual. He was scolding Kurt about leaving our rear door unlocked."

"That's kind of serious, considering the thefts around here lately."

"Right, it would've been, before we learned Kurt was the thief. But it wasn't Kurt's doing. He was crazy careful about things like that. He took his job and his reputation seriously. Or I thought he did."

"That's why you were defending him."

"The door had been left unlocked, but that's because my uncle has the attention span of an over-caffeinated ferret and forgets to set the code."

"You're sure?"

"Positive. It happened Wednesday night, and Kurt hadn't been over here yet. I'd stopped in because I'd left my phone on a shelf when I'd put on my coat earlier. I mentioned the door to Glen on Thursday, but he blamed it on Kurt."

"Decent of you to step in. Seems like the man was already on the edge."

He declined the medal for heroism. "I just told Glen to knock it off. He didn't listen, of course. And now that Kurt was the one stealing, I don't know whose side I should've been on. At any rate, Kurt had a key to every shop that had a theft. He didn't need to leave the doors open and throw suspicion on himself."

"Okay. And otherwise, you haven't seen anything strange near Vi's?"

Derek ran a hand through his thick, wavy hair. "No. I mean, strange is subjective, especially in the afternoon and early evenings. The Hopeful Holidays gang brings in a lot of out-of-towners, plus they have a large cast in costume."

"Speaking of which, who plays the Ghost of Christmas Yet to Come?" The Ramseys and Vita both said there wasn't one. Unlike her sister, perhaps Vita was human and made an occasional error.

"The crew quit using *A Christmas Carol*. It's why Glen can go around impersonating Dickens' ghost without stepping on toes."

"Darn."

"Why do you ask?"

"I've apparently got specters on my mind. I've caught glimpses of someone who fit the phantom's description way more than I'd like."

"Yikes. Now, we do have five different Santa Clauses, if you're looking for any of those."

"Five?"

"They want to cover all the bases. Our regular red-suited ho-ho-ho-er. Then Père Noël, of course, since this was a French settlement. We also have St. Nicholas, who wears blue, an Old Man Winter, and even the surfing Santa who brings toys Down Under."

"How cosmopolitan."

"Somebody isn't a fan," he chuckled, indicating everyone's favorite deceased author. "He wants Père Noël only, but the kids would riot if they didn't have the traditional Santa to beg for gifts."

Another strike against the dealer of fine-ish antiquities. "Are folks really okay with him acting like that?"

Derek smirked. "Most try to ignore him when he gets going. He's a nuisance, and he's crowned himself the King of Main. But does he pose any danger?"

That's the question, isn't it? Could it have been that last unwarranted berating that drove the final nail into Kurt Boulton's coffin?

"Then it's helpful you're here. Youth has its advantages as the rest of us get addled."

"Right, because you're a hundred and seven," he laughed. *A certain shoulder feels one-twenty-five, if we're being truthful.* "I don't think I qualify as youth anymore."

"Did someone say you went to school with Vi's partner, Fran Gill?"

He blushed. *Yep, as I thought. Somebody has a sweet spot.* He'd been too deferential at the cafe yesterday when fair and frazzled

Fran had joined the party. "Have you seen her little girl yet? She couldn't be cuter. And Fran's got her own business and—" He cringed as his uncle, having puttered nearby, caught the words.

"Don't let me keep you from any high and mighty aspirations, son." Heavy on the *son*.

"No, Glen. I'm happy here, and I don't need to get rich."

"Your parents think otherwise."

"And that's why I know I don't need it."

Jude turned to the proprietor. "Your things that were stolen weren't too valuable, right?"

He crossed his arms, less theatric without his waistcoat and ascot. "Everything's valuable, whether the public recognizes it or not. Taking those objects was an assault on our past. How can someone be so crass as to tear it away from where it belongs?" His flushed face looked near to tears, though real or crocodile was up for debate.

Then the front door jingled.

Glen, composure recovered like a switch had flipped, clapped as he spun toward the fresh meat. With a snap, he bid his budding apprentice—er, duster—to follow him.

Derek apologized. "Duty calls."

"Go, share antiquities with the world. I need to get out of your hair."

He followed his uncle, and the two were soon engrossed in over-explaining a Louis XVI-style chair that he could only identify thanks to Vita having one similar. *Wonder how that would look in the camper? Darn, we're decorated in vintage traveler chic. Wrong period.*

He stuffed his hands in his pockets, afraid of clumsily causing more distress to Mr. G. Armquist, and took a last gander at the back of the retail area. A discrete table near the storeroom entrance said 'yes, we want to sell things, but we can't look like we're putting a price on these priceless treasures. How plebeian.' It was polished to a reflective finish, with only an invoice book and calligraphy-style pen lying atop it to take care of the droll monetary side of transactions.

Behind it on the wall, a china cabinet with missing doors served as a waiting room for items needing a tag before joining their brethren on display. A Brownie camera sat on the top shelf, a box for silverware beside it. On the next were two eight-by-ten oil paintings whose frames were probably worth more than the completed art. The left-hand one caught his eye, because it looked Picasso-esque. Glen was still absorbed in his sales pitch, so Jude nonchalantly approached it. He rotated the piece and realized it made much more sense right side up. In its new position, something trapped beneath the painting reflected the overhead lights.

Stacking your precious wares, Mr. Armquist? For shame. A protruding edge showed petite pink petals.

Why does that look so famil—

Oh no.

Jude's heart skipped more beats than approved by nine out of ten cardiologists. In his dream, Josephine had held out that horrible, fractured glass, loaded to the brim with clustered pink flowers, cherry blossoms, the gift from her husband that was used to end her far-too-short life. But it couldn't be, right? They had no way of knowing what was actually on the weapon, and surely some ghost wasn't stopping by his dreams to tell him what her favorite flower was.

The picture frame dropped with a rattle as his jacket pocket blasted Black Sabbath's "Iron Man." Her ringtone should've been Iron Woman, though Vi worked mostly with silver and bronze, but—

The chords clamored again, and the store's occupants glared in his direction. One of them, anyway. But his was a potent glare. Still seeing murdered brides and falling petals, he fumbled to pull out the phone and answer.

"Hey, Vita." That came out higher pitched than usual. He cleared his throat and found his baritone. "What's up?"

"Jude! Where are you?"

Okay, her tone wasn't helping. "I'm at Armquist's Fine Furnishings or whatever this place is called."

"I'll be there in two seconds. I'm by our shop now." The cadence of her words screamed DEFCON 1.

"What's wrong?"

"Audie isn't with you, is she?"

"No, she was going to see your mom."

"I know. It didn't go well. Jude, I don't know where she is."

Chapter 14

Jude had redialed Audie's number seventeen times before he spotted Vita on the sidewalk between the antique store and the boutique.

"She definitely made it to Irina's?" he called out, ignoring the busyness skirting around them.

Vita's toe clipped an uneven cobblestone, and he darted to save her from a face-plant. Her chest heaved from running, and it was the closest he'd ever witnessed a Marik sister come to cursing.

"Vita!"

She pulled herself upright and shook her head to clear it. "I called Mulberry when I hadn't heard from her. She left there abruptly hours ago."

Why are those places always named after trees? What does a mulberry have to do with losing your brain to a horrific disease? If one was being truthful and handling this with the dark humor needed to do so, you'd choose a nut, as irony. Walnut Village. Or The Walnuts. 'I'm going to the 'Nuts, hon, be home as soon as my own mental stability allows.'

Vita was staring at him. *Right. Sorry. Coping mechanism.*

"She didn't say anything to the staff?"

"It sounds like she wasn't in a state to say much."

His jaw clenched tight enough to crack a molar. "Every blasted time."

She tried so hard, and for what? Self-torture.

"Shonda called me, you know, Mom's primary aide? God bless that woman. She was so levelheaded and sad about what happened. She heard Irina getting agitated and had been going in to de-escalate. Jude, Mom's back to not remembering that Ollie's dead and that you're not a gangster, and she said all sorts of awful things to her. Audie finally lost it."

So very not good.

Vi looked him square in the eye with irises almost as deep and swirling as her baby sister's. "She yelled at Mom."

Every nerve ending shorted, followed by a whole series of words that no Marik would approve. *If I'm going to be a thug, I may as well act it.* "Audie doesn't yell."

"Exactly. But when you've gone another ten rounds with your own mother, only to be told again that you've got no sense, that you're a disappointment? And then being forced to relive Oliver's death? I begged her not to go. She didn't have to go." Vita stopped, closed her eyes, and struggled to steady herself. Panic wouldn't help anything. "I've called the few friends she keeps up with nearby. I drove over to the church, and I keep swinging by the house, of course. I don't know where she went."

Or what she's going to do. Vita didn't say it. She didn't need to.

A red-black stain on a boutique floor colored his vision.

"Okay. Okay." Thoughts and fears and phrases tossed around his head like the world's worst salad, and the best he could come up with was 'okay?' This was why Audie led their genealogy hunts; she's a wonder at sorting out the details, getting into others' heads when it seemed they were made of nothing but croutons. *What is with the salad bar references, West? And why can't I think of a single appropriate saint right now?* The effort required to form a coherent sentence topped Sisyphus and his giant rock. "You go back to the house. I'll start hunting. Keep calling. Maybe she'll get annoyed enough at both of us to answer eventually."

Vita nodded, for once at her own loss for words. He gave her a quick hug.

"We'll find her. She'll be okay."

Please, love.

Please be okay.

Chapter 15

The snow stopped, but the clouds would bring darkness before its time, even with the shortest day of the year speeding toward them. He never remembered exactly when the solstice fell. That's what the interwebs were for.

Now if they would only tell him where his wife was.

After the first two hours, he'd quit calling so often. If she didn't want to answer, driving her insane with his personal ringtone wouldn't help. The woman had the patience of a gentle stream—*thank you, Shakespeare and junior year lit class*—unless she was dealing with her mother.

She knew better, and he knew she knew better, which was worse. No one can get under the skin of someone like a parent, and though they all understood what horrible things dementia does to one's mind, the tricks it plays, Audie had too much critical narrative that was simply deleted from her mother's consciousness.

It was too high a mountain for his wife, for anyone, to climb.

She shouldn't have gone. Or she shouldn't have gone alone. But he couldn't go with her, because that just upsets Irina. They learned that one the hard way a few years ago. His mother-in-law had waffled between thinking he was holding her daughter against her will and accusing Audie of cheating on a man who'd been dead for a decade and a half.

Yeah, no wonder she'd run.

He leaned forward to peer out the top of the Jeep's windshield. Not a sliver of blue sky. The Gulf Coast and its warmish waters beckoned. But before that, a certain wife needed to be located or it would be a lonely trip in that camper.

And who would he cook for?

Even though Vita had already checked, he'd twice driven a circuit past the huge and stately St. Peter Catholic Church. He'd swung by the grotto for Rose Philippine Duchesne, the first saint canonized west of the Mississippi. The snow at the grotto was undisturbed, and the woman vacuuming poinsettia leaves around the church altar had seen no one matching Audie's description. He'd loitered in the narthex long enough to ensure Audie hadn't been in a confessional, having begged a priest to listen to her thimbleful of sins in his off-hours. With offenses like curse words that weren't spoken or struggles with the fifth commandment, she wouldn't be assigned more than five Hail Marys as penance.

But no, she wasn't there.

Vita had rung every twenty minutes, updating him that there was no update. She wanted to return to the field herself, but Jude convinced her someone should be at the house. Simon wouldn't be home until Wednesday, and Connor hadn't been drafted to the cause yet.

And if I can't track down my own better half, my Husband Card should be revoked.

Husband. She couldn't very well be sitting in a graveyard with Husband Number One, unless she absconded with Simon's Accord and drove clear across the state. How hard it must've been, burying Oliver in his hometown and not near her own family. But his parents needed it. His mother was a wreck; his father had shut down. They were good people—Jude had met them twice now—but their grief cut so profoundly that they couldn't provide much solace to their widowed daughter-in-law.

Cue Vita and Sister Philomena and a year in the desert.

If there was a desert nearby, he would've headed there next. But no such luck. If this had been one of their usual rural burgs, he might've had a better shot at coming up with a place for her to haunt. In a full-sized city? Would she have gone over to St. Louis, back near their home in the County or to one of her and Oliver's spots? He didn't know them all.

What else didn't he know about her life before him?

He rolled to a stop at the base of the petite hills and picked up his phone. He'd call Vita, ask for a list of places over the river where she might go.

That's when he glimpsed a speck of yellow across the wide park, near the edge of the muddy Missouri.

He tossed the phone, pulled into the parking lot adjacent, and dropped out of the vehicle. Zipping the leather jacket and forgetting his hat, he rushed through the crosswalk too close to a pickup hauling a fresh Christmas tree in its bed.

"Sorry," he waved to the bleating horn without making eye contact. Best not to see if an obscene gesture was coming from someone carrying a religious symbol.

She sat on a bench, snowflakes accenting her duck-colored coat and red knit hat. She could've been the statue of St. Duchesne, motionless as she watched the river sludge meander toward the Mississippi thirty miles east. It wouldn't freeze until late January, if then. In the meantime, it carried bare logs and brown water and the thoughts and sadness of Mrs. Audra West.

"Hey." She said it before he'd come into her field of vision, before he'd uttered a word.

"Hey." He gave her a wide berth, circling like one would a wounded animal. Because she kinda was.

"Vita sounded the alarm, didn't she?" She hadn't looked at him yet. Her new blue gloves rested on her lap.

"Yeah. She heard things didn't go well with your mom."

The muscle twitched along her jaw. "My fault."

"Not so much." He took a step closer. She didn't flinch.

"It was. She can't help it."

"Doesn't make it hurt less."

Two fingers flickered, waving the thought away. "She's probably forgotten all about it. She's waiting for Dad to come home from the store with the Irish cream."

Something special was going into the cocoa tonight, if they ever made it to the house.

He neared the bench. "May I?"

"Of course. It's snowy, though. You'll get wet."

He was already soaked to the bone after hunting. As it appeared, so was she.

"Want to talk about it?"

"No." Shocking. If she even talked about it to Sister Phil, he'd be impressed. "It was more of the same. It shouldn't bother me. She's my mother. I should be the one who's compassionate."

So much history. So much trauma. "You just should've married someone she would've approved of." He tried to get her to smile. No dice.

"Nobody will ever compare to Ollie."

Ouch.

Immediately, she cringed. "In *her* eyes. And he was great, obviously, or we wouldn't have been together. But he's gone." She moved her hand onto his and looked down. "You forgot your gloves."

I left my heart in San Francisco too, but that's not important right now.

"It's awful that I don't visit her more, but I can't do it. Poor Vita."

"Vita doesn't feel that way, love. You know that."

"But she's stuck with the hard stuff while I'm off gallivanting."

"She doesn't think that either."

The side of her mouth pulled back, and she studied her feet.

"You help with logistics. We pay for what we can. There comes a point where God understands. I'm certain of it."

He did not send His only Son to torture her. He sent Him to heal her. Jude didn't need catechism to recognize that much.

After a long minute, she squeezed his bare fingers. "We should go. Vita will be nuts by now."

Vita was nuts several hours ago. If she hadn't called out the National Guard yet, it would be a miracle. There'd be a command center on the lawn of the century-old brick house, complete with enough antennae to contact Neptune.

"If you're sure."

"Yeah. I just needed…" She squinted, watching the water pass. "It doesn't matter. Let's go."

He stood and pulled her with him. She slipped her hand through the crook of his arm, and they walked like old lovers on the cold, wet grass toward the street. As they passed through the crosswalk—more carefully, as there was a spare second to check for traffic—Audie paused, her head turned to the right.

"That's odd, isn't it?"

A grassy area near where the Jeep had been badly parked? He saw nothing except a purple Scion, beyond its prime but probably not qualifying as odd.

"That patch where the snow's melted."

Ah. There was a spot, maybe ten feet in diameter—though it resembled more of an alien head than a circle—where the snow was already gone. The rest wouldn't last long.

"A steam vent?"

"I don't think there are steam pipes under these roads. Wrong era." They neared their vehicle, resembling a reverse dalmatian from the white flakes and black paint job. "I wonder."

"What's that?"

The skinny line between her eyes deepened, but after a moment, she abandoned her survey and climbed into the cab. "I don't know. It's nothing important."

Jude shrugged as he shut her door and headed to the driver's side.

Fine—keep your secrets. But keep them where I can find you.

This woman was taking years off his life.

And yet I'm still a lucky man.

Chapter 16

"If it's all the same to everyone, you can stop tiptoeing around me now."

They hadn't swaddled her in blankets or forced her to soak her feet, but Audie knew Vita was fighting the urge. She wanted to give her a teddy bear and a kiss on the forehead and send her off to bed with warm milk and a cookie. She'd restrained, which was appreciated, but jeez.

A careful breath allowed more of the mental Tetris pattern to fall into place. With it came a truth about the worried looks and the coddling.

I had it coming.

Vita cleared the last of the plates from the table, having tried to keep little sister in one spot like an invalid. She picked up her glass—and Jude's, only to be defiant—and carried them to the sink. Dinner had been a simple affair since they'd gotten back late. But a quick meal made by their hyperlocal chef in an honest-to-goodness kitchen with more than two burners and a full-sized oven was a treat in any case.

"I'm sorry, sweetie." Vita returned and planted that kiss atop her head after all. "I don't mean to smother you. I'm happy you're safe and sound."

Sound? Jude knew better. And that wall she built when her hackles raised and she couldn't be touched? Physically, mentally, or emotionally? Suboptimal for a marriage.

Darn it, Mother. Why can't you forget about the Bailey's and remember my current husband?

She rose from the table and grabbed the dish towel before Vita could, joining said spouse at the sink. She squeezed his biceps, and he winked at her.

A chunk of inner wall fell off. *Good.*

"Should we get out a board game or something?" Vita accepted the towel circumvention and stacked the dry dishes as Audie handed them to her. "You need a true night off. I should've never asked you two to dig Frannie out of the hole she's gotten herself into. She needs help, but we're not the police. Tonight, we'll sit around the fire like settlers without streaming services."

"Sounds good. But before we do, I want to go on one quick outing."

"Nope." Jude said nothing else, but continued scrubbing the pan that had held the roasted garlic.

"I don't mean alone. I've gotten that out of my system. I'd like to talk to Stuart Morrison before this evening's ghost tour."

"Stu? Why on earth would you need to see him?"

"I'm stuck on the many connections between the old story of Josephine Richards and Kurt Boulton's death. With the tie-ins to glass art and the location of the dastardly deed, I'm wondering if more details about what happened—factual details, anyway—might give us a clue where Kurt hid his purloined loot."

The last pot came out of the water, and Jude pulled the stopper on the sink. "So long as I can keep an eye on you, I'm in."

"I promise to never be farther than arm's length. Vi? Care to chat with a certain ghost guide and his hyperactive imagination?"

Her sister studied her like a metalwork-in-progress. Whatever flaws she found must not have been too troublesome.

More likely, she trusted Jude to keep Audie's escapades to a minimum.

And he's *the one who scares Mom.*

"I'll leave the frozen streets to you teenagers."

"We won't be long." Audie placed the coffee carafe in its home, handle properly aligned, and sighed. "I really am sorry about making you both worry. I just needed space after everything."

Over Vita's shoulder, Jude caught her eye, and for the thousandth time that day, she thanked God for him.

'At least I didn't have to track you down in the desert,' his look said. It also repeated his words as they'd driven home from the park. 'As long as you always come back, you do what you need to do. But I'd much prefer to go along. I can give you all the space in the world, but let me be in the orbit, okay?'

Yeah, okay. That she could do.

"It's a disturbing story, isn't it?"

In front of Missouri's first Capitol, Stuart Morrison stood in his hooded cape with a lantern and a handheld sign. They had fifteen minutes before ticket holders would arrive.

Audie's hands squeezed within her pockets, trying to keep the blood flowing, and Jude had actually worn his hat tonight. Black bangs still hung rakishly from under the rows of knitted yarn.

"A powerful man, a lonely bride, a jealous neighbor, and a murder? Disturbing barely covers it."

"Don't forget about the hanging."

A fairy, presumably of the Sugarplum tribe, flitted past, tossing glitter at the trio. She giggled and ran away, a Nutcracker in hot pursuit.

Jude dusted off his jacket. "How could we forget?" He frowned at his gloves, now sparkling under the streetlamp.

Stu's nose crinkled. "I can't imagine executions as entertainment, but they were until much later than modern society would care to admit. The broken neck, the kicking feet, the bulging eyes…"

"We've got the picture." Jude peeked in Audie's direction, wariness from earlier clinging to him like the fairy's tribute.

"Sorry," Stuart grimaced. "Fell into guide mode. What's saddest to me is how much Nathaniel Silvain protested his innocence."

"He was caught red-handed, right?"

"But he insisted he'd found Josephine like that, that he was only holding the bloody glass because he'd pulled it out of her neck himself."

"And no one believed him?"

"It's said he was a good-looking man." He glanced up at Jude, then hurried on. "And though he was married, he was charismatic and popular. It made the community wonder if he might've taken advantage of that with young Josephine. It's impossible to say, two hundred years later. Maybe he was a people-person because his sales required it. You don't sell a lot of goods if folks don't like you." He shook his head. "None of that is going to help find the stuff Boulton stole in this century."

A horse-drawn carriage, animal and occupants snugly wrapped, clomped by on the stone paving. It knocked something loose in Stuart's spirit-filled brain, and he snapped his fingers. "Mabel Ehrand. She may be able to give you more info."

"Does she do tours like yours?"

The concept must've been a funny one. "Good grief, no. But her relatives in town were contemporaries of the Peck brothers and their hardware-store-turned-government-HQ. She's got old papers that might shed some light, if you're willing to risk a visit."

"Risk?"

Stu shrugged. "Mabel is unique. Her late husband owned the IGA up on Fifth Street. A box of ketchup fell off a shelf one day and gave her a nasty concussion. This was years ago, but she's been a bit different since then." Now there's a spectrum of worrisomeness. "Just be cautious. It's like Hansel and Gretel. The situation's hunky-dory until you wake up being baked in an oven."

"Grand." Jude's right eyebrow raised to her. "Sound fun?"

Team West, on the prowl again. Another section of bricks tumbled from her mental wall. "I wouldn't miss it."

A group of four adults neared their corner, checking phones as they tried to decide if the creepy man in the dark hood was their guide for the hereafter or a holiday slasher. He waved them over with his lantern.

"Okay, thanks much, Stuart." Audie slipped her arm through her husband's. "Good luck with the tour."

"Don't you ever get bored telling the same stories?" Jude snuggled her hand in close, taking the arm's-reach agreement seriously.

"Not on your life." The lamp threw shadows over his face, fitting the mood too perfectly. "Or, rather, death."

Mabel can't be any worse than him, can she?

"And, technically, I only repeat every other night. We'll walk south along Main tonight, like when you joined me. Tomorrow, it's north and down through the park near the river."

"Are the tales as good in the other direction?"

"There's no Josephine, but there are plenty of spirits haunting the whole place." The makings of spirit stories, at any rate. "Over that restaurant across the street, an elderly spinster sways a rocking chair for the babies she never had. And down toward Frontier Park, you can still hear three native children playing, hundreds of years after they drowned."

"Lord have mercy."

"They were exploring one of the caves you could get to in that era, long before the founding of St. Charles."

"But how could they drown?"

Stuart nodded down the hill. "The Missouri's bank used to be much higher, edging on what's now Riverside Drive."

"Ranger Quinn did mention that."

"The cavern the kids chose would've been safe any other time of year. The river was in a light flood, though, and picked that afternoon to push through seams in a wall down there."

A shiver unrelated to the cold ran through her, and Jude's arm pulled her in tighter. "How did anyone find out?"

"The ground above it sprang a leak. The waters had to recede before the bodies were recovered."

"What a terrible way to go. I'm surprised they stick around in the afterlife."

The man who made his living from the dead put out his palms. "We all have to go sometime."

Another couple joined the quartet already stamping their feet against the temperature, and Stuart moved to greet them. The hauntings might be ongoing, but his short-and-sweet tours needed to run on schedule.

"Where to?" Jude asked as they left the group to their manufactured frights. "Back to the homestead?"

At the corner of Jefferson, she steered him to the right, down the last block toward Riverside. "I want to check one thing."

"This is your second 'one thing' of the night, you know."

She knew. Between watching her feet on the imperfect stones, she squinted into the dark. Away from Main, the lighting wasn't as bright. She could just make out the lot where Jude had parked earlier on his mission to find her.

What had she been doing, scaring everybody like that? It was selfish, it was cruel, it was—

The sort of reasoning that gets you into these moods in the first place, woman. Terrific. Either her guardian angel or Sister Philomena had joined the conversation. *Figuring you need to hold it together to spare those around you.*

Yeah, I win prizes for holding it together. My heavens, have you met me?

You do your best.

Do I?

Yes.

Do I?

(Silence.)

Thought so.

"What's down here that's so captivating?"

She jumped as Jude interrupted her internal argument. He surveyed her out of the corner of his eye, yet was smart enough not to draw too much attention to his wife's worrisome ways.

On the sidewalks, salt had melted the snow, but most grass glistened with the day's dusting. She stepped off the curb and crossed the road toward the plot they'd noticed earlier, covered only by dormant zoysia.

"Stuart gave me a thought. The river used to come right up near here."

"Hard to believe, isn't it? I guess we can thank the Army Corps that it's way out yonder these days."

"Yonder?"

"I'm being frontiersy."

Alrighty then. "There's a reason for this warm spot. It could be over a cellar or one of those caves."

"Eek. The one with the lost boys?"

"No, Stu had pointed in the other direction. But there could be another."

"Our favorite ranger claimed there weren't too many nearby. You think it's significant for us? The drowning happened long before Josephine's murder."

"I wasn't thinking about the olden days."

Now he did slow his step. "Who are you and what have you done with my wife?"

"Quinn said caves were used as stockrooms. The Lemp Brewery, down in South St. Louis, stored and lagered beer in ones below the factory because they stayed at a cool, constant temperature year round. Same with dug-out cellars."

"Okay…"

"Jude, love, don't you see?"

"Obviously not."

They'd reached the far side of the lot. Thankful for her waterproof boots, she unhooked herself from her spouse and entered the yellow grass. "This area is warmer than anywhere around us, in a region known to have underground hollows, with a cache of antiques missing from a street away and hidden somewhere no one has found."

"Oh! Kurt Boulton's buried treasure." He joined her in the Shmoo-like circle. "How do we find out? Phone the cops and tell them our theory?"

He was generous to call it 'our' theory. The crazier her ideas sounded, the more he'd protect her by backing them up.

St. Jude indeed.

"I don't know if we have enough to get them involved yet. Any suggestions on how to bolster the hunch?" She looked around her, pulling her small and ever-present flashlight from her pocket. It didn't cut far into the shadows. Still better than her cell, though.

Jude pulled out his as well. *Aren't we the prepared little genealogists?* Post-sunset cemetery searches and dimly lit basement files had come in useful at last. "Okay, we know something is going on directly below us. How do we get in?"

Audie turned up the hill and climbed toward the rear of a dark building. Whatever it housed, it must not have evening hours. "Remember those sidewalk doors at the Capitol?"

"The ones that led to my second run-in with the Phantom of the Opera? Difficult to forget."

She flashed the beam around, crossing over leafless bushes, a heap of old timber, and a set of steps that had been recently replaced. Shouldn't there be a—

"There it is!" Jude's light landed on a pair of upward-opening doors between the shrubbery and the stairs.

"A big gold star for Mr. West."

"I'll take as many stars as I can get."

She approached the entrance. "I don't see a padlock."

Jude situated his feet at the frame and reached for the rusty metal handle. It lifted with creaking ease. "Normally, I'd complain that any kid could come down here, fall in, and break his neck."

"It's possible that not all kids are like you were." She inspected the inkwell below them. Another black hole, reminiscent of Belsever's mill last month. Only this one cut straight through the earth. She shaded her eyes from the ambient light and knelt at the frame. A ladder, dusty and unused, led to a narrow tunnel. She lined herself up at the end of the doors and turned to find the melted snow ring. "It travels in the right direction."

"Now do we call the police?"

And there's the dilemma. That look, the one people in authority always gave to the amateur sleuth who claims they've discovered some brilliant clue. She'd had enough patronizing looks, especially today. Did she want another?

On the other hand, she wasn't venturing down those rungs for heck or high water. Literally.

"I guess it's time, yes."

Jude nodded and moved to close the hatchway. Night-roaming gangs of schoolchildren didn't need to be plummeting to their death.

A metallic clunk was followed by his flashlight's laser show as it caught on the door and careened into the abyss.

"For the love of Pete." He exhaled the whole day's aggravation, then dropped the panel on the ground. Taking the top rung of the ladder, he said, "At least it's lighting the way for me."

Audie held her light—and her breath—as Husband Number Two lowered himself into the pit of doom. "Please be careful," she begged between appeals to one of the St. Benedicts. No, not the one with the brown-robed monks... Nursia. St. Benedict of Nursia, patron saint of cavers. He can't be too busy, can he?

From the floor, Jude called up, "Got it."

"Good. Now come up before the trolls get you."

But he didn't, of course. He stayed by the ladder, but turned the light to the tunnel behind him. The hesitation wasn't encouraging.

"Sweetheart? Trolls, goblins, basilisks…"

He moved, but not in the direction she was willing him. "I know. I just want to see something." His voice trailed off as he and the flashlight slipped into the shaft and out of sight.

Okay, St. Ben, you're not off duty, but we're calling in reinforcements.

The sudden crash below, the sharp yelp, and the cloud of dust blasting from the tunnel stopped every mental process except one.

Not again.

Dear sweet Lord, not again.

She threw the flashlight's lanyard over her neck and was on the floor of her worst nightmare before she could think another thought.

Chapter 17

That board must've hit him harder than he thought, because Jude would've sworn he saw a duck-yellow coat scrambling down the ladder into its personal definition of perdition.

"Jude!" the impossible-to-be-his-wife's voice called for him, throttled either by dust or a fear so legitimate that he would've preferred the earth swallow him than make him hear it.

"Over here!" he choked out. Technically, more choking than out. The golden image neared and soon knelt beside where he'd landed on the stone floor.

Her flashlight shone in his eyes, around his face, over his arms, legs, and whatever else she classified as crushable. He reached for the top of his forehead and felt something wet beneath a complete lack of knit.

"I think I lost my hat." Fortunately, it wasn't as cold down here. He did have his own set of stars and constellations to admire, though.

Doctor West must've decided the only serious damage was the bleeding head wound. That was assuring, as he'd had enough of those that his body should just shrug at another.

"What happened?" Unzipping the purse hanging across her torso, she pulled out a tissue and handed him her flashlight. He needed to get his own surgically attached somewhere. "Point this upward, would you?"

She probably wouldn't appreciate that thing you do as a kid, with the light below your chin. Best not to annoy an already high-strung first responder in his hour of need.

"What happened was I made the mistake of trusting a pioneer carpenter to have done the job correctly. I pulled hard on that board," now lying to his right, "to see if it covered any nifty hidey-holes full of Tiffany stained glass."

"And did it?"

"Did the pioneer have good carpentry skills? No. And no hidey-holes either."

She produced a bandage out of the Bag o' Everything and taped it over the cut, evening out the edges. Her jaw clenched so tightly, the twitching muscle could double as the high string on a fiddle. He moved the flashlight and caught her hand.

"I'm all right."

More dabbing, more twitching.

"Audie." He squeezed her wrist. "I'm all right."

She paused, still as a statue, then sat back on her own foot. "You're sure?"

"One hundred percent." He got to his feet, which required a bit of acrobatics, because he wasn't about to let go of her yet. In the gloom, he pulled her into a hug. Her rigid frame softened.

"Now," he said, releasing her only at the arm's length he'd promised, "any idea where my hat and flashlight are?"

She took a step in a direction he hadn't expected and came up with both. A quick tap of the cylinder against her palm and it relit.

"You're handy. I think I'll keep you."

She half-smiled at him. He'd take it.

Audie peered into the pitch blackness ahead of them, now filled with floating dust particles from him disturbing the resident ghosts. He aimed his light that way too.

"Since you're down here…"

She didn't reply. She didn't say no either. He skirted around, gave her a quick glance, and decided to see how this would go. An emergency may have gotten them into the space, but curiosity could keep her there. He started down the tunnel.

This part was certainly man-made. The dampness of the atmosphere turned the stones under them into a hockey rink. He wasn't sure if that was better than pure mud or not. Wood shoring, similar to what had attacked him, lined the walls and ceiling, covered in the toils of ancient spiders. Roots reached down through the dirt above their heads and grabbed at his hair.

He glanced backward once. The duck-yellow coat picked its way through the corridor like it was crossing a minefield. Or maybe playing a game of Operation—if a boot touched the wrong rock, the entire place would explode.

Her long breaths were forced, and the sound reverberated oddly. Whatever kept her breathing was fine with him.

"You with me up there?" she asked, unironically.

He brushed spider silk off his cuff. "Are you kidding? I'm not going anywhere down here alone. It's spooky."

Her catalog of possible underground inhabitants popped to mind. She wasn't wrong. At the very least, the ghosts of those unfortunate native kids may be nearby. What a rotten way to go. Perhaps their spirits don't know what happened to their corporeal forms, and they've been rolling wooden hoops for years without a care in the after-world.

One can hope, anyway.

The dank aroma of air locked away for too long filled his sinuses, and he wondered if this had been a smart move. Even if they weren't asphyxiated, they may never get the smell out of their clothes. He was already starting to mildew. For a young woman's stolen-and-re-stolen art, they risked an awful lot.

But two ribboned pigtails and a freckled nose superseded stale air.

The risk was necessary.

Behind him, Audie yelped and must've slipped, because he was bumped forward on the ad hoc banana peel. Against all odds, they stayed upright.

"That would've earned us a solid nine and a half from the Norwegian judge." It took him too long to register that she still clutched his jacket. In what he could glimpse of her face at this pretzeled angle, those gray marbles of hers had locked into the unknown in front of them like the freight train of inevitability would blow through at any moment.

'Let's see what happens.' Brilliant, Einstein.

"Love, let's go up." This had been an astronomically bad idea. She'd had a troublesome and troubling day. Now in here, where the low ceiling was getting lower and the corridor narrowed bit by bit? They needed to be topside before she realized exactly how uncomfortable she was.

Suffocating.

Suffocated.

He drew in a deep breath himself.

But she shuddered, shook herself loose from her own ties that bind, and stepped out of his grasp. "I think we're almost there."

Almost where—the core of the earth? The River Styx?

She continued on, actually taking the lead though stooping more than necessary for her height. *Alrighty then.*

And they say marriage is boring.

He removed his hat on purpose this time before it provided a free ride to whatever crawly things were awaiting their Uber. He gave it a good whack against his pant leg, making a mental note to rinse it tonight when they got home.

If they got home.

If Godfrey the Goblin didn't decide they'd make a tasty snack.

Tucking the hat in his pocket, he aimed the light forward again. The depth ahead lay unbroken.

"Audie?" His gut turned to ice, and he picked up his pace.

"Wow."

She sounded muffled, farther away than she should've gotten in the zero-point-three seconds he'd looked elsewhere. He slid on the stones as he hustled. "Where are you?"

A circle shined his way like a Cyclops. "Sorry. I wanted to keep moving."

Ah.

The sooner done, the sooner out.

Okay, that I'll go along with that.

"Can you see me?"

"Yeah, I'm coming." He stepped more carefully now, deferring emergency actions for at least another thirty seconds. "What was the wow for?"

When he reached her, he was so relieved it took a second to notice they had a lot more headroom.

"This isn't just a cellar. I think we found one of the caves."

The area was roughly fifteen by fifteen, irregularly shaped, but solid. The walls looked to be limestone, like the riverbed. Heck, it probably *had* been the riverbed at some time. He reached out a hand and touched the slick surface. A rivulet formed beneath his finger, slipping down the rock and carrying calcium deposits to exotic destinations.

But Audie was looking the opposite way. There stood wooden shelving so old Lewis and Clark might've stored their spare paddles on them. At present, they were empty of anything but more dust.

Their lights played about the room until Audie gasped at something more than the particle-filled ether. She pulled him with her to the corner where the cave seemed to end.

In the shadows was a pile of junk that looked as prehistoric as the garbage now coating his lungs. Some of it was cloth that had seen better days, old leather or canvas more tattered than whole. The remainder seemed to be the Kilimanjaro of glass bottles. They ranged from milk jugs to demijohns, each dry as a bone.

Audie crouched at the edge of the heap and extracted one. "These are not modern vintage."

"Do they date back to the frontier era?"

She grinned. "I think it's a better story." She turned over the container and examined the bottom in the light.

"Does it give a company or something?"

She handed it to him, then picked up another. Unlike the first clear one, it was smaller and brown.

"No, but this many bottles stored away, all different sizes and varieties? I think we've got leftovers from Prohibition."

"They've been down here since then?"

She rubbed dirt off the mouth. "When the ban was in effect, enterprising entrepreneurs used whatever they got their hands on to store and sell their bathtub gin and moonshine. It often came with bonus features like blindness, coma, and death thanks to methanol poisoning. But in 1933, when the law was repealed, whoever had run the local speakeasy probably returned to business as usual and didn't need these anymore."

"Too bad they're empties. I could use a stiff drink." *Speaking of which...* "How are you doing?"

She didn't look up at him. "I'm fine."

Liar, but okay.

She moved on before he could pursue additional questioning. "Any guess as to what might be under the canvases?" A cache of stolen antiques, perhaps?

He handed her his flashlight. "Only one way to find out." He approached the heap, hunted for an edge, and said a quick prayer to whichever saint saved people from monsters.

St. George. *He's useful against dragons, isn't he?*

He pulled the canvas off with a flourish—another mistake, another cyclone blasting their eyes. He wiped tears as the dust went everywhere. Through slits, he saw Audie staggering away too.

"Sorry," he coughed. "I've got to stop doing that."

"It's okay." She was waving bits from her intrastellar space. "But we're still out of luck." She returned to examine what had been unveiled: an angled bank of softball-sized rocks.

"Nobody on Main reported their miniature boulder collection stolen, did they?"

"Not that I'm aware of, no." She scratched at her neck and folded her arms, studying the logjam. Or, rather, rockjam.

He dropped the cloth remnant and touched a stone. The one beneath it shifted. "Yikes," he said, hopping backward.

"Maybe don't do that." Her vocal cords had tightened beyond Scrooge's purse strings.

"I didn't mean to."

Another rolled loose.

"Oh dear." That was the lowest-key 'oh dear,' he'd ever heard. Translation: time to panic.

"Let's go."

He hadn't finished the two-word sentence when the post nearest to the rock pile creaked.

Hard. Loud.

And then splintered.

"Uh-oh."

It was like an avalanche as the shelving system, ignored for decades, began to pancake onto itself. As more rocks rolled out, the bottles in their path shattered like firecrackers.

His eyes fell on the one now-visible spot that wasn't limestone, the dirt wall that had been blocked by rubble and under pressure for generations.

It started pouring in toward them.

He grabbed for her arm, tearing her away as the first buckets of soil dumped onto her boots.

"Run!"

She didn't need the encouragement. Together, they scrambled on the slippery floor as the cascade—now combined with freezing water from the river a hundred yards east—chased them like a demon.

And it was outpacing them.

As they hit the corridor, the throat of the beast constricted. A horizontal plank bulged outward and snapped in two just as he got past it. He threw an arm up over his eyes, pushing her faster in front of him.

Another chunk of the shored roof swung down on Audie, knocking her sideways. He tumbled after her, both crashing into the rising flood.

She clawed at a post, trying and failing to find her feet. "Jude!"

If they lived through this, he never wanted to hear that strangled sound again.

He fought for his footing and hooked his arm through hers. "We're almost there. We can make it." He pushed her forward. He knew her eyes were closed, he knew she wasn't looking anymore, and she definitely wasn't in a cave below the city of St. Charles, Missouri.

She was in a collapsing cinder-block school 2400 miles away in the middle of the Lesser Antilles.

And he wouldn't get her back until he got her out.

"There's the ladder! We're almost there. Come on."

Another timber fell, and as it slammed into his left shoulder, his sight exploded like a supernova. The screen went blank, and his stomach fled the country.

"Jude!"

"The ladder." *Stay conscious, keep going, keep going.*

Through a hazy veil, he caught her expression, but all she said was, "Where?"

At least she was looking. He steadied his flashlight, and the metal reflected at them. White fingers grabbed for the rails, and he put a hand at her waist as she climbed. She slipped on the second rung, but he countered and propelled her back up.

"The door's closed!"

Why? "Give it a push. It's not heavy. It'll open, and we'll be out."

She did.

It didn't.

The panic was complete now. She couldn't even say his name as she turned to look down at him with terror-filled eyes.

He couldn't bring her down to the floor, because it might not be a floor in another few seconds. He swung to the side of the ladder, praying it was built better than that first board had been, and climbed alongside her. With his right hand, he reached upward, finding the rough wood. "Push with me."

She blindly obeyed, but it still didn't give. It had been a light panel, half-rotted. It was nothing to lift. Why wouldn't it budge? His left arm howled as he hooked it through the side rail, and another chunk of who knows what hit his back. "Once more, on three. One, two…"

The door gave. Abruptly, freely.

"Go!" He shoved her upward, and with debris battering his lower legs, he pulled himself along the rungs and fell onto the cold, wet lawn.

A couple feet away, Audie knelt on all fours, coughing, hacking, gasping for air and sucking it in faster than her lungs allowed. He rolled to his side, blinded again by pain in that good-for-nothing joint, and belly-crawled toward her.

A furtive movement to their right cleared his vision. Beyond the edge of the building and between the next ran a shadowed, black-robed figure.

The phantom.

A string of curse words that Audie would never approve—if she ever started taking in oxygen—barreled through his mind. He fought the urge to try chasing the man who'd tried to kill them, use whatever strength was left in his beat-up body to tell him what he could do with his spectral presence and attempt at double murder.

But his wife needed him there. And in that decimated spot in the sea, no husband had been able to help.

He wasn't about to leave her now.

Her wool coat, the color of waterfowl caught in oil spills, had been defiled by filth.

"You're okay, love. You're okay." He said it over and over. Her head hung down, dripping, but he could feel her fighting, fighting, to calm herself.

He wondered how far down the litany of saints she was.

St. George—you did not come through.

But it had been a structural collapse, not a fantastic beast. He'd prayed to the wrong saint.

She coughed some more, but her back wasn't heaving as badly. He pushed himself up by one arm into a sitting position, jeans soaked through, and turned her around to sit with him. "Come on, you're all right. It's over. We're out. We're safe."

She reached for his hand and squeezed it like she'd never let go. From the dim light of the parking lot, he saw the tears pouring down her face. "Are you hurt?" Her voice was as gritty as her coat.

"I'm okay." *I'm going to need three bottles of ibuprofen and that stiff drink when we get to Vita's, but I'll live.*

Unlike Oliver, I'll live.

"What happened?" she asked, huddling into his chest from the side.

"I don't know. We touched the pea under the mattress. Somebody should've painted that rock red, so I'd have known not to exist too loudly near it."

"The cave wasn't a cave?"

"Part of it was. Part of it was a poorly shored cellar room."

"Those unlucky kids."

The ghost kids. A blown-out wall and drowned children.

He didn't want to have lived through what they just lived through. If those boys had seen the water pouring in on them and couldn't get out?

She studied the open hatch. "Why did the door stick?"

Stick? *Not exactly.* But there was no reason to freak her out any more.

If that ghost had the gall to show his hood one more time…

"Jude?"

"Probably the frame shifted when the wood below it failed, and it jammed." Wait, was that a— "Do you have your flashlight?" His was lost to the torrent. She handed hers over, and he targeted the side still lying shut. "An actual stick." It was half-in, half-out of the handle.

That blasted ghost.

A whispered prayer escaped her lips, as close to a curse as his wife would ever get. After that, they sat in silence. The bars and restaurants up on Main could've been doing live outdoor karaoke contests with Swiss yodelers; he wouldn't have noticed.

Where was she going to go once all of this sunk in? It promised to be harder to find than the banks of the river.

"Are you sure you're okay?" She asked it, and he'd never been so happy to hear a present-sounding wife.

Stay with me, darling. Stay with me. "Yeah, I'm fine. A little black and blue. I'll match my wardrobe." He struggled onto tired feet and put a hand out to her. "Think you can stand?"

She reached and let him pull, landing her in a bear hug that he refused to release. He murmured sweet nothings in her ear for a full minute, combing webs out of her hair as he stroked it. After an eon or so, she took a single step backward.

"Let's not do that again."

He feigned horror, which wasn't difficult considering the amount of pain he had to draw from. "No more hugging?"

She wiped at her cheeks. "I've told you before, basements should be outlawed."

"Sweetheart, tell me where to sign the petition."

They turned and started the slow walk up Louis Blanchette's Little Hills toward Vita's.

Chapter 18

Audie pulled her feet up under her on Vita's chair by the hearth and opened her laptop. The fireplace crackled thanks to Jude's latent pyromania. That was the only sound in the big house, though, and it suited her fine.

The three of them had attended the earliest Sunday Mass offered at St. Peter's, a quieter affair than the one most families would experience later in the morning. As much as she loved the choir echoing off the high ceilings, the toned-down service provided solace needed by their close-knit trio.

Jude also needed a higher dose of anti-inflammatories, the way he rolled that bad shoulder whenever he thought she wasn't looking.

Last night's chaos—Jude's pain, the dark and horrible confines, the dust and oppressiveness and race for freedom that almost hadn't come… for what? A stockpile of bottles used to slip under Prohibition's radar. They hadn't found Kurt Boulton's ill-gotten gains. They hadn't uncovered Fran's missing Tiffany panel. All they'd learned was how impossible it was going to be to help the young woman and her child. They sat in a city, a couple of cities, actually. Kurt may've put that artwork anywhere.

They'd gained nothing.

Where they'd succeeded was in taking a year off both their lifespans by inhaling ancient grime. It tickled the back of her throat, and she coughed. Rude.

Emotionally and mentally, it had done more damage, but who was she to admit that to anyone other than a specific nun in the Arizona desert? She'd already talked with Sister Philomena, as soon as they'd gotten home from church. Despite the time zone difference, she'd be awake. The world's best listener—okay, she tied with Jude—had supplemented the priest's homily with wisdom of her own.

Has Sister ever panicked a single minute? Never in the seventeen years Audie had known her.

Wonder what that's like.

I knew, once. But it was more than seventeen years ago.

Besides, certain occasions required panic. The Fran-Trent melodrama seemed the right opportunity.

A log popped in the fire, and Audie watched an ember die out on the bricks.

Fitting.

Which shop would Vita have towed Jude into by now? Main Street must be abuzz the last weekend day before Christmas. He wouldn't mind, even though the Wests had agreed to their customary not-spending-much holiday. She could never give him a better gift than the chance to cook a fancy meal for an appreciative family. And stores didn't stock that. Since she herself needed nothing but him, it balanced out.

She opened a blank document and stared at it in a cluttered fog. What was she trying to parse out? And why? This wasn't a case or a job, officially.

But if she didn't work, she'd think. Not a good trade.

Brain dump time. Questions began to fill the page.

Where did Kurt bury his treasure?

Why did he steal something of major value—the Tiffany—after so many neglected opportunities at other stores?

Why didn't he sell his plunder?

Why would he kill himself in a way so counter to suicide statistics?

She backspaced over a line involving a nineteenth-century ghost and her influence. Sister Philomena would not approve of that sort of rumination.

The 'why Kurt did what he did' questions rose to the top, central to unraveling this mess. Was there any possibility he hadn't stolen Fran's piece, even if he was responsible for everything else that went missing?

But no one knew about the $25,000 art, let alone that it hid in plain sight.

The handyman didn't either, and we're still assuming he stumbled across it the night before he left this earth for good.

So does it come down to opportunity if not knowledge? Who had the opportunity? Vita—yikes. Best not to mention she'd made it onto a suspect list, however briefly. Darla—well, the panel was right under her nose, mere feet from her scarves. How about motive? No, there couldn't be—

Oh. Maybe there was.

An image of those two NICU bassinets, full of expensive equipment for her newborn grandbabies, flashed forward. And their parents had just come into unexpected money?

Intriguing. And awful. Vita wouldn't be learning of this theory either.

She pulled up the Missouri court record database. Most days, she disliked it being so easy to find this sort of information, but it had been helpful on several genealogy quests. A search of Darla's name returned nothing. Her husband had two tickets, both for going less than ten miles over the speed limit. So at least the Jameses weren't leading a life of crime.

Or they were good at getting away with it.

Hmm.

For morbid fun, she typed in every person they'd met in the historic district this week, although it must be sacrilege and coal-inviting to search for St. Nicholas and his wife. Nick had been part of a suit in the late '90s. He and the trucking company who employed him were both named in an accident where a small child was seriously injured. The docket entries told her how terrifying it must've been for the present-day ice cream scoopers, but in the end, Nick was exonerated and the company didn't even need to pay court fees. Highway traffic cameras substantiated his claim that the sedan had pulled a stupid move, cutting in front of the semi with no warning to beat him to an exit ramp.

Some people wouldn't realize the value of their lives if you broke it down in crayon.

The results for the next search raised the hair on her neck. Glen Armquist's entry covered two full pages. Hang on, most of those dealt with a guy half his age who enjoyed stalking his significant others.

Swell.

Near the bottom of page two, though, the Ghost-of-Dickens-Mister-Armquist stood up. A couple of years back, the landlord of G. Armquist Fine Antiques had resorted to suing to get the rent paid. Eventually, the suit settled out of court, so the money must've materialized. Derek said his uncle wasn't the Warren Buffet of bookkeeping. Perhaps that's when he brought his nephew on board.

Then wouldn't Glen treat him better? Jude had described the businessman as his usual condescending self during the shop visit yesterday while she was... well, while she was otherwise occupied. Then again, he might not like to admit the Great and Powerful Oz of Antiquities needed assistance. It wasn't a good look for the de facto mayor.

Here was a funny one. The same Glen Armquist had a youthful indiscretion, only he'd been not quite youthful enough to have it hidden in juvenile court docs. At the ripe old age of eighteen, he'd been arrested for shoplifting, at the art museum gift shop of all places. Somebody had told her Glen's father had hoarding tendencies, with Glen and his collections following suit. Did he get sticky fingers whenever near elegance?

Did that say something about the Tiffany?

Trent Gill—now his crimes were many, but unvaried. Moving vehicle citations mostly—so much for learning one's lesson—and one for petty theft.

She opened a second browser window and did a general search for his name. High school yearbooks came up first. He was a handsome boy, she'd give Fran that. There was the girl herself. She looked almost the same as today, but her chestnut hair matched Audie's own.

Should I go blue too? Or teal?

It would give the next visit to Mom more variety.

As she skimmed the yearbooks, finding Trent in no clubs or sports or anything other than a moody shot amongst his classmates, she heard Jude in her head.

'You're doing that thing we tell people not to rely on.'

'There's a time and a place for the interwebs,' she argued in this imaginary conversation. 'Besides, this isn't a job.'

'Right. We're not being paid.'

And that's why low-expense Christmas gifts were the best kind.

A familiar face with glasses and a mop of thick hair popped up on the next page. Forgot Derek was a classmate of Fran's. He was grinning, also a handsome boy who looked like he knew it, holding a trophy at the center of nine other kids. They'd placed first in their division at the state scholar bowl championship. The teenage girls on either side of him seemed enamored with his smile. Well, Nick Ramsey, the ice cream shop owner, said he'd been wealthy and cocky. She checked the index and found him in multiple photos, including one shaking hands with a former governor. He'd written an essay on world hunger or some such impossible problem. Maybe the cockiness hadn't been about his family money after all, but about brains.

She still felt bad that he'd had his heart handed to him in college. But that may've been good, brought him down to earth with the rest of the mortals before he turned into another Uncle Glen.

Jude told her Derek lit up whenever Fran was mentioned. The two might be the best thing that could happen to each other. Audie hadn't known she'd needed her own white knight until he'd appeared. Maybe the same would hold true for Fran and little Lizzie.

It would sure be a step up from Trent.

The fire settled, and she closed the laptop. Retrieving a log from the handcrafted holder, she placed it at the perfect angle atop the others already burning. Her husband wasn't the only West who enjoyed a good flame and could keep it going. She simply chose to let him have that one joy.

He earns it.

That moment on the grass above their almost-tomb... Dirt, mildew, and the questionable air had clung to him as much as she had. But beneath it was the familiar scent of the man she'd love forever. Twenty years ago, she couldn't have conceived of needing a second husband. Not so young, not ever. Yet there he was, her white knight in black clothing.

Yeah, may Fran find the same. And soon.

Chapter 19

"Jude, honey, you're resembling a pack mule."

He adjusted the two small bags on his left forearm and gripped the larger one with his right hand. "It's okay. I'm balanced this way."

And as long as he kept the forearm tucked in, Mr. Cranky Shoulder could deal without an excessive amount of whining. Thank goodness Vi shopped lightly. Or maybe the ibuprofen was still in effect. He needed to write its inventor a thank-you note, send some homemade chili.

At least the cut to his forehead hid itself behind his bangs. A miracle every minute, this holiday.

Church bells tolled 1 p.m. The gray skies were no match for the festive atmosphere of this big local shopping day. Take that, online retailers.

Correction: gigantic soulless conglomerates. There was a difference.

Until Vi had rented the boutique space with Darla and then Fran, she'd been one of those e-shops, along with attending all the in-person fairs she could manage. Good thing she'd maintained the virtual presence, or their current spree—odds and ends for her kids and husband—would've been underfunded this strange season.

Ahead, two giant ice cream cones swayed in the December breeze. Would Vi be easier to lure toward snacky-snacks than her sister? He opened his mouth to ask when she picked up her pace.

"Crud. Somebody's heading up our path to the shop. I'd better go explain the situation."

The 'closed' sign hung on their short fence gate, but a woman had ignored it and was studying the building more than scurrying for a last-minute gift. They crossed toward her—and away from the frozen dairy goodness, dang it—dodging two cars and a host of people trying to travel in every direction except that of the person next to them.

"I'm so sorry, ma'am," Vi called out before he'd gotten through the gate behind her. "I run this shop"—one third of it, anyway—"and we're not open today."

The woman turned. About Vita's age, she was slender, wearing a plaid wool scarf and a hunter-green coat over black slacks. What she didn't wear was either of the two expressions pasted onto most faces: festive and fun or stressed and half-crazed.

Her look was just… troubled. Or sad?

"Oh! Sorry. I didn't—I mean, I saw you're closed. I only wanted…"

Did she know what she wanted? It didn't seem like it.

Then she put out a hand, covered in brown faux leather. "My name is Monica." Vita took her hand, because that's what Vita does. "Monica Boulton."

Ah.

"I'm—I was Kurt's ex-wife."

Troubled. Yeah, nailed it the first time.

"Goodness, honey. I'm so sorry." Vi, who never looked lost, was lost. Her options for comforting hospitality had been stripped from her. "I can't even let you into the building to chat. Blame law enforcement, not me."

"I don't want to go in." She really didn't, at the rate with which those words had spilled out. "I only wanted to see the place. I'm not from here. But the police called our daughter with the news, and I drove in from Indianapolis this morning. It felt like it needed doing."

Would Trenton Gill have done that for his soon-to-be-ex?

"Everybody liked Kurt," Vita said, her voice as much a balm as her sister's. She neglected to mention Glen's opinion, which was for the best.

"They always did." Monica smiled. "It's why we wound up together. I wish it would've ended differently."

"We can never understand why folks do things like this."

She half-waved it away. "I meant us. I wish we had ended differently. Did he tell you he was in the army? At the start of Desert Storm, he was on the ground in Iraq. It did a number on him, something we never saw coming. He returned home changed. My younger self with a child to care for wasn't prepared for it."

Vita realized she'd skipped introductions. Jude offered his sympathies as well.

"I appreciate the kindness. It's been a long time since we split up. I still loved him, if you can believe that, and I never lost hope that he'd get the help he needed."

"What I've known of Kurt over the past two years, he was reserved but eminently capable. Focused."

"That was him. The old him. And it's good to hear. These thefts, though?" She grimaced.

"That floored everyone."

"Us too. Our daughter, Brooke, didn't have contact with him for most of her life—I thought I was protecting her. But a leopard doesn't change his spots, right? I believe the part of him that I fell in love with was there, if damaged by war." She carried the pain in the lines at her eyes. "He was never a bad man. The idea of him being a thief is almost as ridiculous as the notion of him killing himself."

"Like I said, we never know."

This time, she firmly shook her head. "I'm going to sound delusional, but no one will ever convince me that Kurt did that to himself."

"Really?"

"Let alone the drama of how he supposedly did it, he'd had an aunt, his mother's sister, who took her own life when he was a teen. He lived through the devastation she left behind. Yes, she'd been in some tight spots, had her share of heartache, and she couldn't see a way out. But there always is one. Always.

"Kurt and I talked about it a lot when we were dating—we'd gotten married just a few years later, when we were twenty-two. He was adamant nobody should give it a first thought, if only as a kindness to their loved ones." She looked at the building, and her protest solidified. "No way could he do this."

The bloody glass, his fingerprints covering it, the stolen items in his jacket pocket. Jude wouldn't persuade her. He wouldn't have wanted anyone persuading him if the shoe had been on the other foot.

"They say he'd been drinking, and of course, that can alter one's decisions," the ever-diplomatic Vita said. "One of our ladies has a little girl, and he seemed to be looking at her picture when he—"

Monica bit at her lower lip. "I heard. My daughter can't figure out how to take it. Kurt had been trying to get me to negotiate some sort of meeting. We'd been in contact over the past six months, him telling me how he'd quit gambling, quit drinking. He claimed to be stone-cold sober for seven years already."

Jude's face, rarely stone-cold according to the elf he lived with, must've divulged his confusion, because she nodded at him. "I know. That whiskey. I'm only repeating what he told me. Regardless, he wanted to make amends for so much, but my goodness, Brooke is a grown woman now. I passed on the idea. It was her decision."

She wiped at her eye. "I wish she could've known him like he was before. He didn't deserve another rejection. I guess I have no one to blame but myself; I did the damage. But I have great memories of a good man who was honored to serve his country and saw it as protecting Brooke and me. But war is not an honor."

"In Sherman's words, it's hell." Audie would've approved of his remembering.

"Yeah, and it led to the drinking, and for a while, gambling and debts and some less than angelic buddies. But I thought that was behind him." She rewrapped her scarf and smoothed out her coat as if she were ironing the wrinkles from a life that had not gone to plan. "I'm sorry to have bothered you. I needed to think a bit, and this felt like the spot to do it."

Vita reached into her purse and gave her a business card. "My cell is on there. Please, please call me if you want to talk, or if there's anything I can do for you or your girl. Are you staying nearby?"

"I'm driving home tonight. My only tie to the city had been Kurt—he'd moved here after the divorce, to get away from everything, predominantly me." She looked Vi squarely in her eyes. "Given all this happening on your doorstep, I wish you and your family a most peaceful holiday."

Vita dove in for the hug before the poor woman could blink, but her surprised look turned into a soft blush as her eyelids closed and she hugged in return.

"I needed that," she admitted. "Merry Christmas to you both."

Without another word, she took the path to the street and disappeared into the crowds. Had she truly been there? He hadn't shaken her hand—too many bags—but his sister-in-law would know if she'd embraced a specter.

Artistic Vita? Maybe not.

Maybe Monica had been a figment, a ghost. Maybe Josephine had found a friend.

But was she right about her ex and his final moments?

Or was she simply grieving for a first love that went as dismally as it had?

A cold gust cut through Jude's jacket. If they didn't recover that stained glass soon, another little girl was going to lose a parent like Brooke Boulton had. Her blue-haired mother, crushed under the weight of that loss? What would it do to her?

I don't want to find out.

Chapter 20

Monday morning—a workday for those with 'real jobs.' Based on how often strangers asked if the occupation qualified, freelance genealogy must not.

Then don't come crying to us when your third-great-grandmother shows up in multiple cemeteries with four different husbands after being arrested for hustling pool in 1860s West Plains.

Shame—that one would've been fun to research.

As he opened the Jeep's passenger door, Jude yawned like Rip Van Winkle before his long nap.

"Sorry," he said. "I think Vita slipped me decaf. Oh wait, I made the coffee."

Audie stepped onto the running board and pivoted to kiss his cheek. "Lousy excuse for a vacation, isn't it?"

At least he'd slept better than the previous night. Still, too much tossing and turning, none of which was the fault of their cozy attic bedroom. Whenever he'd drifted off, the transparent image of a certain bride, frightened and frightening, reached out to him. He shuddered.

Lord, please give me more useful things to do on the other side than impersonating Casper. Does heaven need any wood chopped?

He closed the door while Audie was fiddling with her seat belt. Fortunately, her mind reading hadn't kicked in for the day. *I blame the coffee.*

When he and Vita had returned from shopping Sunday afternoon, his wife had been disappointed to hear she'd missed Monica Boulton. She hung on each word of their encounter.

Hung.

Sorry, Josephine.

No wonder sleep only came in fits.

He rounded the front of their trusty workhorse, every inch of his body stifling a whimper as he dropped off the curb. Their underground escapade had taken the usual two days to reach maximum soreness. That stupid left shoulder screamed. He waffled between irritation that the collapsing braces had chosen that one to hit and thankfulness that it hadn't demolished the other.

Yesterday, the priest at St. Peter's had lit the final candle on the Advent wreath. In that stunning Romanesque space, he wanted it to offer catharsis, like they were almost to the end of preparations, almost to Christmas Day and the promise of hope and love and peace. But the finish line meant something very different to a blue-haired woman and a pigtailed kindergartner. The Tiffany panel wasn't lost, per se, so does one pray to Anthony or somebody else? Divine intervention would be super-useful.

Sigh.

He climbed into the Jeep and pulled away from the Kleins' curb, turning up the hill toward the north end of St. Charles. "This Mabel knows we're coming, yes?"

Audie gestured to the right at the first stop sign, and he followed her direction with more trust than he had in any GPS. "Vita texted her, because Vita has everybody's cell number on the planet."

"Popular, that sister of yours."

"Mabel's eager to meet us."

"That's worrisome." The folks most excited to see them usually had a mountain of dull tidbits to share and too many free hours to do so. The comfy attic bedroom and a siesta grew more distant by the moment.

"We don't have a choice. If there's a tie between Kurt Boulton's death, the thefts, and Josephine Richards' murder, we need more info. I've searched through the newspaper indices for the area, and there is almost nothing from the 1820s."

"I would've thought Nathaniel's hanging was big news."

"This was the frontier. It must've been a hot topic around town and in the infant legislature, but printed papers were scarce. If we were back East, it would've been a much larger scandal."

"Stuart said Mabel had family here at the time of the murder?"

"Some intrepid pioneers had arrived a year prior to statehood, though most of her kin remained where they'd sprouted. Fortunately for us, it was a period where writing was the sole means of keeping up with far-flung relations. A string of letters passed between the adventurous man who'd moved here and his people in Quebec. Somebody was smart enough to stick the letters in a box so we'd have them today."

"I love an experienced hoarder."

"They're terrific, so long as the walls don't collapse in on us."

She realized what she'd said as soon as she'd said it. He held his breath and surveyed the passenger seat without moving his head. Her gloved hands had clenched in her lap.

That was one bad night. But it could've been worse.

And she knew it more than he did.

In a few minutes, they'd left the well-defined city blocks and entered what used to be rural county land.

"Wow" was the best word he could muster as he pulled before a two-story, Italianate brick house. It had white shutters and what he thought was called a hipped roof, the overhangs supported by ornate wooden brackets. Windows on the first floor were narrow and arched, and the porch was more of a portico than a place to put rockers and sip your morning joe.

Even in winter, the yard was impeccable. A single, elegant wreath with a red velvet ribbon adorned the front door, and candles like those in Vita's boutique sat behind every bit of glass. A strand of clear lights lined the portico's eave, but that was all. Whispering 'mid-nineteenth century Christmas' in a demure and stately manner, the owner felt as he did regarding inflatable Santas in Bermuda shorts driving a reindeer-powered monster truck.

Whose brainchild *was* that thing?

He shook his head as he climbed out, then retrieved the backpack from the trunk. How had he thought they'd get through the holiday break without doing research of some kind?

Audie led the way up a winding concrete path. The snow had melted as the temperature rose to the upper-thirties. She wore one of Becca's old coats left hanging in the hall closet. Vita was dropping the yellow wool at the cleaners before anyone had to be re-traumatized by seeing its current condition.

He missed the yellow.

At the top of the steps—Jude's knees creaking like an archaic roller coaster—the door opened before Audie rang the bell.

"My heavens, if you aren't the spitting image of your sister."

Mabel Ehrand matched her pristine house to a tee—tidy, smart, and well-aged. She had bright green eyes behind stylish glasses and walked with a quad cane that somehow passed for fashionable in her hand. Her short white hair was as dazzling as

Sunday's flakes, none of that battleship gray, and held a curl like it had been born that way. She'd lost a battle for the perfect posture of her youth, but she still looked confident enough in her abilities that she wouldn't be letting anyone put her in some home without a fight.

Stuart had to have been wrong about her flightiness. This woman was at the top of her game, and he had no intention of challenging it.

"Come in out of this weather!" She pulled a burgundy cardigan closer around her thin frame and stepped aside for them to enter. A cat with shiny black fur slipped between her ankles before darting down the hall. "Alistair, that's rude. Please excuse his manners. Anyway, I was so excited to hear from Vita that you'd be stopping by. I miss the hubbub of Main Street at Christmas."

This season's hubbub was a tad overrated. "Do you go listen to the carolers or anything?"

"Honey, I used to be one of the carolers!" Her laugh echoed up a walnut staircase. Evergreen garland with bows to match her sweater spiraled around its banister. She led them into a parlor, already set with a tray of cookies and a coffee service. "Believe it or not, I was a founding member of the Holidays of Hope brigade. All that history down in our district? I thought it would be fun to trot it out for a charitable cause." She motioned them to an antique off-white sofa while she sat opposite in an amber wingback, cane positioned to the side. "I had Sandy run me over some of her apple cider shortbreads when I heard I'd be having company. Would one of you be a dear and pour? My joints have gone rusty, and I wind up making a mess."

Audie picked up the silver urn, filled a china cup, and passed it with a saucer toward Mabel.

"None for me, thanks. The doctors think it's okay, but I'm not taking any chances. If I can stay in this place for another hundred years, that's what I want to do." She considered the treat plate as Jude took the cup and Audie poured another for herself. After the briefest of hesitations, her smart eyes twinkled. "But what's the use of living that long if you can't have a cookie once in a while?"

Audie smiled, put a pair on a cloth napkin, and handed them to their host.

"You aren't involved with the holiday group anymore, Mrs. Ehrand?"

Her nose crinkled. "Mabel, please. I finally retired about five years ago. I don't drive, and it was a hassle for others to fetch me." Unlikely, but Jude figured he'd feel the same at her age. "Plus, certain factors were making it less enjoyable."

Jude's eyebrows raised, and she caught it. There wasn't much this woman didn't catch.

"I'm big on tradition. I mean, look at this place. But some people push too hard. We need to keep the right balance of the old with the modern. If you're going to berate anyone who isn't speaking like they live in Victorian England, you're going to lose both visitors and volunteers."

Mrs. Mabel Ehrand, for instance.

"You couldn't be referring to Glen Armquist, could you?"

She flushed and began to answer, then chose the way of nonviolence. After lifting a cookie to her perfectly colored lips, the cinnamon had its desired effect, and she maintained her even keel. "Mostly, yes. For all of his insistence on Père Noël, he goes off and makes up a ghost of Charles Dickens. Don't get me wrong; I read *A Christmas Carol* each December. But this isn't London, and if he's a gifted author, then I am Mighty Mouse."

At the mention of rodents, two triangular ears and a matching tail appeared from behind a wicker basket by the fireplace. These were white. Alistair's fraternal twin?

"You're not here to listen to me grouse." She placed the half-eaten shortbread beside its partner on an oval side table. Reaching down, she pulled a manila envelope out of the basket and switched on the lamp.

"You're interested in that horrible murder, aren't you? The legislator's young bride done in by the glassmaker?"

"We are. We normally do genealogy research, but for anything like this, we're moths to a flame."

"Family trees? Fascinating. It's a topic for another day, but I should tell you some stories about my own lines. Most of them are mundane—you're born, you grow, you die. But the Yarborough ancestors are everything you'd never want in your DNA. Mad as a pack of hatters."

"The whole branch?"

"One on each limb, as far back as we can find." She turned the opened envelope out onto her lap. "You never know where it's going to hit. I'm glad Martin and I never had children."

She tapped together a neat stack of paper-clipped sheets. Those did not look centuries old.

"When I first inherited the collection, I had it digitized and made copies. I have the originals, but they're in sorry shape, as you can imagine." Thoroughly modern Mabel—nice. She sorted through the sheaf and handed one set to Audie. "This is what you're looking for, I think, but my eyes aren't as sharp as they used to be."

Somehow, Jude doubted that.

Audie read the reproduced envelopes. "These are addressed to a Timothy, from his brother William."

"That's the ones. William came to the frontier from Canada to find his fortune. With his wife and kids, he eventually settled along the river and was employed in the fur trade as a dealer. By the time of these letters, he seemed content with his life. Thank goodness they weren't texting in those days, or we wouldn't know anything from that period." She waved a dismissive hand at the iPhone propped against the lamp. "They're convenient, but not exactly archivable. Of course, we only have William's side of things, because Timothy had room to store the correspondence. Here on the edge of civilization, William did not, so his brother's responses are gone with the wind."

"That shouldn't matter, since what we're looking for are accounts of life here locally." Audie was already skimming with those eagle eyes of hers. "These begin in April 1821."

"Yes, I sorted those out for you. The Richards didn't arrive here until that May."

"Mabel, you're an absolute peach." She'd be hired by West Genealogy in a heartbeat if budget allowed. "Nothing much in this initial letter. The family had made it through their first full winter here and everyone was healthy."

Remember that when you're griping about the camper's wonky plumbing. "There's something to be said for antibiotics and central heating."

Audie's index finger slid down the page. "He apologizes for the long span between notes, but mail was less than reliable during the frozen weather."

Jude leaned closer. The tight script was impossible to read at this angle. "Any discussion of the community in general?"

"Not much. He says the big excitement was from November, when his adopted home was chosen as the temporary capital of the new state until some infant city could be birthed near its center. The assembly would be forming in the coming months."

"That's a start."

Audie set the sheet aside and moved to the next. "This is four weeks later, early May. William is talking about his daughter and son practicing their arithmetic, how Annette is meeting other wives now that the children are in school. They've grown particularly close to the Silvains, Nathaniel and Patrice."

"Jackpot."

"No kidding. Their kids are the same age, so they find it easy to spend time with them. The Silvains have been living here a year longer and have helped them adjust to town life."

"I know it took a village to raise children back then," Jude cringed, "but it doesn't bode well that one turned out to be a murderer."

"It still does. Take a village, I mean, not a murderer." She continued reading. "Here's something. We're in mid-June now. The general assembly has assembled—appropriate—so the neighborhood has a fresh influx of inhabitants. All the boardinghouses are full. Simpson's, next to the Silvain home and workshop, is busting at the seams.

"William writes that the population boom, even if temporary for the summer, was a boost for his business. The demand for fur here was up, and that meant he needn't pay to ship as many items to the east. It was especially beneficial after the fire." That line above her nose appeared as she flipped to the next missive. "I'd forgotten about that."

"What fire?" Jude asked.

"Somewhere, we read about a warehouse going up in flames. That was at the Capitol site, wasn't it?"

"Of course. The one where Clarence Richards was able to stop the bleeding. Earned him a gubernatorial commendation."

"Nice use of the vocab, Watson."

"Thank you, Sherlock." He blushed as he remembered they had an audience for their marital shenanigans. Mabel only winked at him knowingly.

"So this was a bit after the fire, I suppose. William is relieved at how things have turned out. There were hours where their next bite was questionable, because more beaver pelts shouldn't have arrived for weeks. They came into St. Charles from far out west, up the river, but the Missouri was famous for being difficult to navigate."

"Then how did our boy Clarence get material here so fast? I thought Chariton was on the river too."

"It was, but they made better time by road. Seeing the problem, our man of action contacted his constituents and got supplies here pronto. Didn't charge an exorbitant rate or anything."

"How kindhearted of him."

"William doesn't say it, but you can tell he wonders about Clarence's motives. He's glad the day was saved, but it also didn't hurt the fine gentleman's shot at a higher office down the line." She turned to Mabel. "Did he ever succeed? I can't place his name on the governors list."

Her simple hoop earrings reflected the lamp as she shook her head. "Clarence only outlived his murdered wife by three years. He was quite a bit older, and I think politicians then weren't much different from those now. He didn't worry about what doctors said regarding coffee and such things."

Jude stopped himself mid-reach for the silver urn.

"The recent arrivals were the talk of the resident population." Audie was skimming again. "Listen to this. 'As for the legislators, some have brought their families with them. Last Sunday, Annette, the children, and I called on the Silvains. When I checked on the little ones outside, I glimpsed a slender woman walking alone in the garden of the Simpson Boardinghouse. She looked at each flower like if she didn't examine it from every angle, some crucial thing would be missed. Patrice said that was Mrs. Clarence Richards, Josephine, and she'd seen her do that many times. Both Patrice and Nathaniel often speak to her across the fence when taking breaks from the household or workshop. I noted she didn't seem quite happy, and both the ladies laughed at my naivete. They said, of course, she's not happy. Her husband is twice her age, and she's far from home and family.

"'Nathaniel came to my defense, and that of the male species. He stated it couldn't be too terrible. Clarence himself had ordered her a beautiful gift for their upcoming first anniversary: a stained-glass panel with a spring theme. It's her favorite time of year, and he requested the art be full of the flora and fauna that rise from winter's grave. Nathaniel brought it out to show us. Though a work in progress, it was magnificent.' He describes a few details, saying how envious he is of the man's talent."

Giving up and pouring another dose of caffeine, Jude asked, "Mabel, do you know if anything else in those letters expounds on the Richards' relationship?"

"Never in so many words. And there isn't too much about them at all until Nathaniel is charged with Josephine's murder. To this point and ever after, William emphasized how steadfast the Silvains were, so faithful to each other. William saw them as role models. Marriages need those."

"Amen to that."

She smiled at him in approval.

His better half said, "It's especially odd that there'd be such rumblings about Nathaniel and Josephine after she died."

Mabel sat up straighter, leaning forward an inch and touching the collar of her blouse. "I've always thought the same. He had a healthy family and a solid business. Some letters talk about his skill with glass, how Nathaniel loved showing off for the children, letting them serve as tiny apprentices occasionally. He sounded happy with his life. Why would he ruin it?"

"Men have ruined for less."

Alistair or his twin returned. Hold on. Now, it was a tabby. Was Mabel running a cat sanctuary?

Before he could inquire, Audie paused on the fifth letter. "This is dated July 30, 1821. That would be just after Josephine's death."

"Would you read it out loud? I haven't looked at these in a while." Retrieving her cookie, the old woman closed her eyes to improve her hearing.

"'Dear Timothy, I hope this note finds you, Michelle, Mother, and Father doing well. I anxiously await word of our niece or nephew. We pray sweet Michelle remains in robust health and comes through the birth without trouble.'"

Childbirth: required for the propagation of the species, deadly for centuries, still not safe for some populations in their own supposedly advanced country. Jeez.

"'I have news that I must share, though it is tragic and involves a friend. You recall Nathaniel Silvain, the glassmaker? Two nights ago, he was discovered standing over the spouse of one of our state representatives. Mrs. Richards was dead, her throat slashed with a piece of Nathaniel's glass. The husband found the horrid scene when he arrived home that evening, Nathaniel still holding the wicked shard. Those in the boardinghouse who answered Mr.

Richards' cry claim my friend turned white as a sheet and tried to flee. He was tackled before he could reach the rear door. He swore his innocence, but the woman's blood covered his shirt and vest like that of a sacrificial lamb.

"'Obviously, the area is shocked. We are devastated. Annette has been sitting with Nathaniel's wife, Patrice, almost since it happened, as she is beside herself. First, he's a murderer, then the district is drowning in rumors about a relationship between her husband and the lost soul. Patrice has no way to protect her children from the awfulness, and if she survives this tragedy, I will find it a miracle of God's own doing. Nathaniel bides his hours in the jail across from the legislature. I fear the hardware store they meet above may be building his gallows soon.'"

"Oh my goodness." Audie put down the letter and looked up at Mabel, who opened her eyes.

"So upsetting, isn't it?" Not enough to dissuade her from Sandy's confections, as she finished off the treat. "Go on."

"'I knew nothing of the murdered woman personally, only to recognize her by sight. We did not run in the same social circles, of course. But she was difficult to miss: slight, pretty, with dark brown hair hung in natural ringlets. I only had one proper conversation with her. I was walking to see Nathaniel in his shop, and Mrs. Richards was in the garden behind the boardinghouse, once more inspecting those flowers like the Silvains had said she was wont to do. I asked only if she was enjoying such a fine summer day, and she replied she liked to be in the sun while she could—it always gave her a different perspective, even if the view from her window was nearly the same.

"'Many other legislators' wives had been jealous of her beauty. At least, that's what Annette says. Now though? I hear murmurs they prefer their fine lines if it makes them unattractive to scoundrels. I find it impossible to believe, Nathaniel being a scoundrel, but I'll admit to being biased. We don't know why he left Quebec, who he was before he arrived on these banks. The frontier is a strange and wild place, Timothy. Strange and wild.'"

Chapter 21

For a minute, the clock on the mantel made the only sound. Then Mabel requested, "Read the next, please. If I remember correctly, it's from a few weeks later."

Audie reached for her cup, as much for an emotional break as a vocal one, then resumed. "'Dear Timothy.' I'll summarize. Michelle has almost reached her due date and both households are abuzz with anticipation. Then he moves on to less joyful things. 'You recall the sad story I last relayed? Nathaniel has given up his cries of innocence. They'd fallen on deaf ears, and his trial was a quick, sure thing. Every person in the boardinghouse had an alibi, and the dead woman's husband claimed to have not been home since the morning, occupied with the business of government. Although he has never admitted to the crime, yesterday Nathaniel asked for permission to finish a project before he's to be hanged.'"

"He was worried about work?" Interesting priorities.

"Keep reading," Mabel instructed.

"'He had been hired to install a small, stained-glass panel, a rectangular scene of our river and the surrounding hills in autumn, into the base of a banjo clock for the governor's office. This was to take the place of the usual painting included on a clock like that, and of course, avoid the required taxes. He expressed hope his wife could be paid for it, as it was nearly complete. His family will be destitute without their breadwinner.

"'Shocking to most here, Mr. Clarence Richards, husband of the woman killed, supported the appeal. He is holding onto his faith through all of this, and though it's been an obvious strain, he's publicly forgiven Nathaniel and encouraged his fellow congressmen to approve the commission.

"'Some find it distasteful to mount the creation of a murderer in our governor's office, but others are showing mercy. Plus, as I've said, his art is without compare. It will be a striking addition to somewhat shabby quarters, especially when you consider our state is governed from above a dry goods store. Quebec City, we are not.

"'This clock and the anniversary gift from a husband now widowed will be the last of the works Nathaniel Silvain produces on this earth. The trial was fast, and though he plead a pathetic not guilty, he couldn't prove his statement and there was so much evidence against him. His wife did not attend, which was for the best, for she would've had to sit in the gallery and it had already turned into the worst sort of macabre entertainment. He is to be hung on Tuesday next.'"

Audie scrutinized that last line for too long, then set the letter aside.

Yeah.

She lifted the following sheet and braced for more horribleness. Her face softened as she read the introduction. "'Dear brother, I write this with the happiest of hearts as I hear of your precious baby girl. Mother wrote at what must have been the moment of birth, and I cannot be more pleased for you. I only wish I could hold Aurora and spoil her, as you'd wished for my own children. Thanks be to God that Michelle came through the experience well. I hope her health is fully restored before the winter cold comes.'"

"Isn't that swell?"

Audie tapped at the paper. "It is while it lasts. But back to the story. 'I do not wish to dampen the glorious delight in your growing household, so I will only say that my friend Nathaniel has passed from this earth and is a worry for the other side now. I pray he repented; eternal suffering is too much to contemplate. But what were they to do? The frontier is dangerous enough. We cannot live in a place where life is taken without consequence.'"

Audie set the letter on the table with the others and reached for her coffee. She held the cup but didn't drink. "Wow."

"Can you imagine?" Mabel said, obviously imagining. "I feel most sorry for Patrice. Later, William notes she has packed up what few things they owned—much of their property had to be sold to cover debts from Nathaniel's shop—and returned to Quebec with her children. Her family wasn't far from where Timothy lived. William asks that if his brother can think of anything that might help the hapless widow, to pass it along to her parents. Her husband may have been a fiend, but he was beyond the cares of this world."

Consequences, indeed. But not for the right person.

Jude flinched as something rubbed the hem of his jeans.

"Alistair!" Mabel scolded. "That's not polite."

The kitty moved away, its tail swishing. "Hang on—Alistair was solid black. This boy's calico."

"What on earth are you talking about? I only have one kitty." Mabel took the envelope after Audie neatly slid the copies inside like the dutiful archivist she was. "Does that help with what you're researching?"

Research? *Can we get back to the cat of many colors?*

"I don't know if I'd call it research." Audie had either missed the feline funny business—doubtful—or succeeded where he'd failed in ignoring them. "It's more curiosity on my part, which gets me in trouble."

In more ways than one, but he couldn't blame her this time. Quite the story, even viewed two hundred years later. What could any of this tell them about Fran's missing stained glass, though?

"I'm the same way, dear. Don't worry about the trouble and never stop being curious." The woman smiled, then looked down at a ring she wore on her right hand, second finger. "My late husband always said curiosity was a waste. Shows what he knew, doesn't it?"

The ring was antique, burnished gold set with a large, marquise-cut emerald. "Has he been gone long, Mabel?"

She chuckled. "You could say that. It was rather sudden. One minute, he's driving his cab, and the next, he's tumbling out of it with a massive stroke."

This place was owned by a taxi driver? "Someone told us your husband ran a grocery store." He'd been counting on the ketchup-box-to-the-head story to explain the cat situation.

"Different husband, dear. I'd been widowed twice when I met Harry at the IGA."

First hubbies must've had amazing life insurance.

"He died while driving?" Audie asked, a widow who would not be as fiscally fortunate if she found herself in need of a third spouse. All she'd get out of his demise was a high-mileage camper and unresolved family drama. "How awful. Did he cause a wreck?"

"No, the horse stopped, as she'd been taught when the reins went loose."

Jude glanced at his wife. The crease in her brow backed his confusion. "I'm sorry, Mabel, but the horse?"

"She was gorgeous. A Friesian, with that shiny coat? So well behaved."

"Your husband drove one of the tourist carriages."

"He'd pick up tourists occasionally, of course. His usual fare were the men who'd traveled to the district for business, even after the capital moved out west. Those fellows were always too important to walk the few blocks to their boardinghouses. If they would've gotten more exercise, they could've lived a long time."

Mabel winked, and Jude's gut went numb.

With a renewed and especially amiable expression plastered on her face, Audie was stealthily closing up her purse, reaching into her pockets for her gloves. "I'll bet you could've given them a lot of healthy tips, Mabel. May I ask an impertinent question? How old are you?"

Another giggle. She played with the ring. "I'm not holding up that well, but it's kind of you to humor a woman. Last March, I turned seventy-three."

Ah, okay. Oxygen reentered his lungs. "You look wonderful for seventy-three."

"Now, that's one hundred and seventy-three, of course." Another wink. "It's tedious to note the centuries, you know. My mother taught me better than that."

Beneath her purse, Audie caught his knee, which he hadn't realized was bouncing like crazy.

Crazy. *How fitting.*

"It comes down to lifestyle. Exercise, as I said, and how one fuels oneself."

Three pairs of eyes fell on the coffee urn. Two pairs widened.

"And are there certain ingredients that help with that?" His voice cracked, and when she tilted her head at him, he threw in, "I'm asking for my mom."

His mom was well past Brewed Beans of Longevity, having been dead for decades, but their host didn't know that.

The corner of her thin lips curled upward. "This and that."

"Of course," Audie said with the diplomacy of Kissinger. "We wouldn't dream of asking you to disclose your secrets." She looked toward her wrist. "My, it's getting late." Funny, her watch was sitting on the dresser at the Kleins, in need of a battery. "I'm so sorry, but I promised Vita we'd pick up lunch for her."

Mabel Ehrand lifted a cookie from the tray, holding it like Lady Liberty. Upon her movement, a Siamese popped out from beneath her chair.

Okay, had he been there all along? Were these things multiplying in the cushions? Was the wingback some sort of feline nexus?

He really would've accepted any of those answers.

He also really didn't want to know.

"Are you sure you need to leave? There's more I can—"

"You've been so generous, and it would be terrible for us to impose further. Thank you, and if we need copies, we know where to come."

"If you're certain."

An abrupt gasp stopped everyone in mid-motion except Alistair IV. The woman's pupils fixed on Audie's lap with the intensity of a thousand swords.

"What's wrong, Mrs. Ehrand?"

"That. What is that?"

His wife fumbled with her purse, brushing a non-existent crumb from her pants, studying the buttons on her borrowed coat, as utterly lost as he was.

Mabel turned away, shielding her eyes like a solar flare glowed from her sofa. "I can't take it. Put them away. Away!"

"What, Mabel? What?" The only thing she held other than her bag was— "My gloves?"

"That color! I can't stand it. It makes me weak. Put them away, please!" She paled, and for a moment, Jude feared the remarkably old woman was about to follow Hubby Number One—or was it Two?—into a stroke.

"I'm sorry!" The gloves disappeared faster than the cat changed his coat. "I didn't know. You can look now."

Mabel peeked through her fingers, and Audie raised her empty open palms.

Bit by bit, her face regained its healthy pinkness, though her chest continued to labor. "I apologize. I should've mentioned that when you entered."

Jude scanned the room—in all this color, all this elegance, there wasn't a single blue-tinted object. Lots of green, so mixing with yellow was acceptable. Returning to the woman, he couldn't help but notice her hospitable attitude had cooled a few degrees.

How many friends does one lose over seventeen decades because of incompatible fashion choices?

He picked up Audie's cobalt-free hand and backpedaled toward the foyer. Mabel recovered herself enough to follow. Grand.

The tabby got caught in her cane, and Jude panicked, wondering what would happen when the ambulance with the blue lights had to come rescue her. She righted herself as he bumped into the doorframe.

Thank goodness.

The wreath swung as they bumbled out onto the porch.

"Thanks again, and have a merry Christmas!" Still smiling that charmer smile, Audie pulled the door closed while Mabel waved from the end of the hallway. Together, they spun, hustling down the stairs and out to the Jeep. Neither said a word until they were buckled up, on the road, and three blocks away.

"Holy guacamole."

"With extra hot sauce."

"I need to apologize to Stuart."

"We'll send him a plant."

"Send him two. Hold the bluebells."

Chapter 22

"I hope Mabel doesn't decide to take her daily constitutional and find out what blatant liars we are."

Carrying a bag with three hoagies from Marigold's Deli, Audie climbed the hill toward Vita's. Her calves wished the area had been called the Little Flats. But after Sandy's shortbreads and the sandwiches they'd felt compelled to buy, they couldn't complain about the exercise.

"St. Peter can list that sin in my ledger. He and I already have a lot to discuss."

Her personal St. Jude, patron of off-kilter wives and other nonsense, needing to negotiate at the Pearly Gates? The penance from climbing these streets with a battered body should pay off any purgatorial sentence.

It would if I was in charge.

Between her ears rang Sister Philomena's vibrant laugh. 'Thinking you're in charge is half the issue, Audra dear.'

I'm just saying.

They had passed the boutique, crime-scene tape still on the door, then stopped to chat with Darla as she came out of The Doggy Bag with a geriatric but tail-wagging German Shepherd.

"Even if I can't be selling over there," she nodded toward the shop while Leonard lapped at the communal water dish, "I had to get out of the house. Lionel is glued to his easy chair, watching his forty-seventh episode of *Gunsmoke*. One more minute of horses and guns, honey, and I was going to lasso his chip bowl right through that television. And it's a nice one, so I chose to leave instead."

Whether she'd meant to protect the television or the chip bowl was anyone's guess.

Now a few blocks away, Audie continued leading their slow train upward until she realized she'd lost her caboose. Jude had stalled a full house behind her, staring into the middle distance while his right hand rubbed at his left shoulder. The wind blew at his bangs, but he didn't move to fix them.

"There's a bench over here," she said, changing course toward wrought-iron seating that looked inviting while sure to be colder than a glacier to sit on. "Why don't we take a break?"

But he frowned, shaking his head. "No, I'm fine." As he closed the gap, he expounded. "This is where I spotted my phantom that first night. He was lurking by that small green space."

A lot-sized park, not much more than a postage stamp, was fenced in and held a naked oak tree, an arbor covered with leafless vines, and a trio of evergreens clustered at the corner. "He was near those firs."

"How terribly Tannenbaum of him." Or her, or it.

Joining her by the bench, he continued studying the park. "I guess that spot in the center is a koi pond or something in the summer?"

The turf at the middle of the lot was indented. "Let's go see."

They crossed, no traffic or specters in view, and walked through the open gate. A bronze plaque inside named it the Carl and Margaret Scheid Memorial Garden. Presumably, the Scheids' philanthropic venture was more lush in June.

Following pavers to the center, they reached the black-lined circular depression, roughly eight feet wide.

"Must be a fountain." Nozzles angled inward along the perimeter. She would've preferred a nice pair of frolicking cherubs to this modern miniature of the Las Vegas Bellagio, but that would need to be deferred until the Wests had their own memorial garden.

'That's as funny as thinking you're in charge of heaven, sweetheart.' Sister Philomena wasn't wrong.

A dark green panel about two feet square lay flush in the grass. It would've blended in if the fescue weren't yellow. "Think that's access to the pipes?"

"Or the front door for Gned and the Gnome family."

She walked around the circle, wondering who tended the patch since Carl and Margaret were likely beyond pruning duties. *Maybe St. Charles has gardening ghosts too.* She doubted nothing at this point. To skirt past the arbor, she had to step off the path and onto the access panel. It shifted.

Her heart contracted an unhealthily long time as she hopped off sideways.

"Not again."

Jude looked up from a sign he was reading about migratory birds. "What was that?"

The ground keeps trying to eat me. No big deal. She crouched down and touched the panel. It wasn't connected to anything. Yet another death trap. She lifted the edge of the plate, a laser-cut plastic much lighter than she'd expected, and looked down another ladder into another abyss.

Nope. Nope nope nope.

The cloud-filtered sun fell to shadow as Jude's boots appeared in her periphery. "More rabbit holes to dive down? Didn't you get enough with the last one?"

"More than enough." She stood, stepping farther than necessary, and handed him the panel. "Think you can fit that any better? I don't want some child ending up in Wonderland with Alice."

He knelt in the grass and laid the cover at an angle over the chasm. Then he stopped.

"What's wrong?"

Setting aside the plastic square, he put a hand on opposite ends of the cutout and bent his head in. He reached up a hand without looking. "You got your flashlight on you?"

"Sure, it's—" *Oops.* "No, either Vi or the dry cleaner must have it."

"Right." He sat back on one knee and fished out his phone. "Let's see how well our high-tech multi-tool does." Once more, his head disappeared, now taking his arm with it. She liked that arm and hoped it would return someday.

From the hole came a low, slow whistle.

"Honey? You're killing your wife."

"Hang here a second." Without waiting to hear her protest, he swung his legs into the opening, grabbed for the railing with his more functional limb, and disappeared below deck.

"Jude! Things went badly the last time you did this!" But he was out of sight already. "Why don't I stay here?" she mumbled, then twitched as she fought to banish several tight spots—literal and figurative—from her hyped-up mind.

A long minute passed. She called down, "How far does that thing go?"

"I can't hear you," he yelled incongruously.

Another minute before underground footsteps approached. Gnome or husband?

"You still up there?" Oh swell. Husband.

"Unfortunately, yes. Would love for you to be too."

"Sorry." Below, the lean form of one good-looking hubby stepped out of the shadow and into the single shaft of light. In his left hand, he held a fancy pewter ice cream scoop, and in the other, the reel from an antique movie camera. "But I think we can quit searching for Kurt Boulton's hideaway."

Chapter 23

"So it was a cave after all." Vita hugged her coat as a crowd milled across from Scheid Park. Word had reached parts of Main Street, and shopkeepers eager to see their poached possessions were now joining the neighbors drawn by strobing red and blue.

Fortunately, Mabel didn't live nearby.

Law enforcement had been busy at the scene for almost an hour, and little by little, objects surfaced into the cloudy daylight.

A harmonica from the music shop, a pair of green glass earrings from Veronica's Vintage, a set of four china dessert plates painted with delicate pink flowers. Why would someone have stolen any of it, let alone Kurt? He'd worked in these businesses for years. Why plunder now?

Mental break—what a rotten phrase, made rottener by Audie's deep familiarity with it. It was also her only theory for such an abrupt change. By every account, Kurt had suffered more than his share of trials, with struggles only a select population would understand. With the things he must've seen in his wartime service, her heart ached for the man she'd never met. Mix those unresolved traumas with alcohol, the holiday season, and a daughter uninterested in hearing his apologies?

Maybe something snapped. It happened to the best of them. But filching trinkets seemed like a strange outlet.

Jack Frost blew another powerful gust, and Audie situated herself behind her husband.

"Happy to be of service," he said over his shoulder with an exaggerated eye roll. But she caught the corner of a grin as he turned into the worst of it.

The boy could use some more meat on his bones. Leave it to her to find a thin and fit windbreak. Around her, plenty of bodies would've performed the task more than adequately.

None of them could've squeezed down that access hole, though. And then they'd have no reason to be standing there in the first place.

The bystanders formed a rough crescent shape, and without abandoning his duty, Jude gestured to a middle-aged couple at the opposite end of the arc. "I talked to the guy who owns the house next door. This corner became a park because early developers had found the hollow downstairs. It's too awkwardly shaped to be a decent cellar and would've undermined any building above it."

"It sure made an excellent spot to hide things, then." Another dark underground space. Fortunately, one of them didn't have raging claustrophobia.

"And it's only two blocks up from the shop." Vita's voice trailed off as she cocked her head and squinted across the street. Audie's ears perked up.

"What are you thinking?"

Jude clapped his hands. "The Marik sisters mind-reading game. I love this show."

Vita nudged him without taking her hands out of their warm pockets. "I'm wondering why Kurt chose our place to kick back with a bottle. Was it—" She stopped, lowering her volume and turning inward to them. "Was it because the guilt from nicking Fran's expensive glass—his first substantial grab—became too much? Or that it was a convenient spot to sit before depositing that night's take? It may have started as a celebration. We don't know."

"Monica swears he's been clean and sober for seven years, proud of his progress. What threw him that far off the wagon on Thursday?"

Chatter from the park grew louder, and they turned toward the search crew. From out of the hole in the ground came a larger find than most of the others. About thirty inches long and wooden, the odd shape passed more carefully between those below and above.

"The banjo clock," Audie whispered, not as discretely as she'd hoped since she heard the phrase radiating out around her. The piece was turned as it traveled to the next officer in line, the clear glass over its face catching the light. As the flash faded, she glimpsed the rectangular art created and installed by Mr. Nathaniel Silvain, murderer, two hundred years ago.

As it neared the fence, parts of the scene became visible. It lived up to its reputation. The azure Missouri river—*never seen it that blue, but okay*—flowed at the bottom of the landscape. Behind it, the hills of St. Charles rose. Brick and clapboard houses poked from the reds, oranges, and yellows of autumn leaves. She even caught smoke rising from some chimneys. The colors contrasted sharply with the steel gray of this winter day, putting to shame the red velvet bows on the streetlamp beside them.

Jude was leaning forward as if the extra few inches would improve the view. "Man had some talent, didn't he?"

"Looks like." Vita clucked her tongue. "What a waste."

The image of a young father swinging from the gallows made Audie shiver. What a horrible way to go.

Having your throat slashed by a temperamental artist wasn't an ideal way out either.

At a folding table near the crime scene van, a man in uniform sat at a laptop, taking notes on everything that came out of the hole.

"How much more do you think there is?"

"Based on what I saw before we called the cops, they've got to be nearing the end," Jude said. "It wasn't that large of a collection. Except for the banjo clock, Kurt could've slipped most things in his coat pockets or tool kit."

"The clock would've fit in a trash bin. Smuggle it to his car behind the Capitol, then bring it up here. The trees shelter the access hole from the neighbors, especially since he worked at night."

Kurt Boulton had been creative, if nothing else.

"Fran nearly went through the roof when I called to tell her you'd found the cache." Vita gave her scarf another twirl around her neck. "She was itching to get over here to watch, but she's at the vet's today."

"One of the guinea pigs must've had fleas."

Both Mariks turned to Jude, and he raised his eyebrows.

"What? You said Fran was itching."

They groaned in unison, Audie apologizing to her sister. "Forgive me. I married him."

He brushed his blowing hair out of the way to give her the full effect of his hazel eyes.

Serves me right. Knowing she'd never resist his antics and not wishing to encourage him further, she returned to more pressing matters. This time, she made sure her voice was low enough to be covered by the ambient noise.

"How will Fran get the panel from the cops? If it wasn't reported missing, she can't very well show up and claim it."

"We have a plan of sorts," her also-creative sister replied. "The police said they'll put out a list of the recovered items. She's going to tell most of the honest story about a glass panel being taken from her raw materials and her not realizing until the list came out."

Audie's frown must've been more disapproving than worrying, because Vita launched a hushed but speedy defense. "I know, I know. But so long as the art gets to that idiot Trenton, then no harm, no foul. Sort of."

"And I guess Trenton could claim it himself, but then the full story would come out." *To lose Lizzie over this?*

Vita nodded and shook her head concurrently, which took skill. "The worst part is she swears Aunt Earline left that Tiffany to her alone. It sounds like the woman understood a thing or two and recognized what might be coming. She wanted to help her niece-by-marriage."

"Then I wish that letter would've shown up with the will." *Oh Aunt Earline, what a mess.*

What did she and Jude have to leave behind? And to whom? Becca and Connor, she guessed, would be stuck with most of their meager vestiges. A camper full of life's necessities did not make for an exciting inheritance. And their storage unit a couple of miles away held nothing as valuable as an antique banjo clock or mother's pearls, nothing that would help the kids pay off their student loans or remember their dear auntie and uncle with heartwarming fondness.

That Swedish death cleaning book was right: purge and don't be a burden after you're gone.

Now Kate, if they ever found her? Perhaps there'd be something of big brother's that she'd want. A lot of roads needed to be traveled before that would happen, though. *Here's hoping.*

Somebody jostled her arm, and she'd stepped out of their way before she registered her husband as the jostler. "Look. They're coming up."

"For air?"

Vita had gone still. "They can't be finished."

But it certainly looked like they were finished. A petite woman in uniform emerged from the land of the trolls, and somebody gave her a hand off the top rung. Not how she'd expected her shift to go today. Another replaced the lid over the access hole and found the screws to hold it in place.

Keeping the local kids out or the demons below in? Either way, smart idea.

The officials gathered where the documenter typed in the last items. A few silver spoons and a handheld mirror—no stained glass worth over twenty grand.

Vita's stillness had been replaced by full-on agitation. She bounced on her toes as those around them departed. "No, no, no. They don't have everything. Did we miss it?"

"Jude and I have been here from the beginning."

"Then…"

Vi wouldn't have looked more upset if it was Becca left in the lurch. Audie's stomach knotted, and she stepped off the curb to cross the street. "Let's go have a chat."

They reached the park's gate before anyone in uniform remembered that the public should stay thirty feet away. A man who may not shave yet approached the fence with his hands out and as much command as his rookie self could muster.

"You need to step back, please."

Audie hoped her congeniality dial hadn't cracked from the chill. She dialed it up to eleven. "I'm so sorry. We're only wondering if the show is over? It's so cold out here, and we didn't want to wait around if you were done." She flashed him the most sincerity her frozen cheeks allowed. Behind her, a certain husband choked trying to cover a laugh.

"Yes, we've pulled out everything. It'll be cataloged and posted against the owners' names to make their claims in a couple of hours. We recognize people are eager to have their items returned." He scanned all three of them. "You had something taken?"

Vita spoke up. "We're not sure. I'm a partner at the shop where Mr. Boulton died." Her anxious, flustered, sad act could've won an Emmy. Jude always did say the skill was genetic, but this time, she had proper motivation. "We haven't been able to do a decent inventory since our access was limited."

Laying the groundwork for Fran's coming deception… a strategic move, if ethically questionable.

But drop a curly-haired kindergartner into the mix, and the ethics cleared a bit.

An older officer approached. He didn't need to summon his inner authority. "Is there something I can help you folks with?"

I.e., scram, people.

Vi was going for the Oscar now. "I was just asking when we'd be able to get back into our business. I run DFV Boutique down the hill. As crass as it sounds, we must reopen as soon as possible, so we don't miss the last of the holiday rush. Small businesses like ours count on this time of year. *If* they want to finish in the black, that is."

And the award goes to…

"Oh boy." The man grimaced.

Of the many reactions he might've had, that was the least expected.

Jude's tone tightened. "Oh boy, what?"

The policeman motioned to follow him away from the rest of the group. Audie glanced behind her—the gawkers had dwindled now that there was nothing left to be unearthed.

"You are…?"

"Vita Klein. The V in DFV."

He rubbed at his neck as he recognized the name. That couldn't be good. "You haven't gotten a call from Detective Flores yet?"

Vi whipped out her phone and scrolled. She'd been checking nonstop for three days, but an unheard miracle could've occurred in the past hour. "No, nothing."

"Shoot. Well, I'm sorry, but you're not opening soon. The shop is still a crime scene."

"But," Jude asked, "if you found the stolen goods, and they're blocks away from where Mr. Boulton killed himself, shouldn't that wrap up the case?"

The grimace turned into a full cringe, and the officer looked past them to the few remaining stragglers. In the late afternoon light, his eyes told a hundred stories. He'd seen too many things in his years on the force, and giving bad news was a perk left out of the recruiting brochure. "I wish they would've called you. The report came from the Medical Examiner. It's based on a lot of circumstantial evidence, but that's all the doc had to go on."

"Sir?"

"First, the empty whiskey bottle? There was more liquor on him than in him. Mr. Boulton wasn't drunk. He shouldn't have even been tipsy."

"But if he hadn't had a drink in years, his tolerance would've been low?"

The man's shrug was skeptical. "Then there's the cut itself. I don't know if you realize, but suicides by slashing are incredibly rare."

"Strangely, we know."

"The way the cut progressed across his neck, a left-handed person—yes, we verified with his ex-wife—couldn't have done it. The left-to-right motion, the angle, no hesitation marks. No suicide note, no other signs of distress. By itself, none of that's conclusive. But all together?"

Her internal knot frayed under pressure. *Don't say it's worse than we thought. Don't say it while standing next to a velvet bow four days before Christmas...*

He said it. "Kurt Boulton didn't kill himself. He was murdered."

Chapter 24

Audie perched on a stool in what was once a small conservatory at the rear of Simon and Vita's home. Picking up a tool she didn't recognize, she turned it over as she rotated her seat in sixty-degree arcs.

"You're making me dizzy." The bright lamp shone down on the wooden shop bench, Vi hard at work on a Tuesday, leaning over a magnifying glass as one hand gripped gold-colored wires with a pair of tweezers and the other reached for the soldering iron.

Audie stopped spinning, bringing her feet up onto the rungs below her. "Sorry."

"Let me get through this tricky spot here, and you can twirl to your heart's content." Always the big sister.

Staying as still as stone, she watched the delicate operation undertaken by skillful and fine-tuned fingers.

Vi looked so much like Dad, fabricating who knows what down in his basement shop, though it wasn't half as cozy as hers. Organized, sure. The man had spent a long career as an engineer, and you did not disturb his things without permission under pain of death.

But ask and ye shall receive.

Any project his daughters had brought to him, he'd greenlit. Stepping in only where he might suggest ways out of an especially knotty problem or keep them from losing a limb, he'd laugh to their mother that he was winning—their girls had more interest in his pursuits than hers.

Irina had been less than enthusiastic. "Sure, have fun. But don't get oil on your clothes. You are not taking apart that bicycle to count its ball bearings. You will learn how to cook and sew and take care of a household. If you have time for that stuff of your father's, fine. But that's not girls' work."

Whatever.

The year Audie, Vita, and Dad had disassembled the lawn mower had been the beginning of a future librarian's interest in mechanics and an inspiration for teenage Vi as she shifted her focus from interior design to metalcraft. They spent hours learning the proper vocabulary and how the engine operated and which nut to tighten in which pattern. What a shock when a male friend used the phrase "righty tighty, lefty loosey" in college. People didn't innately know this stuff?

That guy should've hung out more in his dad's workshop, 'helping' him and looting his root beer.

Not that she'd do a thing like that.

But she'd done a thing like that.

Every dang time, as Dad would've said.

"I come bearing gifts." Jude's cheery proclamation broke the fragile silence, and Vita paused over her design with a prayer to summon patience. He reddened. "Sorry! Didn't realize you were in the middle of brain surgery." He tiptoed to set a tray on the corner table.

Vita raised her hands, touched the hot knife to the metal once more, then returned the implement to its holder. She also resumed breathing. "There. Good enough for now." She pushed the magnifier away and turned on her own stool. "You," she said to Audie, "can resume spinning. You, Jude, should open a catering business."

Atop the tray was a selection of sandwiches cut into fourths, a bowl of mixed fruit, and three soda bottles.

Root beer.

God love the boy.

"Catering might be fun someday. But West Genealogy LLC has bigger fish to fry until then."

The future overlaid the present as Audie watched her husband of a decade load up the lunch plates with servings for both sisters and himself. In her mind, the sandstone of the Western US towered over the camper—oddly, still the same one with the red-and-white vintage styling. *I don't think they last that long.* Her daydream didn't care. Nearby, the neon sign in a window flashed "Café West."

He'd love the double meaning.

They would get stowable rocking chairs and sit around the fire when their legs were too old to hike or walk cemeteries anymore. They'd take the winters off and drive the country, popping in on Becca in Seattle and Connor in St. Louis, or wherever the kids lived by then. Maybe Simon would be convinced to join them in trailer life. He'd be an easier sell than Vi. She'd go crazy if unable to answer the muse at the instant it called. The suspension on the Jeep wasn't handicraft approved.

Jude doled out the plates, then settled on the plush periwinkle love seat where customers chatted with Vita as she designed their custom baubles. The way his knees creaked anymore—and especially after the underground disaster on Saturday—he'd need a crane to escape its cushions.

"Delicious." Vita's shoulders relaxed as she fell into the sandwich and whatever finishing sauce he'd concocted this go-around. It would never be replicated, they knew that much. Get your tickets now, one night only.

At least it gave him a diversion from ghosts, both the real and dreamed varieties. Thank goodness the Kleins had invested in high-quality kitchenware.

Chimes rang overhead as someone pressed the doorbell out front. Jude tried and failed to rise. "Expecting anyone?"

"No," Vita said, eyeing his attempt. "It may be time to replace that couch."

Audie dropped from her perch and headed for the hallway. "Don't hurt yourself."

In the hall, she passed lines of family photos, many in black and white because her sister was as ethereal in her designs as Jude said Audie herself was in her actions.

The boy was a romantic to the core.

Offset from the middle of the display hung a frame smaller than most others. A sandy-blond man in his mid-twenties, gentle waves in his unruly hair, looked at something the camera hadn't caught. A grin lit the side of his face.

In the early days after the disaster, Vita had waited before broaching the subject. Then she'd asked on a quarterly schedule: would Audie like the photo taken down or prefer to keep it herself? They both remembered what Oliver had been watching—Connor and Becca on the floor on Christmas morning, playing with toys newly delivered from the North Pole and begging their uncle to help with Lego assembly.

No, that snapshot belonged in this house with the rest. Ollie was gone, but the moment caught in each of those photos was gone.

Past. A memory. She continued to the door and its elegant frosted glass. A single figure hovered beyond. Before she touched the knob, the bell rang again.

"I'm sorry!" Fran Gill recoiled like the button had bitten her. "I didn't mean to be impatient." Her knit hat was pulled down, wisps of blue sticking out by her ears, and she twisted at her mittens.

"Come on in, Fran. Get out of this cold."

She wiped boots that may have seen Lincoln give the Gettysburg Address and stepped onto the hardwood floors. Gaping at the foyer like every visitor did, she said, "I'm amazed whenever I walk into this place. It'd be like living in a fairy house." She pried her eyes away from the lantern-shaped light fixture hanging over their heads and asked, "Is Vita here?"

"She's helping Santa's elves. I'll bring you back. Jude made lunch, if you're hungry."

"I can't stay." Agitation filled her voice as she slipped off the hat and the ombre hair leapt to attention with static. She brushed it down. "But I really need to talk to her."

Together, they traveled to the North Pole's satellite workshop.

"Fran!" Vita swallowed a bite and wiped secret sauce off her chin with a napkin. "Did the police call?"

The whole room paused, but Audie knew. Hope sank beneath the tidal wave.

"The list of what they found was published on the department's website." She bit at her lip. "My panel isn't on it."

Jude finally made it to his feet and gestured for Fran to take his spot. She collapsed into the cushions. They wanted to swallow her whole, and it didn't seem like she'd care.

"Sweetheart." Vita climbed off her seat and joined her.

"How can it not be there? Kurt had to have taken it, right? I don't understand." Her eyes welled up, and she wiped at them with aggravation. "I'm sorry. It's my stupid fault. I just had to let you know I've made a decision."

Uh-oh.

"I'm going to the cops and telling them what I did, so they'll look harder for the Tiffany."

"But Lizzie—"

"Lizzie shouldn't be living with a thief." Now the flood walls burst, tears landing on the bib of her overalls, worn today over a grass green t-shirt covered in a certain red-nosed reindeer. She leaned forward, elbows on her knees, face buried in her hands, hiding from the universe.

Vita dragged the young mother into a hug. "You're not a thief. You took something that was supposed to be yours."

Fran sobbed. "I took it to be spiteful."

"You loved the artistry, the craftsmanship."

"I did," she sniffled.

"His aunt said it was yours."

"She did," she nodded, one-eighth ounce of dignity restored.

"Darling, I know the law is the law, but nobody else would label you a flat-out thief."

Jude disappeared for a minute and returned with a glass of water. Fran accepted it with shaky fingers. "But what am I going to do? If that panel isn't found, I'm in the same trouble. If I turn myself in now, it might go better."

Vita cringed. "I'm not sure what to tell you. You heard the latest about Kurt?"

"That he'd been killed?" She shuddered. "And I walked in right after, apparently."

"Thank the stars you weren't earlier. But if he was murdered, it changes the story, doesn't it?"

"Oh! Someone had to be in the shop with him."

Jude sat on Vita's abandoned stool. "Maybe that someone took the panel, and it never was Kurt?"

"No, it was taken the night before."

"Oops. Memory lapse." Jude frowned with the irritation of a man with too many plots to keep straight and too little sleep. Being haunted by murdered brides had that effect.

"Do you think he could've sold it already?" Vita looked sick.

"That would've been awfully fast." But it wasn't out of the realm of possibility. "Had anything weird happened in the couple of days before all this? Kurt was found late Thursday night. Who manned the shop that day?"

"I did until three," Vita said, "then I left to go grocery shopping and get back here for supper." She almost laughed, nodding to Jude. "Not that I cooked."

He winked at her, and she melted, as usual.

Good thing Simon and Vi were solid.

"Who relieved you?"

"Darla, and she was there until closing."

"Right, her grandson's pageant. Fran, you stopped in before the store opened on Thursday. That's when you were going to pick up the Tiffany panel to return it to Trent?"

She snagged a tissue from the box on the end table. "My shift at the vet's started at nine. I planned to swing by and grab the piece. I wanted to drop it off at Trent's before work, because I worried about it sitting in my car." *Ironic.*

"So I headed straight to my squares file, flipped to the blue-greens, and had a panic attack. I must've sorted through that thing a thousand times. But I had to leave, or I'd be late to the clinic. I couldn't tell you what animals we saw that day, I was such a wreck."

"And when you came back that night?"

Her red-splotched face winced. "I didn't expect to run into anyone. I was going to tear the place apart, thinking I must've hidden it somewhere else and forgotten. It's the holidays, Lizzie just got over a virus, school is always wanting volunteers for the kids' parties, I'm finishing commissions…"

"Then there's a gaggle of us blocking the way."

She shrugged. "Couldn't do much at that point, so I acted like nothing was wrong. But never in a million years did I imagine I'd find…" She shook her head and pulled at one of the silver studs on her earlobe.

Moving on. "How about Wednesday? Were you at the boutique?"

"Darla worked the morning, and I came in later. We had a decent business—somebody bought two pairs of Vita's earrings. Darla sold a bunch of scarves to a woman panicking over her shopping list. She'd admired one of my suncatchers, and her daughter picked it up for her when she wasn't looking."

"Did any of those folks hang around your workbench?"

"Not really. I was at the register to ring everyone out, but it's got a straight view from Vita's station to my area. I don't think I could've been distracted enough to miss someone messing with my supplies."

"What about any business-type visitors? Did you see Kurt that day?"

"We rarely did, unless we were there way past closing." The group fell into silence as Fran's eyes scrunched up, studying the tools hanging from pegboard above Vita's bench. "No, the rest of that day was calm. Not like the dust-up on Tuesday."

"Oh?"

She waved it away. "It wasn't anything. I worked at the vet's in the morning and came to the boutique about two. Vita left—that might've been when you guys were coming into town?—and I went into the kitchen to heat my lunch. The bells rang, and it was Derek. He was dropping off that flyer about the Christmas potluck for the Main Street shop owners."

Vi moaned. "I forgot about that. Guess I need to make something."

Jude side-eyed her.

"I wasn't going to ask you. It's not even your party."

"Woman, please."

One corner of Fran's mouth lifted at the exchange. Better than nothing. "Anyway, we were talking and in comes Glen."

"The Ghost of Charles Dickens?"

Fran's smirk said what she thought about that. "He was being his usual self. Derek handing out store-bought invitations was an embarrassment. He wanted them hand-inked with real gold and sealed with wax, then dropped in our boxes by a Victorian mail carrier."

"That fellow needs a hobby."

"He has one. He's competing for the crown at the Most Annoying Man Pageant."

Jude wrinkled his nose. "I'd hate to see the evening gown competition."

That was an image they could've done without.

"The microwave dinged, and I went to grab my lunch. I didn't care if either of those two saw me eating. When I came back, Glen was already out the door, probably off to his next unwanted engagement, and Derek was at your station, Vi, checking out the bracelets."

"He should've bought one."

"If I'd known we would be closed for so long, I'd have given a better sales pitch." She looked truly sorry.

Vita smiled. "I don't think it would've taken much with that boy."

She blushed, the first sign of happiness they'd seen. "He's so different than he was in school. That girl in college must've steamrolled his heart to rewire him like that."

Audie kept turning something over in her head, and Jude caught it. "What are you thinking?"

Six eyes turned to her. *Thanks for the subtlety, dear.* "Derek was alone for a bit in the shop? There weren't any other customers milling around?"

"No, the place was empty or Glen's tantrum would've been embarrassing."

Vi folded her arms. "He'd have shut his trap if the public came in. He has too much of a show to put on to look bad in front of the guests."

"But Derek couldn't have taken the glass, if it's what you're thinking." She was quick on the objection. "First, I was in the kitchen less than a minute, and Glen was with him for most of the time." *If they were in cahoots, though...* "More than that, the panel was still there that day when I closed at 7:30."

Ah. That's a hiccup. "All right. I just can't figure out why the art wasn't with the rest of the loot. And they didn't find it at his apartment or in his car, so it doesn't leave us much of anywhere, does it?"

The silence this time was weighty. Soul-crushingly weighty.

"Fran." Vita picked up her hand. "Don't go confessing yet. Trent has no idea you don't have it, right? So we've got until Thursday to meet his deadline?" Audie caught the 'we.' "I'm sure we'll come up with something before then."

The girl didn't believe a word coming out of Vita's mouth, but she humored her anyway. That was best. Vi wasn't one to take no for an answer. "I guess it doesn't hurt anything but the ulcer I'm getting." She glanced at the clock on the wall. "I've got to get Lizzie from school soon, and I need to come up with something for dinner."

"No, you don't." Jude made off with the tray of extra sandwiches and returned with a paper plate wrapped high in aluminum foil. "Dinner's on me."

He'd make more for the household if necessary. If one went hungry with him around, it was their own darn fault.

"Thank you so much." She took the food, and fresh tears threatened. "I don't know what I'd do without friends like you." She hugged Vita, then escaped the clutches of the cushions with relative ease. *Youth.* The hugs continued to Jude and, at last, Audie.

"Just take care of your girl, okay? As one of our school nuns used to say, all will be well."

"If a nun said it, who am I to argue?" Fran pulled the knit over her blue hair and studded ear. "I'll call you if I have any brainstorms." She'd never hoped so much for a rainy forecast. Vita walked her down the hallway toward the front of the house.

"That was sweet," Audie said, stepping across to her handsome hubby and getting in on the hugging action. "You don't believe in letting damsels be in distress, do you?"

He rubbed her back. "It's against my religion."

She turned her head upward and kissed him. "This is a disaster, isn't it?"

"Quantifiably so, yes."

Jude settled onto the arm of the couch, and she retook her seat. "Here we thought we'd done our job when you uncovered the buried treasure. Now it's like we hit reset. We may need to root out Kurt's killer to find the most important bit."

"It throws everything on its side."

Spirits. Murders. Jealousy. Shards of glass and blood and hangings and thefts. Antiques and desperate women and destitute children, if not dead ones.

A Christmas Carol this wasn't. To have Scrooge wake up on December twenty-fifth, full of joy and love and goodwill to men? It took the miracles of the night before, the labor of all three ghosts.

They had phantoms aplenty, including the ghoul haunting her husband. With that much spectral activity, surely it could end well for their downtrodden, blue-haired shop clerk. Isn't that how Dickens would've written it?

Then why was the ghost of the author himself the one leaving her with the most chills?

Chapter 25

It was a sad fact that the warmth dripping from every sappy holiday commercial couldn't raise the actual temperature on the sidewalks of St. Charles. Well, what did she want for late December? At least Audie had her own coat again. Becca's was nice, but the girl was also four inches taller. It was like playing dress-up as a child in Mom's clothes.

How can Bec not need a winter coat in Seattle?

It probably wasn't a matter of need. She's twenty-three. A legitimate adult salary steadily replaced the remnants of impoverished college days.

Except ramen. Add some fish and voilà—a legit grown-up dish. Cooking what you knew, using fresh catches from Puget Sound... how much better could life get?

Becca and her father were both due big hugs when they flew in together tomorrow night. And it would do a world of good for Vita after this awful week.

As Audie walked, snuggled beside her husband on the downward slope, the bitter air stabbed at her bones. Jude would say she needed more insulation, but this polar vortex nonsense had no business being this far south.

She shuddered at the thought of January. Jude's aching joints already had him proposing they camp on the Gulf Coast for part of the winter. Fortunately, when you live with your house on your back, you go wherever your turtle feet can take you.

"Miss I-need-some-air-to-think, you should be swamped with new ideas by now." His knuckles were showing through the pockets of the leather coat. He'd broken down and accepted the fleece-lined trapper hat, ear flaps included, that Vita had thrust at him as they'd left the house.

"Yeah, this was a bad idea. My brain cells have turned to creamsicles."

For a Tuesday afternoon, the historic district was hopping. Universities were out on break now, some of the high schools, too. People able to take two weeks from the office were already on day four, and the silly shoppers who'd thought starting after Sunday would give them fewer crowds to deal with? Surprise!

At the corner of Main and Jefferson, they waited as a slow-moving and eternal line of cars passed.

"Eight," Jude said.

"Tiny reindeer?"

"Vehicles wearing antlers, so yes, kinda." A pickup truck sporting a big red nose on its grill rolled by. "They even have Rudolph as their trusty guide."

"Wonder how he did in the Reindeer Game qualifiers this season."

He snagged her hand as a break in the procession approached. Dragging her into the breach, they reached the other side just as an impatient Toyota raced past them.

"Do they know they're driving a first-generation Prius?" he shouted toward the receding car. A rope of silver garland flapped from inside the trunk.

Audie split from her husband to avoid crashing into a mother carrying twenty-seven bags and the small hands of forty-three children. Or maybe they were a family of octopi, and that's why it looked like a thousand arms were in the mix.

"This place is dangerous today," Jude said as they merged back together.

Ahead on the left, a certain brown campaign hat floated near the sign for the First Capitol Site.

"Ranger Thackeray!"

The hat turned their way as they broke through the horde. The Missouri State Park rep clapped his gloved hands. "My favorite local historians."

"You're only saying that because I'm Vita's sister."

"I never show favoritism when history's on the line. Vita's wonderful, but I get the feeling one of you is a bit more hardcore where the past is concerned."

Jude burst out laughing, then tried half-heartedly to swallow it. "Sorry. But hardcore is too perfect."

She rolled her eyes. "Yes, census records fear me."

Her partner-in-crime agreed with too much exuberance. "That is not untrue." He was right, of course.

"What are you doing standing here in this? The lovely Edith lock you out until you fix that door?"

"I'm failing to drum up business. Edith had some shopping to finish, so a volunteer is manning the fort. I've got him stacking books and trying not to look bored. Tons of people around, but we won't rope many tourists inside until Boxing Day. Everybody's too busy playing elf."

"We just met a driver who could use a lesson on the meaning of the season."

Quinn cringed. "The one with garland fishing for street trout? I've seen that car go by three times. I think he's trying to will a parking space into existence. There's plenty down along Riverside. If he thinks he's nabbing a curb up here, he'd better pray for a Christmas miracle."

"Hope springs eternal."

He shook his head as the tenth reindeer rolled past, then brightened. "Hey, I was going to call Vi on my lunch break. You finding Kurt's cache yesterday is the talk of the town."

"It was a happy accident, but we're glad it helped."

"You need to go see it."

"We'd love to."

Jude nodded while also asking, "See what?"

"The banjo clock." The ranger pointed to the upper floor. "A detective delivered it to us this morning, and I've got it hanging in its rightful spot."

"Any thoughts on beefed-up security?"

"The state was none too pleased about our break-in, so they parted with a few bucks for more surveillance cameras. We have better coverage of the stairs now, and as that's the only access unless you're coming down the chimney, I guess it's an improvement."

Jude clutched his chest. "No chimney view?"

"Hey, if Santa decides he needs to come in and sit a spell Thursday night, mi casa es su casa. But don't pillage our stuff and don't expect cookies."

Another gust tried to remove the ranger's hat. Audie turned to her better half. "I need to either go see a clock or mug somebody for their hot chocolate."

"As I'm a state-certified law enforcement officer, I suggest you start with the clock." Quinn checked his belt for his keys. "With it being a slow news day, I'll let you head up by yourselves."

"What if we're in league with the burglar?"

"Or Santa?"

"If you are, you're doing a terrible job, showing the police your buried treasure. Not very skilled at this, are you?"

"We're practicing catch-and-release robbery."

Quinn laughed, handing over a single key. "Through the passage, up the stairs. Lock up behind you on your way out. If I find anything amiss, I'll track down Vita. Seems like she'd be one to dole out wrath if need be."

True.

Poor Simon.

"Got it. See you shortly."

They hurried through the carriageway, then up the creaking steps. Audie unlocked the door and relished the relative warmth inside.

"Let's stay here and melt a second, okay?"

Jude stamped his feet, and a shiver ran the length of his body. "If you insist." They stood once more at the rear of the lower legislative chamber. "Sure hard to picture this loaded with men in the heat of summer, isn't it?"

"I bet it smells better now."

Tingling inched up her toes. She wriggled them within her boots—yep, all piggies accounted for.

"The clock is in the Senate room?" Jude headed to the left around the benches, but she caught his arm.

"Governor's office. This way."

"Perfect, you passed the test. I was worried your little gray cells froze out there."

"Not sure how they could, with ten thousand unanswered questions poking at them right now."

He paused, studying the rows of seating. "I guess it would've been awkward to hang that clock in here, within sight of the murdered woman's husband. I can't imagine debating laws while looking at art created by the man who killed my wife."

"Speaking as your wife, please stop trying to imagine. And Clarence accounts for several of the unanswered questions."

"How's that?" He gestured for her to lead the way down the hall to the big guy's office.

"Two hundred years has made their situation fairly…"

"Wraithish?"

"I was going to say vague. The young bride with a husband twice her age, her quiet meanderings in the garden. I can't help picturing her as sad. But I'm also viewing it through a modern lens."

"I get it. There's evidence he was doing some things right: representing his home county, helping after that warehouse fire, granting a crumb of mercy on Nathaniel's family after the, uh, incident."

Audie bit her tongue. A weird vibe about a man so far removed from her in time meant nothing. But did good deeds demonstrate anything either? It was horrifying, the number of people they'd run across who claimed to be the very face of morality, yet were devils behind closed doors. Josephine told Mabel's distant relation that she needed a change of perspective to see a thing fully. The bygone decades had created too much haze for a clear view now.

Jude was talking. "I wonder what happened to that stained-glass pane Nathaniel gave Clarence the day of the murder."

"The anniversary present? I'd forgotten about that."

He stopped again. "Your brain did freeze."

"You call me Eagle Eye, not Elephant Eye. I do forget stuff on occasion."

"Twice a marriage. I'll note this in the logbook later."

The governor's domain appeared as it had a few days earlier and nothing like the posh one in today's Jefferson City.

The first Missouri government had been *built* above a hardware store and a carpenter shop—how fitting.

"Would you look at that?"

Audie followed Jude's gaze. On the wall opposite the entrance, behind and to the left of Governor Alexander McNair's desk, hung the restored treasure. In the afternoon light filtered by the western windows beside it, the face of the banjo clock glowed. The polished red-hued wood could've been assembled yesterday.

No wonder Quinn Thackeray was proud to show it off.

The crowning glory, by far, was the stained glass. Inserted into the rectangular box at the base of the inverted banjo shape, every color in the scene glistened. She neared the clock, happy to have no mass of onlookers nor law enforcement personnel between her and it this time. She'd never been on a boat on this river, but looking at the warm colors, she wondered if the view would be much different this October.

Jude joined her, leaning in to inspect the scene. "I'll give it to Nathaniel Silvain. He was talented."

"Was being the operative word."

"You know, I've been thinking about this, and not because I'm ghost-obsessed." He stepped to the large desk and settled onto its edge, legs stretched out. "There's one thing I can't figure out. How did Nathaniel kill Josephine with a shard of his glass? Why did he have it on him? He wasn't in his own shop. None of his work was in the house yet since he'd just delivered the first to Clarence at the Capitol that day. It's such a weird choice in weapon. Did he carry it with him like a rabbit's foot? After Stuart's melodrama, that seems unwise." He mocked diving into his coat. "'Oh no, I'm going to sneeze and need my handkerchief.'" His hand returned, index finger hidden. "'Drat! I forgot about my lucky shard!'"

She laughed despite herself. "I've been wondering the same thing. They found Josephine near the kitchen—wouldn't knives have been handier? Or, if he was in a rage, a lamp or letter opener? Why not simply hit her? Why go straight to slitting her throat?" She ran her fingertips over the lead between colors.

Jude shrugged. "Artistic temperament?" He stood from the desk and wandered to the bookcase on the far wall, weary of the guessing game. She didn't blame him.

From the streets below, "Bring a Torch, Jeanette Isabella" arose, and Audie peeked down from their crow's nest. Carolers, a trio of two women and one brave man, lilted the song in its original language. Harmonies made the tune as full as the ladies' hoop skirts, but they could've been singing the lyrics to "Here Comes Peter Cottontail" for all the French she knew.

The top of Quinn's hat still lingered near the museum entrance. If he was looking to bring in visitors, it wasn't going well.

She returned to the clock and considered the composed landscape. The colors at the edges of the rectangle were darker, more intense than the ones at the center. How did he get that effect? Different shades of glass? Something backing it to darken the hues? Fran would've known.

Maybe I need Josephine's change in perspective.

A knob on the side must open the rectangular box, so whatever a person wanted to tuck away in 1821 could be tucked behind hidden hinges. Before she opened it, she pulled out her recovered flashlight—wouldn't Jeanette Isabella be proud?—and took one more look at the front of the glass art.

The mini Mag clattered onto the planked floor.

"Audie?"

"Holy moley." She scooped up the light and aimed it at the center of the glass. Then she inched to the right and back to the left.

Boots echoed off the high ceiling. "What is it?"

Side to side, she ran the beam. On the outside edges, the autumn leaves and blue water of the Missouri glistened vividly. But in the middle?

Jude's breath caught. "Wow."

A different scene emerged. Gone were *les petites côtes*, those hills filled with smoking chimneys and clapboard homes. In their place were the pale pinks and whites of a cherry blossom ring, enclosing a miniature bluebird. Beneath it, strange runes were written in tiny black loops.

"Hold that," she said, releasing the flashlight in Jude's direction with the hope that his reflexes had thawed. It didn't hit the floor, so attaboy. She turned the knob on the side of the box and swung the door outward. A thin wooden panel hid the glass. "Could you aim the beam in here, please?" The edges of the wood lit up. It looked like it sat on a rail. She touched her fingertips to the antique, and the panel began to slide. Removing it carefully, she handed it to Jude in exchange for the light.

Then gasped.

The sun from those western windows poured through, painting her hand as it passed through the glass. This entire piece of art was a different image, darker at the edges and brighter at the center. The autumn colors were so bold on the opposite side because back here, red-orange licks of fire formed a border that lightened toward the middle. On either side, two brown, flat-tailed mammals faced inward, both adorned with top hats. Who knew beavers were so fashion-conscious? At the midpoint, though, was what she'd seen from the front: a cherry blossom wreath and a bluebird. Vinework swooped in and out of the blossoms, tying the flames to the blooms.

"This is dark for our boy, Nathaniel."

"Considering he created it while awaiting execution?" Jude loomed at her shoulder, but she wasn't willing to give up her prime viewing spot yet.

What was that in the vines? She played with distance, those readers coming sooner rather than later. In the foliage, a dozen tiny symbols came into focus, made from the leaves of the flowers. All alike, they appeared to be an early version of the dollar sign. *Think, woman.* Her mental card catalog flipped. United States currency had used the symbol since 1785, so it wasn't an anachronism.

At the six o'clock position, a pair of the symbols merged to create the tip of a flaming tongue. The arrow-like apex aimed at the breast of the delicate bird. Between the blue feathers and the images that Audie could only compare to hell, two initials were plainly inscribed.

C.R.

She clenched the flashlight so as not to drop it again. "Oh my gosh."

Beavers and top hats, flames and money...

"Aud?"

The bluebird, the perfect trademark of Josephine's beloved spring—of Josephine herself—trapped by blazing greed, her husband's initials cutting toward her from the inferno itself.

"The warehouse fire," she exhaled.

"Yeah?"

"The one where Clarence saved the day."

"I got that, yes. What are you seeing?"

She traded places with him, taking the flashlight and shining it over the second plate of the dichroic concoction. When the icons coalesced, he stumbled backward as if burned himself.

"Right? The fire wasn't an accident."

"No," he shook his head, black bangs flying. "Not that. They're cherry blossoms. Cherry."

His natural tan had drained, replaced by Frosty's. "Oh my goodness. Your dream."

"Why would I dream of cherry blossoms, and here they are?"

There are more things in heaven and earth, Horatio, than are dreamt of in your philosophy. She never thought the Bard had meant an actual dream, but here they were.

"We need more information on that gift and on the fire."

"Newspaper archives?"

"They were scant out here in the Wild West, remember?" But they had to get a first-hand account, details from a source who lived through the drama. "We need Mabel Ehrand."

Chapter 26

"Dichroic glass." In the passenger seat beside him, Audie wagged her head as they took the last turn toward Mabel's. "Five days ago, I'd never heard of it. Now it may be the key to solving a murder."

"One everyone considered solved. To be speaking from the grave like that, with a master-level technique, all because nobody would believe the story of a powerless man?" *Dang.* "I wish we didn't have to count on our friend with the head injury for fact-checking, though."

"Not her, merely her letters. It's too bad she doesn't claim to be a bit older. We might've gotten an eyewitness to the murder itself."

Was that too bad? In front of the white-shuttered brick beauty, he eased the Jeep to the curb. A horn blared, Doppler-style, as he opened his door without scanning for moving vehicles.

"Yeah, that one's on me," he said to his wife's startled look. He rounded the bumper and joined her on the walk.

"Please stop that," she muttered at him as they hurried up to the porch stairs. "I have no interest in collecting husbands like Mabel."

Jude took the steps by twos and pressed the doorbell. "Your gloves!"

"Stowed in the car."

"Smart." Although Mrs. Ehrand probably had x-ray vision on top of the rest of it.

A long minute passed. Audie peeked through the narrow sidelight. "Think she's out?"

"Of her mind, yes?"

Then the doorknob turned, and Jude's heart contracted. *Does x-ray vision come with ultra-hearing? Is it a two-fer package?* The homeowner opened the door a crack, peeking with a single eye while one of the many Alistairs analyzed them from her feet.

Audie fell on her sword. "Mabel, we're so sorry to show up like this unannounced."

The supercentenarian's stern appraisal stopped any further begging. He nudged his wife's elbow. "Present for inspection," he hissed into her hair.

She pulled her hands from her pockets: thin, pale, and freezing, but most importantly, bare.

After an uncomfortably thorough once-over of Jude, the woman's entire demeanor softened, and she opened the door wide like the queen of hospitality. "No problem, dears. I'm glad to see you back so soon."

He followed Audie into the hall, dodging a feline tail. "We can't stay." Nor eat, nor get trapped in the vortex swirling around this house and its inhabitants. "But those letters you showed us? May we give them another quick peek? Did you put them away already?"

"I was just going to do that. Come into the den. I'm so glad they're of help." She led them down the hallway, past the parlor and into an impeccably kept office. A carved mahogany desk sat on a round Moroccan rug, the mocha-colored wood grain setting off the greens and ivories of the floor covering.

There was nary a navy nor robin's egg in sight, let alone a decent cerulean.

From the desktop, she picked up the familiar manila envelope and handed it to Audie.

"You two look flushed. Is that from the cold or something exciting happening in the old town tonight?" The twinkle relit her eyes.

"We—" *We what?* "We discovered an unusual bit of history down at the Capitol and would love some first-hand corroboration."

"Sounds juicy."

"It could be, though it's really old." Audie cringed. It was only twenty-seven years senior to Mabel herself, apparently. "I mean, it wouldn't affect anyone nowadays. It might answer another mystery."

The woman and her cane hobbled to the leather chair behind the desk, settling into it. "Nothing is ever simple when it comes to old mysteries."

Preach, sister.

Audie slid the copied letters onto the surface and began sorting. He hovered over her shoulder until she frowned up at him.

"Yes, dear."

Before he stepped too far away, she handed him the second of the piles.

"You start with those. I remember skimming a description of the anniversary gift Nathaniel had made for the two Richards."

"Lovebirds that they were," he mumbled. "When was that?"

"It should've been right before the murder, late July. He'd shown it to William and Annette when it was nearing completion. I need to see what he said about it."

He took the letters and thumbed through them. Mabel was certainly an organized head case. As he found the correct dates, his speed-reading wife, already on her third missal, straightened up with a paper in hand.

"Here. This is where William talks about the fire for the first time." She summarized as her finger followed the old cursive. "It happened two days before, at the end of June. All the season's pelts burned. They blame it on lightning, because a summer storm had just popped up. With the local economy relying on the fur trade, men had rushed to save the structure. For a short while, there was worry that Pierre Chevenard might've died in the disaster."

"Who the heck is Pierre What's-his-name?"

More skimming. "The man who ran the warehouse. A bachelor, he owned and lived in the building. He acted as security guard too."

"That didn't go well."

"He'd gone to the tavern past his usual time to get his supper. A trapper had been traveling through, and their dealings had run long. Pierre rushed back when word came that his business and bedroom were burning to the ground."

"Bad night for Monsieur Chevenard."

"Bad night for everybody." She moved on to the next letter. "William is beside himself. He writes a couple of days later, far sooner than usual, pleading for guidance from his brother. The weight of the loss has hit, and he's beginning to panic. His livelihood is dead in the water for a month or more until the pelts can be replaced. He's fearful of not being able to feed his family."

Mabel steepled her fingers. "The frontier had folks living on the margin."

If anyone would know, it would be Mabel.

"Wow, another letter that same week."

"I'll bet he's asking for money." *Typical.* Not that his own family would've lent him a penny if he'd been dying, but his kin weren't typical. Thank heavens for small mercies.

Audie brought this one closer to the lamp to read, and her finger slowed its pace along the calligraphy. "It's good news. A legislator, Clarence Richards, has summoned up a miracle. Apparently, several had been trying to get their constituents' furs to St. Charles, but he won the race. Three wagonloads, mostly beaver but some otter and mink, arrived that afternoon. As word spread, the community that had fought to save the warehouse raced to see if the rumor was true. Then they carried our boy Clarence and his wagon teams straight to the tavern."

"I'll bet he never paid for another meal his entire term in the Legislature. What a guy."

But Audie was looking at him—or rather, at the rear lobe of his brain, because that stare penetrated well beyond the surface. "Jude, six days. How far is it from here to Chariton County?"

He pulled out his phone and tapped. "With the modern road system, 160 miles. I don't have a way to see what the path was like in 1821."

"But wagons only moved ten to twenty miles per day. That's eight minimum from Richards' home base to here. And it doesn't account for gathering up the merchandise before they could head east." Her focus came forward to his eyes. "How did he get them here so quickly?"

The sickening truth was universally understood, but the words emerged from Mabel's assured voice. "He knew they'd be needed." Her face lit up like Sirius. "He set the fire."

"Holy cow." Jude folded his arms and leaned against a bookshelf overloaded with volumes on the Civil War, the Victorian Age, the Roaring Twenties. Mabel must enjoy reliving her youth.

"Convenient, isn't it, that the warehouse keeper was away later than normal right as a storm was about to hit?"

"So the two had a deal?"

"Clarence needed to be a hero. Who cared about a farmer from central Missouri? But if he rescued the birthplace of an infant government?"

"Fast track for a future election." Jude turned to his wife. "So, the clock. Nathaniel knew?"

Behind the desk, their host straightened. "What clock?"

Audie explained what they'd found on the back of the decorative glass.

"How clever!" Mabel wouldn't have looked giddier if one of the Alistairs had had kittens.

"Jude, did you find that description?"

"Whoops, sorry. Got caught in the moment." He picked up the letter dated July 26, 1821. "Here's where he describes the artwork Nathaniel created for Clarence."

"Details, please." Audie put her hands to the desk. Even from the side, he could see her forehead ridged in concentration.

"A spring scene, he says. Blossoming cherry trees, surrounded by honeysuckle vines. He was considering adding a bluebird, because that was Mrs. Richards' favorite." He looked up. "We know he finished and delivered it to Clarence at noon the day of the murder. Both Nathaniel and Clarence stated that in court."

"And Clarence claimed to have been away from the boardinghouse until late, when he found Nathaniel and his dearly departed wife."

"That means the glass Clarence said was the murder weapon—"

"Exactly." Audie rubbed the bridge of her nose. "It couldn't have been there. If Clarence was telling the truth about where he was, there's no way for Nathaniel to have used it as a scalpel before the rep arrived home."

"Yet no one listened to Nathaniel."

A mini light bulb must've exploded in Audie's cerebellum, because she was digging through the letters like a dog after a bone. "I should be fired. I should've read these more closely the first time."

"We're self-employed, dear. You'd have to fire yourself."

"I'll start the paperwork." She drew out a note and reviewed the first few paragraphs. "Here it is. This was written a week after Josephine's death. 'I visited Nathaniel. I can hardly bear to see him locked up, so distraught and helpless. He paces his cell like a caged animal, desperate for word of his family, which I gave, of course. No one considers his protests of innocence, and he's losing hope. I begged him to tell me anything I might do in his aid. I feel he knows more, but won't say outright for fear of how things may go for his wife. He would only relay a short story.

"'Two days before Mrs. Richards' death, Patrice made a soup for the boardinghouse landlady who'd taken ill. She sent Nathaniel to deliver it. He entered through the front and walked toward the kitchen at the rear. There, he found Mrs. Richards standing beside the garden door, which was open but a crack. She jumped when he came in, but he quietly brought the soup to the cook and then joined her. Through the opening, he could see a pair of men, one being her husband and the other Chevenard, the owner of the destroyed warehouse. Mr. Richards handed Chevenard an envelope, and they shook hands.

"'Nathaniel said he would've been less surprised if it had been the other way around, politicians known for making side deals that would line their pockets. The men were parting ways, and Nathaniel hurried to close the door. Before he could, it flew from his hand. Another boarder was returning by the back entrance. He gave a hearty "good morning," and Clarence looked up to see them in the doorway.'"

Jude's gut twisted for the soon-to-be victims. "Clarence realized they witnessed the money exchange. It's no gigantic leap that it was for the fire."

"No wonder Mr. Silvain wanted to finish the clock," Audie said, livid that she hadn't paid better attention earlier, that no one had paid attention to Nathaniel at all. "He understood he'd be hung, because he'd never win against a man with power. He saw this as a way to leave his side of the story, that he hadn't killed her, even if it didn't matter in the long run."

"So he mimics what he made for Josephine, adding the beavers and Dante's Inferno around it to tie in the warehouse fire. He includes her bluebird at the center, sacrificed on an altar by her own husband to the gods of greed." Jude looked at Sherlock with renewed awe, though he'd refrain from calling her that. For now. "You justified Nathaniel Silvain's cries of innocence by noticing what others hadn't."

"There's no way I'm the first person in two hundred years to see it. But they never had the other parts of the picture."

Literally.

"What about our present-day thief?"

Both Wests turned to Mabel, who was glowing with more vigor than caroling could've ever offered.

"I mean, maybe that's why Mr. Boulton stole it? He realized it could be worth something."

"None of the other items"—*well, not quite none*—"were worth anything, though."

She nodded. "Exactly."

"Mabel, you've lost me."

"The others were supposed to deflect attention away from the clock."

For a minute, the only sound came from a well-concealed cat, color and breed unknown.

"Interesting idea." Audie squinted at the mental jigsaw puzzle. "But most of its value is in its history. It's a decoration in a reconstructed frontier office, not worth much more than a desk or bookcase. Plus, as the property of a government site, it would've been tricky to sell."

"Hmm. You're right. Then maybe he simply enjoyed having these things in his possession." She looked around her own antique-filled room. "I'd understand that. Made him feel cozy. Complete."

"I need to think," Audie said with a sigh. "Thank you so much for the help, Mabel."

Was it help or was it more muddied water? The first lines of a letter caught his eye as Jude returned the papers to the envelope. It was from two months post-hanging. "Well, crud."

She stepped nearer. "What did you find?"

"A sad epilogue. William says Patrice is packing to return to her parents with the children, and he himself spends hours by the river, trying to sort it all. Winter struggles are coming soon, and he can't help dwelling on his friend's fate. But he also can't prove the truth."

"And no one would've believed him if he tried," Mabel said. "A lowly fur trader, going up against a legislator? He'd be swinging alongside Nathaniel's corpse by the end of the week."

Ick.

"Mabel, we appreciate you letting us barge in like this."

"You're always welcome." Pending color palette, that is. "If you're staying past Christmas, bring over Vita. I'll make some snacks, and—"

"We'll do our best." Jude hooked into Audie's arm and gently tugged her toward the hallway.

For once, his good sense triumphed over his taste buds.

"Nathaniel Silvain was framed." The cab of the Jeep was taking forever to warm.

"By the real murderer who killed his own wife."

"And hung an innocent man, leaving a woman and two children helpless on a brutal frontier."

"Dear Lord."

Audie studied her cobalt blue gloves as she pulled them over her frozen fingers. "Nathaniel was brilliant. In one hidden artwork, he indicates the weapon, the murderer, and the motive."

"Not brilliant enough to save his neck." The steering wheel flexed as his grip tightened. "I guess the centerpiece in the clock couldn't have been the actual weapon from Josephine's gift, right? That would've been evidence or something?"

"Was CSI Frontier Missouri that fastidious? But no, I doubt it was the impromptu knife. I wonder what happened to it. Echoing the bluebird and the cherry blossom in the backing panel tells the same story, though."

"Who would've thought glass could testify to someone's innocence?"

"It'll be difficult to do anything to clear Nathaniel's name, but we can give it a shot."

The afternoon light continued to fade. Christmas decorations on timers began illuminating rooftops as the clock rolled 4:30. The car's heater must've been drowning out the hamster wheel in his wife's skull, as she'd fallen silent. "Nickel for your thoughts?"

"They're not worth that much." She toyed with the tassels of her scarf. "It boils down to people in power and those who have none. Clarence was an elected legislator in a brand-new state, with an attractive young bride on his arm. He thinks can get away with anything. And he does, or Patrice wouldn't have been widowed.

"What if that power difference is the cause of our present mess? We know Kurt Boulton was murdered, but we're still trying to hang those thefts on him." *Hang.* Unfortunate word choice. "Because of what, a few baubles left in his pockets? If the whiskey was forced on him, those probably were too. The tie-ins to the legend, the glass art, the shard as a weapon—it seems more and more like a melodramatic frame-up, doesn't it? And once again, we've got someone taking advantage of a vulnerable man and getting away with it."

"But what was the crime before Kurt's death? Just the thefts? With most of the stuff being worth so little, why would the killer stoop to murder to cover up?"

"I don't know. I can't help thinking, who have we met who's overly zealous and steeped in history?"

"How about the entire town? It's a giant mug of history tea." Jude tapped his fingers as he counted. "We have ghosts and carolers dressing like it's the 1800s. We have a park ranger who could recite every word of the Missouri Compromise. Shop owners can tell you the date when each brick was placed a couple of centuries ago. Vita, Fran, Darla—they're all into it and wouldn't want anyone pooh-poohing their fair city."

"I thought we'd cleared my sister, which is important since she's housing us. But how many on your list can quickly put a value on any item, are driven to collect it no matter its worth, and refuse to suffer fools in violation of his personal outlook?"

Jude pulled up to a stoplight, and turned to her, the red painting her ivory white face.

"Yeah," she said. "Glen Armquist. And we have no way to prove it."

Chapter 27

The next morning passed twice as fast and twice as slowly. An image of construction paper rings slipped through Jude's memory, the way they'd mark off the last days until Christmas in primary school. Every twenty-four hours lasted a week.

And here we are, trapped in another time continuum. We're supposed to be working *in the past, not living there* and *in the present* and *in some purgatorial central ground simultaneously.*

We're not supposed to be working at all.

Holiday vacation, anyone?

And me without my swim trunks.

A fresh wave of dark clouds made the afternoon appear much later than three o'clock, yet Christmas Eve seemed a month away. He wished it was true, for Fran's sake. Vita, upset but resigned, said her young partner had called and planned to turn herself in that night. Yesterday hadn't moved them any further in untangling her knotted web, and she clung to the hope it'd go better if she admitted to taking the Tiffany before Trent reported it. After a morning shift at the vet, she'd be helping Derek at the antique shop. Glen closed for the year as of noon, and his nephew had been assigned clean-up duties after the holiday rush. *Some rush.* Lizzie was with Trent's mom today, anyway. No use hanging around the apartment, picking up her toys and crying.

Glen. The concept of him being a thief and a murderer didn't jive. Despite his shoplifting mischief decades ago, Audie agreed it felt wrong. But she couldn't get past it. Maybe he'd always been unable to resist pretty shiny things. But slicing a man's throat to take it?

A tremor ran up his spine, and he rose from the Kleins' kitchen table where he'd been losing against himself on a crossword puzzle. More caffeine beckoned.

Vita was out delivering orders to customers since shop pickup had been nixed. What a ruined season for the three entrepreneurs. It's hard enough to be an artist; a murder and a string of thefts were an unnecessary monkey wrench.

Unless one of *them* was the murderer. Darla's reaction to Fran's stolen and re-stolen artwork had been... odd. Antsy, agitated. Obviously, she would've been upset by the news. Like Vi, she cared about Fran almost as a child—

Children—the preemie grandbabies. That couldn't be the answer, could it? Darla's daughter and son-in-law coming into mysterious money to pay the medical bills—did she sell the Tiffany and create her own miracle?

But he'd watched her consoling Frannie after finding Kurt's body. The love she showed for her husband, her friends and neighbors, even the household pet...

It wouldn't be the first time you were fooled, son.

The last two months stood in stark evidence of that.

But if he suspected Darla James, he may as well suspect the entire citizenry of St. Charles. Vita trusted her. He should too.

So the city population it is. To start, he could scratch the short ones off the list for playing the Phantom.

Assuming that was a real person and not something less substantial.

Lord, have mercy on a confused man.

He looked down and realized he still stood with the pot of coffee in one hand and an empty mug in the other. As he poured the bean juice, he heard Audie shift by the fire in the living room. When he'd peeked in earlier, she'd been studying the flames hard enough to burn her retinas. The answers resided somewhere within that hearth.

He'd better add more wood.

He set the cup down and pulled his coat off the wall peg. It was precipitating again, that snow-sleet combo the meteorologists loved to call a wintry mix. *Some sort of granola blend courtesy of Jack Frost.* Wonderful gift, providing a lingering aftertaste of black ice, car accidents, and traffic jams.

Frost should've hung onto his receipt.

Where was I? Right. Firewood.

He laced his boots and stepped onto the back porch. Simon and Connor had taken his fun away: most of the wood waited in stacked quarters on the steel log rack. How was he supposed to do any deep thinking? Hang on—a couple of unsplit chunks sat off to the side. He turned them over and saw why they'd been rejected. Bug trails everywhere. Wouldn't burn worth a darn, and Vita would murder him in a particularly creative way if he escorted termites into her house.

But it gave him something to swing at.

He opened the door to the shed and pulled out the axe propped beside the hibernating lawn mower. At the wood pile, he set a log onto a pair of concrete blocks and lined himself up. Bringing the chopper around behind him, he swung overhead like Lizzie Borden.

The satisfying whack comforted his soul, but his left shoulder howled. Unlike Miss Borden, there would not be thirty-nine more.

I've had enough of you lately. You know I won't stop. Why bother fussing?

Tugging the blade edge out of the wood, he reset the target. *Whack.* Lizzie Borden. Lizzie Gill—Fran's daughter caught in the cross fire. They had no time. Fran would be exposed for stealing what she was sure was hers, and she'd lose custody in a heartbeat. He couldn't imagine. They should smuggle both of them out of town, hidden in the camper's under-bed storage.

What's a few felonies amongst friends? *Whack.*

But isn't it a crime for this to have happened in the first place? The Tiffany was supposed to be Fran's, so Trent was just being a jerk. He had no interest in raising his daughter. He only wanted to get revenge on his wife.

It was all a horrible game.

Whack.

A game. A fractured thought splintered from his brain, and he paused, leaning on the handle's knob and staring at the halved wood chunk. He tried to lure the idea forward, let it settle into place, but it refused.

Without movement, the chill sunk its claws into his skin, and he pulled the knit cap out of his pocket. He'd last worn it after leaving Mabel's yesterday, when they'd unraveled a distressing scenario for a crime that occurred two centuries ago.

That had been a frame-up. A game.

Did it help the present-day drama? Tie it together somehow?

Weird what one thinks about while chopping wood.

Hey, dummy, what say you think about getting some more physical therapy on those beat-up joints of yours?

For the eighteenth round? Not going to fix anything more than it had in the past. The damage was done.

And not only to the shoulder.

Jeez. Dramatic much?

Not that his conscience was wrong. Here they were, sharing another holiday with Audie's family. He loved them. He appreciated them. He was so, so grateful for them.

Would there ever be a member of his own around that table? The one possibility was so remote as to be laughable. Maybe Kate's got a family by now. He smiled and went for a second log. That would be wild. Uncle Jude. Well, he was already Uncle Jude, but those kids were older when he joined the fun. To have flesh-and-blood nieces and nephews?

He would be such a bad influence.

He grinned and swung, missing entirely. No points for that one.

Points. Games again. What was this random fixation on games?

Was it Dickens' line about how people love to play games at Christmas? Vita was at grandmaster level on Scrabble, so nobody would take her on except him. Audie had given up ages ago. He never won, but it was fun and Vi bribed him with a killer eggnog—killer for his liver, at any rate—so who cared?

Family. Connections. The games played between siblings? No, not that either. At least the Marik sisters had inherited most of the positive traits in the clan, not the crazy ones.

Poor Derek. If Glen Armquist had gotten his hoarding gene from his father, his nephew better purge house now before it took root there too.

But that still wasn't it. What was the tie to games?

The murder. The thefts. Kurt's murder was made to mimic a suicide, to fool them, to frame him for the burgling.

Or he actually *was* the thief and somebody found out. There was a scuffle, and he was killed by accident. The other person panicked, grabbed the first thing they saw, and created an impromptu suicide.

But wow, staging with the alcohol? Or had Kurt tumbled from the long-sober wagon at that exact moment, even if he wasn't sloshed at the time of death? That seemed… coincidental. A little too much, if you'd ask Sherlock in there by the fire.

Wait, she denies being Sherlock. Eagle Eye, then.

Let's say it wasn't a crime of passion or panic. Framing somebody to get away with something else—that might be considered a game?

Then what was the goal of it? And who was the somebody?

Whack.

Persons unknown stole almost-worthless items from every store possible over a couple of months. They happily squirreled it aside for funsies until they came across the Tiffany stained glass. With their sticky fingers on that high score, the game ended. They could sell the art and collect their winnings.

Jude studied the axe where it stuck from the log.

Why would someone make up a game like this?

Boredom.

Who would be that bored?

Option A: an older person who retired from their career without a plan to open an ice cream store. Thankfully, that left St. Nick and Idelle out of the running, because their pistachio had been amazing. How about Darla's husband, Lionel? No, his TV marathons kept him as busy as he wanted to be.

Okay, Option B: a drone who's over-smart and under-occupied, under-utilized, under-challenged. Someone doing jobs beneath their education and drive.

He yanked the head free.

A person who needed the challenge of stealing to stay stimulated, the adrenaline of cat-and-mouse. Somebody masquerading as someone they weren't, hiding their spots, because the leopard hadn't changed and wasn't about to.

Spots. Circles.

Petals. Flowers.

White. Not pink.

White.

Never pink.

White!

Oh my Lord.

He dropped the handle and bolted for the house. Flinging open the door, he found Audie at the sink with her water glass. It splashed as she jumped. "It wasn't cherries!"

"What?" She set the glass on the counter and pulled a towel from the oven handle.

"At the shop, the antique shop." He knew he was going too fast. He tried to take a breath and slow it down, but hiccuped instead. "At Glen Armquist's shop, I saw something half-hidden that I thought had cherry blossoms on it. But I had cherry blossoms on my mind after that dream with Josephine. They weren't cherries. They were magnolias."

Audie paled, the towel frozen between her fingers. "You're sure?"

He nodded so hard he felt like a bobblehead. "So Josephine wasn't showing up in my dreams in some literal sense, which is a relief because I was starting to worry. But I forgot all about the piece at the store, because that's the day you—" *Well, you know.* "I thought it was another knick-knack to be priced for sale. But I just remembered. Magnolias, Audie. Magnolias!"

In unison, they said, "I think I know who did it."

She darted toward the mudroom. "Let me get my coat."

"I'll bring the car around front."

Narrowly missing a marble-topped accent table and its variegated plum poinsettia, he dashed through the house.

There wasn't a minute to lose.

Chapter 28

Jude threw the Jeep into park one block above Main Street. The patron saint of open curbs must've been on his side today, though the bumper encroached on a fire hydrant's personal space by a half-inch. Here's hoping any first responders were busy with holiday prep and not wandering St. Charles with a measuring tape.

Audie was already out of the car as he fought with his seat belt. Too much coffee, too many nerves. "Would you hang on a second?"

At last, it came undone. He flung aside the vinyl strap and dropped out. Even with a light snow, last-minute shoppers flooded every inch of the historic district.

"Glen closes early on a day like this?"

"He goes straight to the spa each December twenty-third, has a standing appointment. Vita said he thinks procrastinators don't appreciate his quality merchandise. To them, it's a check in a box."

"As iffy as his finances sound, it would also be a check in his bank account."

A chorus listing the gifts her true love gave to her echoed through an alleyway, accompanied by joyous laughter from Sandy's cafe. In a gap between buildings, he caught sight of The Doggy Bag. Customers streaming in and out all had wagging tails, pups and humans alike.

The only store closed already must be where they were headed. Well, that and DFV Boutique.

The concrete walk lifted and fell like the New Madrid fault, and Jude tripped twice as they scurried to the rear door of G. Armquist Fine Antiques. A brick as old as the state propped it open about a foot.

Audie started to slip sideways through the gap, and he caught her arm, whispering, "If Derek's the killer—"

"Fran is in there. We have no choice."

There's always a choice, rarely a good one.

"Then let me go first."

She hesitated, but recognized a losing battle.

He entered a dim storage area, every tendon in his body taut enough to spring him straight over that muddy river and into the next county. The smell of items that had lived a full life hit him, reminiscent of too many census books and microfiche boxes. Sounds from the showroom overlaid the track created by twelve drummers drumming nearby.

But it was two men's voices where there should've been Fran's.

He bent to Audie's ear. "Glen should be tissue-deep in a Swedish massage by now."

She squinted, which somehow improved her hearing. "He sure doesn't sound relaxed."

"I don't care if you've got three wise men and a dozen shepherd swearing beside the manger," said Dickens' ghost. "You're up to something, Derek, and you need to come clean."

Jude crept in further, stepping around a dragon's horde of old bronze bells and crystal lamps courtesy of Great-Aunt Lilith. On a card table with two folding chairs sat a camera whose antiquity bordered on insulting, as he'd had one of those as a child. It still had a flashbulb attached.

Focus. If the guys came in here and caught them sneaking? He'd think of something. Or Audie would. Or they'd blame Vita somehow; she wouldn't mind. If Fran was inside, they had to hustle her out pronto and go talk to the police.

Did they have enough to get the authorities involved? Questionable. But the story was sounding stronger the longer it spin-dried inside his skull.

First, they had to figure out the current kerfuffle before dear uncle ruined everything.

"Glen, please calm down." So Fran was there. Crud. "We're cleaning, like you wanted."

"That's not what I meant."

"Then what are you talking about?"

The guardian of questionable collectibles was losing his patience. "Fran, I'm sorry, but this doesn't involve you."

Jude rolled his eyes. Never a smart thing to say to anyone, especially a stressed-out woman on the brink.

He tiptoed around a trio of camera tripods—would that make it a nonopod? Somebody must've recently emptied their photographer father's studio.

Then a figure stepped right in front of him, and his heart rocketed straight to Neptune.

Wait, I recognize that hair.

A full-length mirror on a swivel stand rested near the wall, showing him how ridiculous they looked playing spy versus spy.

But it was also convenient. He could see into the showroom without sticking his neck out.

Of course, that meant they could see him too. He backpedaled into the shadows, almost taking out the wife at his heels. He cringed a silent apology. She waved it off, intent on the conversation.

"You're judging him like you do everybody, Glen,"

"Uncle, aren't you supposed to be somewhere? Please, you need a break. That's where these crazy ideas are coming from." The younger man sounded so sincere, so unlike a thief or a murderer.

Remember the acting lessons your sincere young man was taking to 'meet people?'

Right.

In the mirror, Derek and Fran stood near the business desk. Opposite, with his hands on his hips, was the spirit of Charles Dickens in his modern-day duds, no pocket watch or waistcoat to adjust pompously.

His whole demeanor projected the attitude, though. It must be the beard.

"Derek, I ran through your numbers this morning, like I should've done months ago. I may not be the best businessman, but I sure never had a year this bad until you took over the books. Your accounting is what polite company would call creative."

"Bookkeeping methods have changed since you started doing them. I—"

"Keep it up. I don't believe a word. And what's with all the lurking around town the past couple of months? I called down to Wax & Wicks. You never placed an order with them. One more lie. I guess the thefts and your sneaking are a coincidence?"

"You think I'm the thief? I was walking. Shopping. Not sneaking. And how would you know that if you weren't out yourself?"

Hold on—was their hoarder the Ghost of Christmas Future after all, the phantom presence lurking around every corner?

No, that ghostie could've played point guard for the Bulls. Mr. Dickens here needed stilts to reach the dude's shoulders.

"You think I'm crazy," the antique dealer said. "Everybody does. But this is stacking up in a way I never dreamt possible from my own sister's son." It was the first time he came across as a person and not a caricature of his own making. Jude's respect for the man rose a quarter-notch. "So before you stand in my shop, telling me to go away, I want to know: did you have something to do with Kurt's death?"

"Glen!"

"Fran, I'm not talking to you! You've got enough problems on your own. He may be my nephew, but that doesn't mean he can't be a fraud and a scammer."

Derek's face had tightened, along with his tone. "You're prejudiced because of things that happened years ago."

"I've seen too many leopards. They never change their spots."

And there it is again.

"You're wrong, Glen. Now please leave."

The older man opened his mouth twice before finding any words. "We'll be revisiting your employment after the holiday, because I don't trust you anymore. Frannie, if you have a brain in your tie-dyed head, you'll come with me."

How to Win Friends and Influence People, a self-help book by G. Armquist.

She, of course, folded her arms and didn't budge. In his aggravated flurry, the older man wheeled around too fast and ran into a large trash bin behind him. He stumbled and only caught himself by grabbing onto the repurposed armoire. It gave him a zoomed-in view of the stock waiting for display. He clambered to his feet like a spider on roller skates, but something in that pile grabbed his eyes and wouldn't let go.

Derek stepped toward him. "For both of our sakes, you need to leave now."

The man instead reached to the middle shelf.

Jude jumped as Audie surfaced under his arm to get a better angle on the mirror.

"Turn around," she hissed, willing Dickens into a marionette. He did block the best view.

Aud must have strings hidden somewhere, because he did shift their way but as unsteadily as those creepy dolls. In an awful imitation of the toy, his mouth had dropped open as if its hinge broke, his eyes wide as a shark's. In his hands was something about the size of a record album. He held it like it was the crown jewels of Imperial Russia.

Jude half-expected Audie's voice to emerge from his lips, but it was all Glen, moderated into an awestruck whisper. "Where on earth did you get this?"

A ceiling spotlight struck the square and projected a hand-laid magnolia tree into full and stunning bloom.

Fran's Tiffany panel.

The air in the room crystallized, more fragile than the artwork.

"How did—?" Fran took a step, her feet working as ineffectively as her words. "Where did—?"

Derek looked from the glass to his relation to Fran. "What is that?"

When Fran dragged her eyes away from the missing art—the thing that promised to steal her child from her—they ricocheted between the two men, unable to find a safe place to settle.

The long-time purveyor of fine antiquities quivered. "How did this get here?"

"It's mine," Fran said simply. "One of you took it from our shop?"

"What? No, not me." Derek's hand went to his chest. "Him! He must've taken it. He planted it so—"

The accused spoke slower now, shock replacing outrage. "This is genuine, isn't it?" Fran's lips pulled straight as an arrow. "It's worth thousands. Tens of thousands."

She nodded. "I know. But it's mine. Or Trent's. I have his aunt's will to prove it." She fought a hundred inner battles as the gears spun. "It was stolen the night before Kurt died."

She turned on Glen. "You were there that day, yelling at Derek about something stupid like you always do. You recognized what it's worth. You came back that evening and took it."

"I didn't. I wouldn't." The argument had slipped from his tone, replaced only with disbelief and awe. He gawked at the panel as if it were the *Pietà*, finally setting it down on the large desk before he could drop it. Audie exhaled. *Amen, sister.* He looked up at Derek, jumbled facts connecting between his ears. "You were alone when I left, with Fran in the kitchen. And the next night, I see you with Kurt out on the street, only hours before he's murdered."

"You didn't see us." Through the mirrored reflection, a weird glint flickered in Derek's eyes, magnified by his glasses. His voice had changed now too. "You scolded us. Like children."

Oh no.

He shifted around the rear of the desk, his gaze laser-focused on his employer. "You think you have that right, with me, with Kurt, with Fran. Everyone is below you. But what are you? Going around pretending to be something you're not while you gather your little treasures, your mounds of useless trash. You're nothing but ego."

The gun glinted in his palm, pulled from under the desktop where it must be kept in case of robbery.

Ironic.

Also, Mr. Vikander must've added some magic lessons to his acting classes, as fast as that sleight-of-hand had been. Jude would've applauded if Lizzie Gill's mom wasn't now standing at the wrong end of the barrel.

Audie stiffened against his ribs.

"I thought wrapping Boulton into the local legend would be poetic. You, Uncle, should've appreciated that. But it complicated things. I know better now. One bullet in the right spot, and your guilt over killing him will be another bit of history."

"You're going to frame me for Kurt's murder like you framed him for the thefts?" He paled, the bluster gone. He was now just a middle-aged man in way over his head. "How did you get into all those buildings?"

"A surprising variety of websites sell lock-picking sets." Not that surprising, really.

"But why? For a couple of bucks? You got more than that embezzling from me."

Derek snickered, and Jude wished he hadn't heard it. If a sound could be crooked, this one was. "None of this was for the money. I wanted to see how long the challenge would last."

The challenge. The game.

Brooke Boulton's father was dead because Derek Vikander had gotten bored.

"And what about me?"

A cherub-faced, blue-haired mother stared at the second man to betray her of late.

"Your Tiffany wound up being the grand prize, didn't it? I couldn't work here this long and not spot the good stuff when I saw it on Wednesday." She blinked, understanding the situation too well, and he rolled his eyes. "You actually believed I was interested?"

Gone were the tears of earlier in the week. Her chin raised to whatever he'd say next. "What happens now?" Lizzie's mom may have lost the chess match, but she wouldn't lay down her queen.

He waved the gun with a shrug, and it was all Jude could do not to go slug the boy. "You were overcome thinking about your own thieving ways and losing your kid, and remembered there's a river out there. I tried to stop you, of course, meek and mild and reformed, but it was too late. I'll be distraught for a while, then I'll sell the panel and leave this lousy city."

Audie grabbed Jude's arm. *I know, love.*

But then he realized she didn't want consoling. He swung in time to see the dark flowy figure swooshing in past the card table.

Jude reeled backward, running into the tripods. The racket had everyone in the room jumping in his direction except Derek, who now aimed the gun at his mother's brother. A brilliant flash of light bounced off the mirror, and Jude landed on the tiles, blinded. A crash, shouts, and a gunshot rang out in chorus.

"Audie!"

Scrambling to his feet, he staggered as fast as he could into the showroom, blinking for a long minute before the blinding white faded to a decent aperture.

Glen Armquist sat on his rear on the floor, his back supported by a Queen Anne fainting couch. Too bad he missed the seat. Audie had Fran by the sleeve, dragging her out of the way. And behind the desk, amongst a wealth of shattered glass fragments, lay Derek Vikander, out cold. The Ghost of Christmas Yet to Come loomed over him.

With a flourish, the Ghost whisked off his hood. Holding the gun, a tall Black man in his late thirties, somehow familiar, pivoted toward them.

The weapon disappeared into his robes when he read their faces. "Sorry about that." He gave Derek a calm, collected appraisal. "He's okay. Nobody got shot."

"Thanks to you," Glen muttered. He made no effort to stand. He did shift, pulling a squashed flower arrangement from under his seat.

The stranger again reached into his garment, and Jude stepped between him and the girls. But Audie slipped beneath his arm.

"You've done your mother proud, Ronald."

"Ronald?" The phantom grinned at Jude's reaction, as did his own wife. *Fine. But whoever heard of a wraith named Ronald? Maybe it's Wronald…*

Out came a slim wallet, opening to a shield and a law enforcement ID card. "Tell Mom that, would you? Now that the grandkids are around, my sister and I are has-beens."

"Would anyone care to share what's going on?" *And why I'm always the last to know?*

The man verified that Derek wasn't stirring, then reached out a hand. "Ronald James. I'm an undercover detective with the St. Charles County Police Department."

"And Darla's oldest child."

That explained a lot. He had her nose and cheekbones, though not her love of colors.

"I've been investigating the thefts, and then after Kurt turned up dead, his murder."

"But we thought it was a suicide at first, didn't we?"

The policeman shook his head. "Suicide never fit. We weren't letting the trail go cold on other possibilities while the medical examiner did her thing. And Kurt being the thief didn't fit either. I knew when those thefts occurred and where Kurt was at those times. It wasn't him. But we didn't start homing in on Vikander until Glen accidentally let on to Mom that his annual profits were unusually low. Before then, I'd been gathering intel wherever and whenever. She was a terrific source on this case. We hadn't known about Fran's stolen art until you told her and she told me."

"That's why she was so out of sorts. It makes so much more sense than her being a suspect."

Ronald James let out an unauthoritative laugh, but he couldn't help it. It was in his genes. "Mom as a thief, that's rich. I shudder to see what she'd say if she ever heard those words put together. No, she came straight to me when you clued her in about the Tiffany. I get that you didn't want to report it, Fran, but we needed to be on the lookout for something so valuable. It threw Mom for a loop. She was horrified it had been kept in the shop." Bowing to Jude, he beat his own chest with his fist. "Mea culpa, though, for freaking you out with my prowling."

"I'm guessing you didn't lock us underground in that collapsing cave, then."

He chuckled. "That would be our buddy here, after he decided you were getting too close to the truth. If I'd stuck around after opening the cellar door, my cover would've been blown."

A tiny sob escaped Fran, unable to hold that firm upper lip a minute longer. "My Tiffany."

Oh.

The piece was in pieces, ruined, shattered, like her life. But some of those tears fell for the lost artwork itself, one creator to another.

"Please." Glen struggled to his feet. "Even with a gun to my head, I wasn't letting anything happen to that." He reached beneath the sofa and pulled out the intact panel. He laid it delicately on the desk once more. "When Derek fired, it hit the collection of kerosene lamps I bought off an estate sale."

Jude scanned the floor, grateful to find no flammable liquid. Detective James was on his cell, calling in the cavalry. An ambulance siren neared.

"He'll be fine. I had to knock him out to get him handled."

"Nothing he didn't deserve," Fran sniffed. "I can't believe I bought his changed-man routine. Maybe I'm really not a fit mother."

Audie twirled, squaring all five-feet-two of her before the woman and boring straight into her brain. *Good, she pulls that on folks other than me.* "Fran Gill, you take that back right now, because if I have to tell Vita you're talking that way?"

Fran wanted to step away from the intensity in those gray marbles, but she was either frozen in place or too scared to move. She stammered out a hoarse "Yes, ma'am."

Audie held her look for another five beats before nodding her approval. "Great. I'm glad we've got that out of the way."

Jude stepped aside as the two ladies moved toward the storeroom. It probably wouldn't be profitable for customers to see the proprietor's nephew escorted out the front entrance, handcuffed to a stretcher. He glanced at the Tiffany panel one more time, then caught a reflection off something in the armoire. Approaching the shelf, he carefully extracted another framed glass artwork from the to-sell pile. Obviously not a Tiffany, the pink petals shook him straight to his core.

There were cherry blossoms after all?

"Hey, Glen," he called as the man followed the conga line toward his own storage area. "How long have you had this?"

"Just since Monday."

The week had been nuts, but his first trip to the shop had been on Sunday. He couldn't have possibly seen this before. Despite his muddied memories, it really had been Fran's magnolia he'd noticed that afternoon, however briefly. "Where did you get it? Another estate sale?"

The shop's owner reentered his personal playground. "No, the seller came in with it. Doesn't happen a lot."

"What did he look like?" Jude found himself holding his breath.

"She." That didn't help his oxygen levels. "Soft-spoken, reserved, but pretty. Thin with this kind of old-fashioned hairdo. You don't see a lot of ringlets these days. We had a brief chat about how someone reworked this section." Surprisingly graceful fingers pointed at a group of lead lines. "It must've been broken. Excellent restoration job, though, because the colors nearly match. See? They never found the corner, because that area was definitely created later."

Jude hadn't even noticed. Hidden amongst the blossoms, the corner looked to be a barely different shade. *Oh my gosh.* Was that—"A bluebird?"

"Isn't it divine? I thought the repairing glazier added it as a clever signature. The lady said she found this in her mother's things. The mother's family had lived nearby when she received it as a gift, so the daughter thought it should return to where it started. I paid her, and that was that." He admired his purchase anew. "It's a stunning old piece."

Jude rubbed the initials etched into the added corner, millimeters from the bird's fragile wings. He was relieved that his wife wasn't inside to see his hand shake.

N.S.

Old. Stunning.

"You can say that again."

Chapter 29

The aromas wafting out of the kitchen filled every square inch of the Klein house and probably each house for a two-block radius. Sage and celery, pork and apples, cinnamon and cranberries and fresh bread—the full warmth of heaven was being dished onto platters. Not a member of today's cook line, Audie surveyed the dining room table and adjusted a red cloth napkin in its gold ring, set at an angle on the china her mother had brought out on holidays.

Vita said that if the Wests ever settled in one spot, she'd split the set with her. There wasn't much use for a gravy boat in the camper.

But Vita's place would always be their home away from home. She could keep the china.

The five o'clock Christmas Eve vigil had been sacred and comforting and packed to the gills. The family had sat in the pew for forty-five minutes before Mass even started, but the choir was prepared. When they opened with "Do You Hear What I Hear," both Marik sisters needed tissues. Jude reached an arm around Audie, Simon patted Vita's knee. Becca and Connor, at the end near the aisle, stole peeks up and behind to the loft like when they were small, trying to glimpse the singers leading the call-and-response anthem.

Were she and Vita ever that young? *Yes, and we'd done the same, sitting between our parents a million years ago in a church across the river.* It had taken the patience of a thousand saints to keep Audie from squirming, while her ten-year-older sister had at least pretended to be proper and pious. To focus on the prayers and long readings was so hard, but she tried, because after it was over, they'd be bundled into the station wagon and arrive at the doorstep of Christmas itself—Grandma and Grandpa's. The homemade Polish sausage would beckon to them the second they'd hit the driveway, much like it was doing now.

Audie assumed it was a genetic thing. She'd love to see the DNA confirmation, though.

Based on the test bite he'd offered his eager aunt ten minutes ago, Connor had nailed it. It could never be identical to Grandpa's recipe, but it shouldn't be. It's Connor's turn now.

The tradition continues.

They'd delivered a poinsettia to Mabel, across her threshold because the Cat of Many Colors and the fear of a fashion faux pas had even the Man in Black too nervous to step inside. Trinkets bought from Darla and Fran went to the proprietors of Lucy's Lix and The Doggy Bag. To Stuart, they gifted a set of extra-warm gloves and a matching scarf. Without his roaming ghosts, they wouldn't have come to know Josephine so well, and that might've changed everything for the worse.

She shifted a tilted fork and shivered. Moving on.

They'd also accompanied Simon and Vita to see Mother again, because Audie couldn't bear the idea that their combined meltdown over the weekend might've been the last holiday with her.

A fatalistic view of things? *Yep, we're Eastern European all right.*

The extra callers had kept Irina distracted, and the visit had gone infinitely better. Now, she might've thought they were the magi themselves, but Audie would take it as a win. At the rear of Mulberry Gardens' private gathering room, Jude had clutched her hand like she dangled from the edge of a cliff, ready to drag her away from the precipice when needed.

Santa had better be bringing extra gifts for that man's stocking. He'd need to be beatified to rank any higher on the Nice List.

And yet, he was beating himself up that he hadn't seen through Derek Vikander from the start.

"That shows how skilled of an actor he is," she'd tried to reassure him. "I don't think he ever needed a lesson to learn that trick. It's a special trait of sociopaths. He just had to find his motivation."

Vita, Fran, and Darla had been able to open the store for six hours today, cleared by the police at last. They caught a flurry of late shoppers plus ones who'd heard about the drama and descended on them in droves. Most of those came from the other shops themselves, along with the entire Holidays of Hope crew.

Noticeably absent was a certain Ghost of Charles Dickens, who'd skipped the spa and gone straight to Florida for some much-needed vacay. After seeing the beauty of that Tiffany panel he would never own, holding it in his hands, one wondered if he'd reflect on his Scroogeness and come home a changed man.

Charles Dickens would've believed it possible. She should too. Who's to argue with the man who remade Christmas?

Ranger Quinn Thackeray had stopped by the boutique right as they were counting out the till. He had a meeting scheduled with the First Capitol's historic researcher on Monday. He planned to present their findings about Clarence Richards and see what she might authenticate.

"In the meantime," Quinn had said, "I noticed that framed commendation is well past schedule for some cleaning. Unfortunately, it's difficult to get on the restoration docket right now, so it might be down for a bit." He shrugged. And grinned.

Jude's midnight encounters with the specter continued to replay in her head. Not Darla's son, though Darla may be deputized as an honorary sleuth for any future St. Charles stumpers. No, it was Josephine, reaching out with that cherry blossom glass, nagging at Jude until it sat so clearly that he subconsciously noticed Fran's missing inheritance. The murdered bride helped them find her own justice while saving another struggling woman from a terrible fate.

Was it real? Jude couldn't say. A certain Victorian writer may have had a thought about it. Either way, she turned out to be a very helpful ghost.

God bless us indeed.

The doorbell rang. "I'll get it," Audie called into the kitchen. The group in there was too close and crowded for her liking, and they hadn't heard the bell anyway. She walked through the hall, automatically touching Ollie's picture, and opened the door with the jingle bells hanging from the knob.

"Fran!"

Peeking out from under the gray wool coat was a red sparkly sweater and black skirt, tights, and ankle boots. Her hair was a dramatic green ombré now. Somebody had needed a change.

When had she had time to do that?

Vita always had said parents didn't sleep. *We could be 2 a.m. pen pals.*

The best part of the artist's ensemble was the tiny pixie standing beside her, gripping her hem and looking up shyly at the stranger.

"And Lizzie! It's so nice to meet you. Come in out of the cold." She opened the door wide, and they stepped inside.

Unlike her last trip to this foyer, Fran shone like a thousand tree toppers. Then the full wave of miracles being worked in the oven and on all four stove burners reached her nose. "Shoot, did I interrupt dinner?"

"No, the cooks are finishing up. Are you going somewhere? We've got enough food here to feed an army." Another Lithuanian thing.

And a Jude thing.

"It smells amazing, but we can't stay. Besides, I already owe you guys so much for the boost you've given Santa."

That had been an awesome shopping trip, overfilling a cart for little Lizzie and sneaking in a few extra surprises for her mom. Audie missed the days of doing the same for Connor and Becca.

Oops, the glassmaker was still talking. "We wanted to share some good news." She unzipped a pocket of her purse and then several more as she searched for something that apparently wasn't the three colored sharpies, two hair ties, or a partridge in a pear tree.

Okay, no fowl emerged, but nothing would've been surprising after this week. Audie made goofy faces at Lizzie while they waited. The child braved eye contact at last, then giggled and hid in the collar of her coat. The animated character on its pink sleeves predated its wearer, but the material remained in perfect condition.

"Eureka!" The envelope Fran handed over was slit open and addressed to Mr. and Mrs. Trenton Gill. Audie slid out the letter.

"'My dear Trenton and his lovely wife Fran,'" she read out loud, her heart already fluttering with where this was going. "'After further consideration, I am leaving the Tiffany panel to Fran alone. I am of sound enough mind and body, Trenton, to know you may question this decision. But you've found a wonderful partner in life and a loving, beautiful mother for your child. She should be your star, not a piece of glass you might only view as a dollar sign.'" *Aunt Earline, you're a peach.* "'Her artwork rivals what we've seen on our travels, and I regret not being here to see what she will become. It is hers to do with as she likes. I am not so naive to think its value might not be worth something to her someday, but I hope it's not because of anything you ever did, Nephew. These are my wishes, pursuant to my last will and testament.'" The date was inscribed beside the smooth, flowing signature of Earline Crandall, two witnesses, a lawyer, and a notary.

Fran beamed brighter than Jeanette Isabella's torch.

The feeling was contagious. "Where did you find it?"

"Can you believe Trent's mom found it while she was watching Liz at his apartment?" She glanced down at her daughter, currently enraptured by the wonders that were Vita and Simon's abode, and lowered her voice. "I'm kind of shocked she handed it over so quickly, but she was super nice about it. That'll help down the road." Grandmas are still grandmas, even after divorce. "I drove straight to the lawyer, who confirmed it was the document he was missing and that it was valid. Then I dropped in on Daddy at the office." That must've been an exciting conversation. "He panicked. Admitted he'd convinced a cousin to nick it way back when they got the will from the safe, then he hid it out of spite." She rolled her eyes. It would take more than Trenton Gill's spitefulness to knock the vibrancy out of this girl's hair.

"Fran, I couldn't be happier for you two. Vita will be over the moon when she hears."

"I wish I had time to tell her myself, but like always, we're running late. My neighbor friend who watches Lizzie sometimes invited us and a bunch of other singletons to her place for games and snack food. A Friendsgiving, Christmas style."

Back in the conversation, Lizzie's eyes opened so wide they glittered. "Penny has a kitty!"

The first words out of that itty-bitty mouth were as adorable as the child who spoke them.

"She does?" Audie crouched down in front of her. "What's her name?"

"Blanchette. She's black and white and furry and she climbs on my head if I'm watching cartoons."

"I can see why. That's an adorable head you have, nice and comfy. Will you wish Blanchette a merry Christmas for me?"

She nodded, her fingers going up to her mouth. Then she whispered, "I got her a toy mouse, but don't tell her it's from me."

Audie put her finger to her lips. "I won't say a word. Besides, I don't speak cat."

Lizzie looked at her funny, then laughed as all children do when the adults have started acting like children. Audie stood, hearing the first serving dishes land on the dining room table. Before she knew it, she was enveloped in a hug, eye to hair with the middle layer of greenness.

"I can't thank you and Jude and Vita enough for everything you did. You saved us."

Oh Lord. Where'd I put that tissue after Mass? "I'm thrilled we could help. You two have a wonderful Christmas, okay?"

Sugarplums already danced a jitterbug under Lizzie's pigtails. Her mother just said, "We most certainly will."

Audie closed the door behind them, and leaned against it for a moment, staring down the line of photos, their family history in mismatched frames. From the kitchen, laughter arose from what sounded like a scuffle over fingerling potatoes. She pushed off of the door, slowed only enough to touch her finger to Oliver's cheek again, and continued toward the living with a smile.

Poor Audie and Jude, always finding themselves in the thick of things. (Of course, it's their own fault for agreeing to star in a mystery series.)

More works by Laurie Alberswerth will be available soon! The series is best enjoyed in the following order:

Bones & Bloodlines
Grain & Gravestones
Kin & Curses
Myrrh & Mayhem

Coming soon
Crypts & Crawdads
Books 6 & 7: Titles in-work!

Want to be in the know for all things West-erly? Sign up for the newsletter at **LaurieAlberswerth.com**! You'll be part of the fun crowd plus receive a FREE download of Audie's trusty binder for their first adventure, *Bones & Bloodlines*.

Dear Reader,

On behalf of Jude, Audie, Vita, and Mabel's cats, **thank you** for coming along on the fourth adventure in this series. Your kind words and support of the first three books make me hope we're onto something here.

If this story kept you entertained, please drop a review on Amazon and Goodreads. **Those ratings and one-liners about what you enjoyed are how other readers decide whether to take a chance on a new-to-them author.** I'd like all the mystery lovers to join the West-ern army, wouldn't you? We're a fun crowd.

If you haven't already, please subscribe to my monthly newsletter at **LaurieAlberswerth.com**. You'll get inside scoops on upcoming releases and other tidbits from the writerly life. It'll be a great chat around the campfire, and I'll provide all the virtual marshmallows. (BYORS—bring your own roasting stick.) See you there!

Your partner in all things murdery,

Laurie

About the Author

Laurie Alberswerth was certain "ENG" stood for English, not Engineering, when she checked the box for a college major. Funny story. Yet somehow, the writing bug survived four years of heat transfer and machine design, followed by a two-decade career as a Mechanical Stress Analyst.

That bug, like the cockroach, could survive a nuclear war.

A St. Louis native, the days and nights spent at Missouri state parks were fuel to the campfire when setting Jude and Audie West on their mystery-solving journey. And who knew the family-tree workbook purchased for her husband on their first anniversary (what else does one do for a "paper" gift?) would lead to so much time spent in libraries and courthouses, fighting with more microfilm than all the spies at MI6?

Laurie's own heritage—Lithuanian, Slovakian, and German—is a source of deep-rooted traditions and soul-satisfying (if not heart-healthy) food. She may or may not have two great-great-grandmothers who may or may not have independently hidden the body of a husband in the dirt floor of a basement.

But it's okay. They were bad guys.

Made in the USA
Monee, IL
15 September 2025

24689377R00177